WAR PAINT

WAR PAINT

Tom Wakefield

St. Martin's Press
New York

Library of Congress Cataloging-in-Publication Data

Wakefield, Tom.
War paint / Tom Wakefield.
p.   cm.
ISBN 0-312-11094-4
1. World War, 1939–1945—England—Fiction.
2. Women teachers—England—Fiction.
3. Villages—England—Fiction.   I. Title.
PR6037.A374W37   1994
823′.914—dc20   94-800   CIP

First published in Great Britain by
Constable and Company Ltd.

First U.S. Edition: July 1994
10 9 8 7 6 5 4 3 2 1

For K.

'It is said that many autobiographies by prominent figures in this period were "ghosted" – that is, written by someone other than the ostensible author. This is sometimes avowed on the title page, where the book is described as written in collaboration with a professional author. It is more often not avowed.'

A. J. P. Taylor
English History 1914 – 1945
Revised Bibliography.

'He said all was fair in love and war. I have always thought it an immoral saying.'
'It means the opposite of what it says. But why say all is unfair in love and war? We all know it.'

I. Compton Burnett.

WAR PAINT

1

At a quarter past eleven this morning, Miss Roper was killed by a mail van. The van had swerved to avoid a roving alsatian dog, the vehicle had mounted the pavement for just a couple of yards or so – but the few yards were enough to destroy Miss Roper. She died instantly.

Sad news travels quickly in a small town and information is usually detailed and precise. I had planned to make mince pies about now – most of the joy of Christmas for me is in the preparation. I put up the decorations yesterday, but now – at a quarter to one, just two hours after Miss Roper's death – I've decided to take them all down. I can start the mince pies later.

Yes, I must take down the streamers, remove the fairy lights from the tree, put away the paper chains, the cardboard silver bells, and the orange and red lanterns. I'll just leave the few sprays of holly where they are. I really don't know what my daughter and grandchildren will think, but . . . but, I need to . . . to . . . to honour Miss Roper.

It's not as though I knew her as well enough as I wanted to: it was very hard to get to know your teacher well in 1943. Or was it 1942? All the classes were so large, huge they were, so huge that it took the teacher at least fifteen or twenty minutes to call the attendance register.

I was turned thirteen and in my last year of school. It was a girl's secondary school. Later they called it a secondary modern school. I have to laugh a little, it's just that there was so little that was modern in that place. They were harsh, austere times. Our town seemed more important then than it is now. Perhaps it was because we only produced two things. Coal and food.

Just looking from our classroom window, I could see a potato field, a pit-stack, and, not far from the edge of the playground, a pine forest. Our school had seven classrooms. Six of the rooms were divided by thin wooden partitions which could be pushed back to form larger areas (I believe the Japanese still build their houses in this way). The seventh classroom, the top class, Miss Roper's class, was apart from the main building. It looked like an army barracks hut – in fact, I think that is what it had originally been – but now, instead of preparing young men for war, it housed forty-six adolescent girls and their teacher.

It wasn't only our classroom that was separate from the main building. Miss Roper was too. She was the only teacher who was unmarried. She must have been over twenty-four and few women in our town were unmarried at that age. And, although such things were taboo for us, Miss Roper's lips were painted cyclamen red and when she moved about the classroom, we would breathe in deeply to catch a whiff of her 'Soir de Paris' perfume. She was well over five and a half feet in height, but chose to wear high-heeled shoes which made her seem as tall as a pine tree. She wore long, dangling purple ear-rings which hung from pierced ear-lobes like fuchsia blossoms.

She moved in gazelle-like slow motion. Graceful and assured. The ear-rings would swing this way and that – the wide brow, the long neck, the deep blue eyes. Oh, these features were not framed by frizzy or permed hair. No, Miss Roper's long dark brown tresses were plaited and twirled round and round her skull to form the most perfect bun on the top of her head. There was never a wisp of hair or a pin out of place.

Mrs Chaplin – our headmistress – must have respected Miss Roper or admired her teaching skills, because she would never have tolerated ear-rings, lipstick, nail varnish, or sanded legs from any other teacher. Or perhaps it was because Miss Roper was the only teacher who could play the piano in assembly and teach singing as well as everything else.

Miss Roper was daring in other ways. She did not bow her

8

head during prayers, but sat bolt upright. Eyes wide open. She would not allow any other teacher, not even Mrs Chaplin, to inflict any physical punishment on girls in her class. 'Rapped knuckles bruise tender minds. Bruised minds never recover.' She would never appoint class prefects. 'I am paid, albeit badly, to serve and teach you all. Help and co-operation must be voluntary, not ordered by me. Prefects would be better placed in a police force rather than a school.'

At some time during the day all the other classes were variably noisy. Miss Roper never had cause to shout or shriek for order because she had discipline. Yes, yes, ours was a willing submission.

I shall never forget that first term. Until that mellow September I had never realized how beautiful our surroundings were. No other teacher had ever taken us out of the classroom, but on Thursday afternoons, she would replace her high-heeled shoes with lace-ups.

'Check your clothes, girls, coats buttoned properly. Janet dear,' she spoke to me, 'are my seams straight?' She would display the calves of her legs: the seams were never crooked. We all knew that Miss Roper wore no stockings, we all knew that her legs were sanded and that the 'seam' was drawn in with a brown eyebrow pencil, yet we granted her this foible, whereas our generosity would not have been proffered to any other woman attempting such a pretence.

On our timetable this weekly jaunt was written in as 'botany' and 'rural science studies'. I can see us all now, trailing after her along the canal towpath. She would sometimes pause and turn about, beckon us with a wrist that clattered on account of the bracelets that encircled it.

'Gather round, girls, gather about me. No, don't go too near the water's edge.' She would point out flowers and name them in such a way that you would remember them for ever.

'The tall, stately pink flowers are called willow-herb. I always think that they look like pink church spires. Pink church spires. They, like harebells, poppies, coltsfoot and cowslip, should not be picked: they are not meant to adorn the insides of houses. Remove

9

these wild flowers from their birthplace, snatch them from their roots and they are dead within hours. Easily murdered.'

Not only was she concerned with what lived on the canal banks, but also with what was in the canal itself. She would greet the fisherman. 'Good afternoon, Mr Harper, I see you have your keep-net in the water. Could it be that our girls have brought you luck? I wonder if you would be so kind as to lift the net out of the water and just hold it up for us. Just for a few seconds? Thank you, so very kind of you.'

He held the net up for Miss Roper and it was as though she were doing him a favour; he held it up for her, not for us. 'The silver fish with the flecks of bright orange near its fin is a roach. And that pale green fish, the one with the three dark green stripes on its sides — that is a perch. Such lovely colours, mankind has never improved on nature as far as colouring is concerned. They are freshwater fish and they are edible. Like many beautiful creatures, they can be eaten.'

Later, *en route* back to school, she stopped and paused near a field of potatoes. What in God's name could she say about a field of potatoes? I'm sure we all wondered but obeyed her unquestioningly.

'Assemble yourselves tidily, girls. Make a tableau. Some of you sitting, some kneeling, some standing. Those of you with scarves may wave them when I give you a sign.'

There were five or six Land Army girls gathering the crop. They looked like women dressed as men. It was this human landscape that Miss Roper was interested in.

'Now girls, when you are ready.' She called out loud and clear in a high piping tone so that the Land Army girls stopped their back-breaking occupation and looked in our direction. Miss Roper pointed towards them, her arm fully stretched. 'Three cheers for working women. Ready, girls? Hip-hip hoo-ray. Hip-hip hoo-ray. Hip-hip hoo-ray.' Some of us waved our scarves. The workers didn't seem embarrassed by our support, not at all, they waved their respects to us all. Then Miss Roper said, 'A woman's place is not necessarily in the home, girls. A woman's place is only where she decides it should be.'

'Just like wild flowers, Miss Roper?' I ventured.

'Yes, yes, Janet. I'm grateful for your insight. Servitude is close to imprisonment for so many wives – these things will change. Must change.'

By November of that year, winter closed in on us – viciously and quickly. There were terrible frosts and harsh cold winds that tore through our gloves and pixie-hoods and made our fingers and ears ache. During the dinner hour, unless it rained or snowed, no girls were allowed inside the school buildings. We would return to our afternoon classes chilled to our bones – heads and feet raw and numb. Spirits dejected.

Ah-ha, what a miracle worker that Miss Roper was. 'Girls, I've had a few words with our head-teacher, Mrs Chaplin, and both she and I feel that as you are top class girls, we should allow you all to make a great, personal, sacrifice and give up your dinner recreation time during the winter months. Only if you wish to, mind. From now on, any girl that wishes to stay in class may do so. I shall be here – and will be supervising our "knitting for victory sessions".'

There was not a single girl in that class who stayed outside. We sat in groups and chatted quietly whilst our needles clicked. We produced scarves and balaclavas as though we were on an assembly line.

Our labours were rewarded. 'Girls, I have brought in my personal gramophone and for twenty or thirty minutes we can sing accompaniment to the star performers on the records.'

Miss Roper would wind up the machine and we sang 'Don't sit under the Apple Tree', 'The White Cliffs of Dover', 'Paper Doll', and a song which could hardly be suitable for teenage girls – 'Can't Help Lovin' that Man of Mine'.

We sang above the noise that was going on outside. Four or five Italian prisoners of war were sawing down pine trees and piling them in pagoda-like stacks. It seemed strange to me that a pine tree should become a pit-prop and even more strange that these men, captives in patchwork uniforms, should be outside our classroom. From time to time, one of them would stop working

11

and applaud our artistry, but Miss Roper appeared to ignore this appreciation.

Towards the early part of December, she introduced us to a strange new record. 'Girls, I am going to let you hear the greatest male singer in the world.' Before she did this, she wrote the words of the song on the blackboard, 'Come Back to Sorrento'. The recording was in Italian and Miss Roper pointed out the English version to us as the melody progressed. We learned it quickly and within a few days it had become part of our repertoire.

Nearer Christmas, we abandoned our records and practised carol singing. The shepherds, angels, King Wenceslas and Royal David's City seemed a poor substitute for our previous gramophone-aided offerings. Perhaps Miss Roper sensed this.

'Girls, I think we could have "Come Back to Sorrento". You have all worked so hard today. Janet, dear,' (she spoke to me) 'it's a little stuffy in here. Open the windows on your side, yes, open all of them. Let's have a little air. Breathe in deeply, girls. Intercostal Diaphragmatic. All great singers breathe in that way. Fill your lungs. That's it. I'll turn up the volume on the player, it will encourage you all to sing with more vigour.'

She turned up that player very loud; we chorused accompaniment to the greatest tenor on earth and I should think they must have heard us a mile away. As the record ended and our singing stopped, one of the Italians ventured right up to the open window. He had a weather-beaten complexion, black, curly hair and soft dark brown eyes. He was short of stature and he reminded me a bit of Tyrone Power.

Miss Roper switched off the player which had begun to make a clicking noise. The silence was quite eerie. We had no idea what the man was going to do, he just stood there at the window and stared at Miss Roper as though there were no tomorrow. And, what's more, she stared back. His face was now without expression but his eyes spoke. Not to us, but to Miss Roper.

Tears trickled down his cheeks. I'd never seen a man cry before. He did not speak but raised his right hand and slowly pushed it through the window opening. In his grasp, he held a huge branch of holly cuttings. None of us girls dared accept an offering from an enemy, and in any event, the gift wasn't meant for one of us.

We watched Miss Roper leave her desk. She seemed to float between the chair spaces. She took the holly from him with both hands and winced as the prickles punctured her skin. She placed the holly on a nearby desk-top, then, turning quickly to face the window, she put both her hands on the black curls, leaned forward – and kissed the man on the forehead with her cyclamen-red lips. He took her hands in his and held them for a moment . . .

Afterwards we sang 'The Holly and the Ivy' as though nothing had happened, but of course, it had, as we could still see the tiny spottles of blood on Miss Roper's hands . . . and now she's dead. Gone.

The last time I saw her was not much more than a couple of months ago. She was coming down the library steps as I was going up them. I greeted her; she nodded a response – she could be brutally economical in social exchanges at times. I attempted conversation.

'Such a lovely autumn, Miss Roper. I've just come back from my holidays. I went to Italy.'

'I've never been abroad.' Her statement hardly invited further discussion, but I persisted.

'I went to Tuscany. I don't think that I have ever been anywhere quite so lovely.'

She answered me flatly. 'Well, everywhere is different.' And then she looked down at me and spoke in slow, dreamy, reflective tones. 'If I had chosen to go to Italy, I think that I would have toured the lakes. Orta, Como, Garda, Maggiore – the landscape mirrored in the waters must be . . . must be . . . oh, so dramatic . . . breathtaking . . . full of illusions . . . What an autumn that would be. And even in winter, the evergreens so dark and forbidding, changeable skies, the firs . . . and the holly . . .'

She smiled in imagined reminiscence. Or was it? I'll never know. She excused herself gently, there was a bus to catch, she was past the age of rushing.

Presto! Presto! Presto! I mustn't dwell on this any longer. Be busy. See to the mincemeat. Mmm, it smells good. It should do.

13

Ingredients: a pound of cooking apples peeled and finely chopped, 12 ounces of raisins, 8 ounces of sultanas, pink church spires, soft brown eyes, soft brown sugar, grated rind of lemon, 'Soir de Paris' perfume, cinnamon, cyclamen-red lipstick, half a nutmeg, a gramophone, chopped almonds, working women, 8 ounces of currants, sanded legs, Como, Maggiore, Sorrento, shredded suet, mixed spices, purple ear-rings. Stir well.

The holly and the ivy, when they are both full grown . . . la-la-la-la-la . . . the holly bears the crown, with the . . . He couldn't. He couldn't have loved Miss Roper as much as I did. Light gas. Very low flame. Let the mixture simmer. Let it simmer for a long time.

2

'Yes, yes, it is a shock . . . Mmm . . . yes, we heard the news this morning. No, we haven't told Mrs Chaplin yet . . . No . . . we didn't want to upset her. Yes . . . Miss Roper was here the day before yesterday. She was always a diligent visitor if nothing else. Who shall I say telephoned?'

'Janet Read.'

'Ah yes, you have visited here. I remember now.'

'No, don't say that. No, say that Janet Haycock called. Mrs Chaplin knows me better by my maiden name.'

'You are not a relative then?'

'No, I'm an ex-pupil. A friend. A close friend of Mrs Chaplin and Miss Roper.'

'Well, thank you for calling, Mrs er . . .?'

'Haycock. Janet Haycock.'

'Ah yes. We will let Mrs Chaplin know about this all in good time. We don't want to spoil her Christmas, do we?'

'I think that she should be informed. Christmas or not.'

'At this moment Mrs . . . Mrs Haycock, she is . . . how can I put it? She is sweetly asleep . . . just a few yards away from here in the rest lounge. If you could see the contented expression on her face . . . It would be cruel to wake her . . . and even more cruel to wake her with such alarming news.'

'Would you mind if I came over? I mean . . . could I tell her?'

'Not today, I'm afraid. We keep to set visiting times for non-relatives. From two to three in the afternoon on Tuesdays and

15

Fridays. No, not on Sundays, this home and all in it are the Lord's freehold on that day.'

'The Lord's freehold?'

'We are in His Fellowship on that day, I am afraid there are no leases. Yes, yes, I'll see that she is told – as I have said before – all in good time, all in good time. I won't waken her now. Thank you for calling, Mrs Haycock – er, I'm sorry . . . Mrs Read. Thank you. Goodbye.'

Silly cow – the Lord's freehold. If this place were His freehold He'd become an atheist. I'm not asleep, I'm just sitting here in this lukewarm lounge with my eyes closed. The other two old women are watching the television. It's a video-tape of some earnest-looking woman dressed as though she were a cowboy singing religious songs. At the moment, she is half-way through cherishing the old rugged cross, her voice is adenoidal and her delivery is rampantly insincere. They've trundled me in here to persecute me with this and yet the cow wouldn't let Janet Haycock come over to see me. Lord's freehold? Lord's prison more like.

So . . . so . . . Kay Roper is dead. Dear Kay . . . gone from us . . . gone from me. But I've always felt that people are around you for as long as you choose to remember them. There's no fear that I could ever forget Kay Roper. Thankfully, the thought of her transports me out of this present aged, dependent, arthritic state I'm now in. If you have a mind and memory, then imprisonment is impossible.

I'm travelling. Fools would say that my mind was rambling, but my journey is direct and uncluttered. There is a sharp rapping on my door, nothing timid about the knock. I know it is my new teacher, so desperately needed – a pianist, and properly qualified – new to the area. I arrange my desk as befits the status of a head-teacher and sit behind it. I have to convey to her that it is a privilege for her to be working for me – that she needs me more than I need her. Dear God, I do need her. We are so short of good teaching skills here, my poor girls . . . There is so little for . . .

'Come in. Come in.' I stand as she enters and try to stop

16

showing my surprise. Or was it concern? I thrust my hand forward. 'Miss Roper?' She nods and takes my hand. I release the hold first. 'Do sit down, Miss Roper.' This is an order and a request. I have already seated myself before she is settled. I need time to study her. Her appearance and demeanour fill me with the same worries as gas-masks or air-raid warnings. I am insecure but feel thrilled; externally, I remain calm. 'Would you like to tell me a little about yourself, Miss Roper? You are from the north, I believe – although I denote no accent. No give-away burr in your voice that might indicate a specific region.'

'I decided to discard it from my fifteenth or sixteenth year – my accent, I mean, not my birthplace. You would know the last piece of information from my application form. I thought that I had filled in the sections on special skills and teaching aptitudes with some degree of care. I believe I included the section on "other interests" with equal attention.'

'I was thinking of human details, Miss Roper.'

'With respect, Mrs Chaplin – I think you mean personal details.'

Whatever else Kay Roper was offering at our first meeting, it was clear that she felt no respect for my status, and if I sat on it, she would kick me off it. I had now appraised her appearance and come to terms with the fact that she did not look like a teacher. Not in any shape or form. For some odd reason I was reminded of flamingoes, so bright, so colourful and somehow slightly ill at ease. (When this wretched war is over and we can open and let light shine out, I hope that zoos remain closed. They are no place for flamingoes to flourish.) Can this woman flourish here? Ought I to attempt to modify her brightness?

'Yes, I probably do mean personal details, Miss Roper. Perhaps I could help if there were some difficulties on a domestic level? I mean with regard to accommodation and . . .

'No, no, thank you, it is most kind of you to think of it, most kind. I am already well settled. My father arrived here shortly before me. He has bought a terraced house in Padmore. It is one of three.'

'Does your mother like it?'

'I like it, Mrs Chaplin. My mother is dead.'

17

'I'm sorry. Most of the houses in the outlying villages are colliery-owned – Padmore is no exception. Has your mother been gone for . . .?'

'Dead long? Yes, she died when I was fifteen – round about the time I decided to discard all trace of accent. I assume that most of the girls here are from mining backgrounds?'

'Oh yes, eighty per cent. Perhaps more.'

'It is good then that my father and I live amongst them. I don't think that one can divide cultural and educational needs, do you?'

'I'm er . . . I don't think that I have had time to dwell on that issue very much, Miss Roper – very remiss of me. Before I go through your timetable and show you your classroom, I'm afraid I do have to make some personal observations. I beg of you, please, please, do not think . . .'

I watched the muscles twitch about her neck and jaw, felt her tension – yes, tension, not anger. She interrupted me. She raised her hand and I caught a flash of blood-red nail varnish before she let it rest in her lap.

'I believe that you are about to make some observations about my appearance. Before you do, Mrs Chaplin, I must state that I cannot – will not shed a single trace of my style.'

Miss Roper's 'style' was irreconcilable with the image of any fellow colleagues in those harsh, uniform times. Admittedly, some teachers wore face powder and a trace of lipstick, but Miss Roper's face had been created entirely by herself. She must have spent hours painting it on; it always seemed more suitable for stage lighting than daylight.

'Please, please, do not take offence.' My voice must have registered some degree of beseeching because Kay answered my plea without any trace of rancour.

'Mrs Chaplin, I understand your position. You are not in any personal sense responsible for the social climate which seems to dictate that all should dress in as drab a manner as possible. I could not exist in such clothing. Indeed, I would prefer to tour the streets in a fringe of leaves . . . or even go naked in the world.'

'I'm sure that will not be necessary, Miss Roper. Your clothing is . . . er, unusual and . . . er, somewhat vivid for these parts, but I would not ask you to change it for our sake. There are some accessories however . . .'

She smiled and nodded knowingly. Oh, that sad smile . . . that look of deadening pitiful defiance.

'You mean these?' She flicked one of her long ear-rings with a forefinger so that it swung to and fro. Then she shook her head. 'They are as much a part of me, Mrs Chaplin, as the wedding-ring on your finger is a part of you. Your wedding-ring declares your married state and these ear-rings fluttering free about my face remind me that I am single and unbonded. Quite simply, I cannot be without them.'

'Ear-rings are banned in this school, Miss Roper, just as they are in other schools, not on grounds of aesthetics, but of safety. You must know, Miss Roper, that the gentler sex can be just as boisterous in play as boys are – there have been cases of girls losing their ear-lobes, something that I would not like to happen to any of our girls here.'

'Do let me point out that I am not a pupil here, Mrs Chaplin. I am sure you will agree that it is right and proper that distances and differences exist between teacher and pupil and I do assure you that there is no question of my entering boisterous games either with pupils or with fellow members of staff.'

She turned her gaze from me and looked at a huge vase of flowers which I had placed on top of a filing cabinet near the right-hand side of my desk. 'Ah, bluebells, bluebells, oh . . . how delightful . . .' Her voice seemed to trail and eventually fade away with a pensive mood that suggested our previous conversation had been beneath our intellect.

'Yes, they have such a lovely, distinctive scent too,' I observed.

'Oh, I'm so glad that you like perfume, Mrs Chaplin. I'm never without it.'

'I prefer it on flowers, Miss Roper.' I said this emptily with a defeated expression – and then looked helplessly into her eyes, and we both laughed and laughed and laughed.

Eventually, I managed to say, 'We need you here, Miss Roper – we need you.'

'I am here to work hard for you, Mrs Chaplin. I shall do my

utmost never to be absent, never to be late, and – to use a somewhat new cinematic expression – you will not regret making allowances for my glorious Technicolor.'

I always wondered if Kay might use less make-up with the passage of time, but the coloured layers were always there – even after she left us. Oh hell, I hope they've left it on her, she would want to be buried with it or burnt with it, or whatever they choose to do with the body. Such redundant things, dead bodies . . . Ah good, they've taken the other two old girls out . . . Wash them . . . feed them . . . toilet them . . . stifle them. Keep my eyes closed and they'll leave me alone. There, they've gone, so has the old rugged cross. Now it is well-dressed carollers who look as though they have just come from a Rotary Club meeting. I don't mind this so much – all these mouths opening and shutting like great draw-bridges. I can see the fillings in that tenor's molars and I'll swear I can see his damned tonsils. Yes, they have gone. I can speak freely now. If they hear me above the television carols, they'll put it down to dementia.

I have started talking to myself. Not just transferring my thoughts into a silent language, most people do that. Oh no, I speak out loud as though I am speaking to a friend who is partially deaf.

'I must confess, I am more surprised with regard to your progress here. You know all the girls in your class so well, and your control over your pupils appears to be effortless. Most teachers here have very real problems keeping order – given the size of classes and our meagre resources, this doesn't surprise me. Yet, by the raising of your index finger, you manage to achieve both quietness and the attention of your girls. I really don't know how you do it – I'm full of admiration and, yes, gratitude.'

'I am happy here, Mrs Chaplin. I'm fond of the girls and enjoy my job. I am paid more than many of the hard-working miners here, and those poor Bevin Boys are paid a pittance for working

20

day and night. In all truth, you ought not to feel grateful towards me – I am merely doing my job as well as I can. Could there be other reasons for your waterfall of goodwill and kindness?'

I did not answer her. Professionally, I could not answer, but of course she was right – my gratitude was based not just in what she had done for the children, but in what she had done for me. I had been in the head-teacher position (Head-teacher? Such a terrible word. It sounds more suitable for a cannibal than an educator) – let's see – yes, I had been in the role for about eighteen months or so. One of the disappointed competing candidates for the position was my deputy, Mrs Pickett.

She had been sure of getting the position; she viewed it as an inheritance. 'I have given ten years of my life to this school.' My appointment grafted a degree of bitterness on to her nature and mind which seemed to colour many of her actions. I do believe that she enjoyed purveying fright and fear amongst our pupils in the line of her duties.

She held that she was responsible for the tone and discipline of the school. If girls had misbehaved they were sent to her for punishments or sanctions. Weak teachers relied on her – and word was put about that she 'ran' the school. Any ideas that I put forward she would cleverly belittle, so that my own self-esteem was low when Miss Roper arrived. Kay Roper recognized Elaine Pickett's qualities when they were formally introduced. In physical terms the two teachers could not have represented greater contrasts in womanhood. There was not a great deal of space in that staff room and when those two met it was as though the two of them took up all of it. The rest of us present might just as well not have been there.

Elaine Pickett was a short, broad-shouldered, stocky woman of forty-two. A large head rested on a neck which was barely existent. All her facial features were small – tiny pursed lips that formed a cupid's bow of lasting disapproval, beady green eyes, tightly permed auburn hair that sprang about her head and ears like coiled wire. She made no attempt to disguise her contempt for Kay as she gazed up into the deep blue eyes.

'Welcome, welcome, Miss Roper. I assume you are starting

21

tomorrow?' Mrs Pickett's eyes travelled down from Kay's eyes, past her beads, the breasts jutting from behind the pale lemon blouse, over her double-pleated floral skirt, the brightly sanded legs – they seemed to flicker with pain as the high-heeled shoes came into view. Then she raised her head quickly, smiled brightly and thrust her hand forward. 'I look forward to meeting you tomorrow, then.'

'In wartime, Mrs Pickett, we are constantly reminded that today is just as important as tomorrow. This is not a time for standing around. I am sure that you will be relieved to hear that I intend to commence working this morning.' Kay referred to her wrist-watch. 'In about twenty minutes from now I shall greet my class.' Kay looked down at Mrs Pickett, who was dressed in varying shades of brown. 'I believe my pupils have been in your charge pending my arrival. No doubt you will be relieved to attend to your other pressing duties.'

'I'm used to holding the fort, Miss Roper.'

Elaine Pickett's retort was sharp. The rest of us held our breath. I knew that Mrs Pickett was working up to a counter-attack; she was a mistress of studied insult. Pupils and staff members had been cowed and wounded by any number of them. She began to make loud sniffing noises as though she had detected a gas leak.

'You may not know that high-heeled shoes damage all our wooden floors here. Our educational authority does have a ruling on them.'

She sniffed and glared meaningfully at Kay's black, shiny, patent leather creations.

I have to admit that I knew of no such ruling with regard to fashionable footwear, but I kept silent. I think it has always been one of my faults. Diplomacy sometimes verges on delinquency.

'Sometimes, Mrs Chaplin,' Kay would say, 'sometimes we must piddle against the wind and suffer the consequences.'

I thought that Kay might cede to this first onslaught from Mrs Pickett – after all, they had only just met. But no, Kay did not display any anxiety or traces of humility, she just nodded and smiled.

Mrs Pickett gasped as Kay kicked off one shoe and then another. Kay stooped and picked up the shoes and held them aloft in one hand. Even without shoes, Kay still towered above her assailant. I noticed that Kay's feet were somewhat large by usual standards, but this had not stopped her painting her toe-nails a dazzling shade of pillar-box red.

Elaine Pickett viewed these coloured appendages with an expression of horror and dismay. Her voice rasped, quietly venomous. 'Surely, Miss Roper, you are not going to teach your class in bare feet? Parents will think that we have employed Dorothy Lamour.'

I can hear Kay's voice now – and still it brings a chuckle to this creaking frame I call my body. 'These are hard times, Mrs Pickett. Times when personal sacrifices need to be made for the common good. Times when ordinary conventions must be put to the test. Times when we must all question anew our outlook and our tastes. Do you have a flower garden, Mrs Pickett?'

'A flower garden?' Mrs Pickett had become somewhat deflated with exasperation but recovered. 'Of course, yes, I do have a presentable garden – but I really cannot see what this has . . .'

'Ah, pull them up. Make the sacrifice. Where your dahlias bloom, plant cabbages. Let Brussels sprouts grow in your lupin and delphinium beds. Cultivate potatoes around your rose-bushes. I seek to compensate for this absence of colour on our domestic landscape by carrying it about on my body.'

A few of the teachers had begun to giggle and titter as Kay defeated Elaine with patriotic strategy. For one sickening moment I thought that Elaine was going to strike her. Kay continued in an undaunted manner.

'I shall walk bare-foot through this building but replace my shoes to negotiate the playground. As you know, the floor of my teaching hut is of stone: a four-pound shell could not penetrate its solidity. Fortunately, I am light of foot so that I am assured my heels will make no impression.'

Kay turned to leave and Mrs Pickett snorted and sniffed like some hungry sow. Kay's scent – her 'Soir de Paris' – was all about us. Before she left the room she asked Mrs Pickett whether or not she suffered from asthma and said that if she did, she might try considering some exercises in breathing control.

Control! I wish that I had more control over these arthritic leg joints and knotted fingers. I'd get across this room like a shot and switch off that bloody television. Now, if you please, that adenoidal cow-girl religious tart from America is singing 'At the end of the day just kneel and pray . . .' If I could kneel, I'd pray to be able to get up off my knees. I do wish they would let me sit in the bay window. I think they like to keep us hidden as though we were all a frightful sight. If they would just draw back the curtains I could look out on to the street. More than half my life was spent without television – I long to look out on the street and see real people and create my own stories from what I see.

There is always a drama of one kind or another in a street. There is always something unfolding if you pick out the details.

'Miss Roper's floral skirt is so colourful, and what is more, it matches her downstairs curtains. So inventive. So original.'

I do believe they are intent on crushing us all here, those two evangelical maids who think they have a passport to heaven because they are caring for a few elderly women. Gentlewomen they call us – suits their book. I'm not a gentlewoman. I'm a . . . I'm a . . . I'm a common woman and I'm damned if I'll let them chloroform the life out of me with their know-all comfort through the Lord philosophy. Their Lord is not my Lord and they are well paid for caring. They couldn't abide Kay calling here to see me and I'm sure they are glad she is gone. No bully ever got the better of Kay no matter how subtly they were dressed. Subtly dressed?

'Did you know that Miss Roper is still bare-legged in the middle of winter? Look carefully at the seams on the backs of her legs and you will see that they are drawn on with a brown eyebrow pencil.'

I always wondered how Kay managed to do this. A contortionist could not have achieved such a convincing graphic hosiery unaided. She could hardly have asked her father to pencil them in, and as far as I knew, she never had any other close women friends. Nor was she involved in any romance.

24

In the first few months people did speculate that courtship would soon come her way on account of her vivid and colourful appearance and friendly personality. If she did receive offers they must have been swiftly rejected: to my knowledge she never had a beau. Up until the war I suppose most women were expected to be subservient to men. I can't imagine Kay being subservient to anybody. 'I never give in to bullies, Mrs Chaplin. If you give in to a bully you are lost. Bullies need power – that is what this war is about, it is about a power-crazed bully. They tend to call themselves leaders. On a smaller scale, in a less advertised arena, I must tell you that I am not afraid of Mrs Pickett.'

It didn't take Kay much longer than six months to relieve Mrs Pickett of her power. Ah, dear Kay – she did not retain the power for herself, she passed it on to me. In the first few months she outwitted Mrs Pickett by making her coarse attacks look absurd. Mrs Pickett often exuded a broad smile when she addressed Kay.

'A little bird has told me that you are quite a picture-goer, Miss Roper – at least twice a week, I'm told. I marvel that there is sufficient choice available to meet the high artistic standards that you set yourself. For my own part, I cannot see any charm in Errol Flynn or Hopalong Cassidy.'

'Not surprising, Mrs Pickett. You have never sailed on a pirate ship or ridden a horse.'

'Have you? Have you done either of those things, Miss Roper?'

'No, no, no. I have only travelled in such a manner in my imaginings.'

'These are hardly the times to let ourselves be ruled by fancy, Miss Roper.' (Again, that horrible smile.)

'My reasons for visiting the cinema go well beyond the film stars – or even beyond the content of the film.'

'Miss Roper, surely you do not go to the cinema for the social intercourse? I must tell you that some of the worst elements of the town . . .'

'I go to the cinema for my research, Mrs Pickett.'

'Research?' Mrs Pickett grinned and sniffed triumph.

'I am writing a book. It is called *The Flashing Smile: a history of dentures in the cinema from 1933 to the present day.*'

Mrs Pickett's jaw hung in suspended disbelief for a few moments then clattered shut. Two of the teachers present stopped their knitting and began to laugh and Mrs Pickett left the staff room, her face flushed beetroot scarlet with shame and anger.

I wondered how long it would be before Mrs Pickett launched a counter-offensive. There seemed to be a lull in the military manoeuvres, both protagonists appearing to be invisible to one another. Then, on a very cold day in early October, Mrs Pickett made a strike that Van Runstedt could not have bettered.

'There!' Mrs Pickett heaved a sigh of satisfaction as she entered the staff room. She wafted the cane about the air as though it were some gorgeous fan before hanging it behind the book-shelf. 'Those girls will not complain about cold hands any more. I have given them something that will soon warm them up.'

'What girls are they, Mrs Pickett?' I could not keep the trace of dismay and concern out of my voice.

'Janet Haycock and Linda Miller. I believe they are in your class, Miss Roper.'

'They are in my class, Mrs Pickett. Both are excellent pupils. What crime – it must be a crime – what terrible thing have they done?'

'They have disobeyed rules and I have made an example of them.'

'Er . . . er . . . What have they been . . .' I faltered weakly.

'I was returning from carrying out my usual duty of patrolling the inside of the school during lunch break and I must say that I was pleased to find all the rooms clear of girls. Vigilance has its rewards. On passing the wash-room, I noticed that the door was open and I distinctly remembered closing that door when I began my rounds.'

'How perceptive of you,' Miss Roper observed flatly.

'I stood and scanned the cloakroom. I stood quite still – and my ears soon detected breathing sounds. The culprits were sitting – no, hiding – behind the door. Apparently, they had been in there reading throughout the lunch-time. It wasn't just a case of breaking rules, but a case of sly attitudes and deceit. I caned them both, one stroke on each hand – and I made sure to punish them in the hall so that other girls could witness it from outside.'

Miss Roper got up from her chair and left the staff room quietly. She seemed to be unaffected by Mrs Pickett's version of the events. Mrs Pickett settled herself into the chair that Miss Roper had vacated and began to tell us the details of the forthcoming Harvest Festival that she was organizing for her church. Before she had completed a bit about the artistic merits of vegetable decoration, Miss Roper returned.

She stood in the middle of the staff room, not more than two yards from Mrs Pickett, and patted the bun on top of her head. She spoke above Mrs Pickett in a loud, forceful voice that bore no trace of hysteria.

'I have just inspected four hands. Each hand not yet fully grown to womanly maturity – not yet worn and calloused by hard work and household drudgery. Four hands that look in worse shape than those of their working mothers. The hands are grossly swollen, purple and scarlet bruises cause the skin to blush in pain.'

'It is transient, Miss Roper. Physical punishment is transient – a short, sharp shock. What is good for boys is good enough for girls – you have said as much yourself on several occasions. Nobody has ever said to me that caning did any harm.' Mrs Pickett spoke out lightly as though the event had taken place a decade ago.

'Caning is good for neither boys nor girls. It is a psychopathic action.' Kay submitted this view as though it were evidential fact.

'A psycho – what?' Mrs Pickett giggled.

'A psychopath, Mrs Pickett. A psychopath is someone who can injure someone else and not feel any sense of remorse or guilt.'

'Surely, Miss Roper, you do not believe that by doing my duty I have not hurt myself more than those girls?'

For an answer Kay reached behind the book-shelf and took out the cane. I held my breath as she held it high above her head. Was she going to strike Mrs Pickett? Kay then moved swiftly, showing a physical strength which surprised all of us.

She snapped the cane into four or five small pieces, using only the strength of her wrists. This done, she handed the cane handle to Mrs Pickett. Mrs Pickett glared at the object. What had once represented extreme power had now become something ludicrous.

'I know that you are a great admirer of Miss Bette Davis, Miss Roper, but such cheap histrionics ought not to be displayed in a school. Worse still, your conduct is unprofessional.'

Mrs Pickett cast the cane handle toward the waste-paper basket and glanced about her, bringing in the other teachers as witnesses to this fact. She behaved as if I did not exist – this, at least, was not unusual.

'It will be my duty to see that this matter is taken higher. I intend to report you to the educational authority.'

She asked one of the teachers to pass her a copy of the *News Chronicle*, signifying that the matter was over. Here, she was mistaken.

'I shall welcome such action. You may report me to George VI for all I care. I would remind you, Mrs Pickett, that this is still a democratic country – I will have my say in matters that concern the welfare of my pupils, and will take full account of my actions taken on their behalf. Furthermore, if you ever cane a girl in my class again, I can assure you that there will be two charges to be met in our local magistrates' court.'

'Two charges?' I enquired weakly.

'Yes, two, Mrs Chaplin. I shall be bringing a charge of assault against Mrs Pickett – acting on behalf of parents – and no doubt Mrs Pickett will be bringing a similar one against me with regard to her own person.'

Kay then looked up at the staff-room clock, which seemed to be ticking louder than usual during the ensuing silence.

'I'm going to collect my girls. Lessons should have started five minutes ago. I don't want them braving this cold any longer. There are more than a few families in my class who cannot afford to have a sick child lingering at home.'

As Kay left the staff room the other teachers followed her with more speed than was usual. This was a small gesture of rebellion: nobody ever left before Mrs Pickett as a rule. I was left sitting opposite my deputy, whom I still feared. Then I seemed to act out of character. I leaned forward and retrieved the cane handle and gathered up the other broken pieces.

'Well?' Mrs Pickett's one-word question asked so many things.

I remember looking at her as I might have looked at someone who had pushed in front of me in the fish queue.

'There will be no more caning in this school, not whilst I am headmistress. I regard the matter as closed.'

She opened her mouth as if to speak and then closed it.

'Mrs Jennings has to visit the doctor this afternoon. She believes she is pregnant – I did mention it to you. I am sure that you won't want to keep her class waiting, Mrs Pickett.'

I watched her plod away from me. I was no longer afraid of her, and from that moment I was not just a head-teacher in status and salary. I had also become one in practice.

I want to go to the toilet and now this choir on television are singing 'O Come all ye Faithful' as though they have plums stuck in the back of their throats. It's going to take me at least five minutes to get to the lavatory; each step feels as though I am treading on broken glass. They do such a tut-tut-tut here if you make a mistake. I hope I'll get there in time.

When Kay used to visit me here she would always accompany me to the lavatory. That sort of thing never worried her – and on my worst days she'd even wipe my bottom for me. We had a good laugh in there only last week. Kay couldn't find the toilet paper and I pointed to this crinoline-skirted doll. Kay looked puzzled. I'm sure she only picked it up to humour me – she gasped when she saw that the roll was secreted up the doll's skirt.

'Do you think this is historically authentic, Ivy dearest? It must have been uncomfortable for them if they carried it around with them like this.' She laughed somewhat gruffly but cleared me up unfussily, carefully, tenderly.

Dear Kay, dear Kay, you must stay about me – stay with me. If all else goes I still need my memories. I think I'll make it . . . I think I'll get there in time . . . I won't let my own body humiliate me . . . I'll get there.

3

My daughter Louise, my son-in-law, and my granddaughter Rachel are all sitting in the lounge. It being Christmas Eve, there is a choice of films. They are watching *The Sound of Music*. We took a vote, as I wanted to see *The Wizard of Oz*. The result was three to one against my choice so I'm retired to the kitchen to clear up the wreckage of our finished meal. It saddens me to see so much food left over and I'm wrapping bits and pieces in foil paper and storing them in the refrigerator. I don't think my actions are based in prudence but – but in what is now historical background. My generation were reared on 'Waste Not, Want Not'.

Nobody seemed to take umbrage about the denuded decorations. I told them all about Miss Roper. They murmured empty-sounding sympathy, 'Oh dear', 'How sad', 'What a shame', but not much more.

My granddaughter is attending university, studying for a degree in economics. I was quite close to her when she was a little girl, but this last decade has distanced me not just in years, but in feelings. ('There's nothing wrong in debt, Nan. All good businesses thrive on it, it doesn't mean that you are making a loss. I rather like it without the paper chains and streamers, this holly gives the room a chic appeal. Minimalism in furnishing is coming back. Why not get rid of that sideboard? I'd like to be able to boast a trendy granny.')

My family, such as it is, seems incapable of entering any distress that does not apply directly to them. We ate the roast pork, roast potatoes and parsnips, greens . . . and discussed their worlds. My world – outside the meal set before them – was redundant. Tomorrow, I eat with them in their home. Christmas has now become an exercise in family virtue which I dislike. I have trained myself to have no expectations beyond the meal itself. There is nothing beyond the preparation and eating of food except disappointment.

Hardly anyone has touched the apple sauce. Perhaps I can use it for a pie-filling or have it with some rice pudding. My friend Linda Miller loves apple pie – mmm, I love the smell of apples.

I'm back with Miss Roper again: it's no effort to return to her and the recall is not in any way blurred. I suppose the rationing of food placed an extra value upon it. Miss Roper brought a creative presence to polite forms of scavenging.

Our village then consisted of five or six long terraces of houses that were built near the Number Five pit by the coal owners in the late 1890s. The doors opened right out on to the pavement and individuality was restricted to which house had the cleanest front doorstep. The front door was never – or hardly ever – used for entrance so that life, as neighbours know it, all took place in the back-yards.

Miss Roper and her father had taken one of three houses that stood alone in a cul-de-sac near the edge of the village. The cul-de-sac was untarmacked and had no street name – a sign near its entrance read 'Unadopted'. No other teacher had been known to live amongst mining families in this way – and all our mothers adored her because she was different. They nicknamed her King-fisher on account of her multi-coloured complexion and bright clothing. (Yes, there is enough apple sauce here to make a pie.)

'I wonder if you would kindly let Janet accompany me on an errand this afternoon, Mrs Haycock? I am taking one or two girls to visit the vicar.'

'The vicar? I never knew you were a church-goer, Miss Roper. I'd have expected you to be chapel if anything. The singing is so much better in a chapel – although church or chapel doesn't interest me or my husband over-much.'

'Ah, no, Mrs Haycock, it has nothing to do with services or

attendance. I can praise God in your back garden more easily than I could in one of those buildings. No, I am leading a small deputation to the minister on behalf of my girls.'

My mother didn't ask what the deputation was about, she just nodded to me and I put my coat on. Miss Roper always got this unquestioning support from the working women of the village. She was a trusted friend in times of trouble or distress; her outward appearance did not lessen their trust in her. She was an independent mascot of understanding as far as they were concerned.

The vicarage was the only house of substance in the village. It must have contained at least six bedrooms and was set in large grounds. The Reverend Jenks opened the door after repeated knockings from Miss Roper. He looked at her and at us as if our presence had alarmed him.

'Oh, I expect you have come to call on my wife. She's not at home, I'm afraid, but I can tell you that the WVS meeting is cancelled for this afternoon – in any event, I fear there is no surplus clothing left. Such a cold day for October, don't you think?' He made as if to close the door, but Miss Roper answered his question rapidly and then quickly posed one for him.

'I don't feel the cold and these girls of my class are well clad. It was you I wanted to speak with, Reverend – just a few words?'

'Ahem, ahem, I am very busy at the moment. There is . . .' The Reverend Jenks always seemed uncomfortable in the presence of the opposite sex. I often wondered how he had managed to organize his marriage, as the feminine gender was regarded by him as something quite alien – you would never have thought that a woman could have produced him.

'I will only keep you a few minutes, Reverend. No – the matter will take seconds. It is about a surplus that I wish to speak. Not a surplus of clothes, but a surplus of apples.'

'Apples, Miss Roper?' The Reverend Jenks' eyes widened in surprise as if he were referring to some exotic, foreign fruit.

'Oh Reverend, I don't wish to take a forbidden fruit, I won't play Eve to your Adam. I promise you we will pick nothing from your trees – not even a leaf. If we could just remove the windfalls from the ground . . . Could we?'

'Well, er . . . my wife does like to watch the tits feeding.' One of the girls began to giggle at his choice of words, but Miss Roper froze the humour from her with a studied glare.

'We will only take what we can carry, Reverend.' Miss Roper saw no shame in pleading. 'I give you my word there will be plenty left over for the blue, great, tom and coal . . . these are all varieties of tits, girls.'

'Oh, very well. See that you are not there for too long. It's not something I want to encourage for the future – I don't want to set a pattern.'

He closed the door very quickly – in just the same way as some seaside landladies had closed doors on small evacuee children from our village.

Miss Roper beckoned us after her. 'Follow me, girls, this way – follow me. No doubt somewhere you might have heard the story of the miracle of the loaves and fishes. I wonder if the Reverend Jenks knows it?' She made a derogatory grunting noise after she had spoken his name. 'We have a much smaller task ahead. We do not have five thousand to feed – only forty, or just over. It will not take a miracle to achieve our goal . . . just a little application. Quickly, girls, quickly.'

She led us through the large orchard of apple trees. Their boughs, heavily laden with fruit, seemed to groan under the weight. Some of the apples touched the ground but remained attached to the tree – so great was the yield of fruit. One of the girls nudged me with her elbow and nodded towards Miss Roper's progress. She seemed to be having some problems in walking and her posture and balance looked awry. This was most unusual for her.

'Last night, girls, I saw Claudette Colbert, a fine actress – beautiful eyes, perfect bone structure – but her posture? Hunched shoulders, arms and hands that look as though they are about to take flight and the gait of an injured duck out of water.'

We all wondered if Miss Roper was being imitative – she was walking in an extremely odd way. Her bizarre progress came to a halt when we were well out of sight of the vicarage. I couldn't see how we were going to carry forty apples or more between us, but did not have the heart to torpedo Miss Roper's heart with doubt.

'Now, girls, avoid any apples that are bruised or blemished – and if you should accidentally knock any apples off the trees as you are gleaning the windfalls, do not hesitate to add them to our crop. Before we begin, I have a private matter to attend to ... Would you all turn south? That's it, girls – look in the direction of the steeple, concentrate on the cock, keep your gaze steadfast until I give you the all-clear.'

Miss Roper had positioned herself behind some sparse foliage as she spoke. We all faced the steeple and burned with curiosity. Was Miss Roper going to piddle in the vicar's orchard?

For some reason, I could not believe that someone as adorable as Miss Roper was capable of bodily functions, at least not the ones that some people might think vulgar. If I turned very quickly the other girls would not notice and, in terms of esteem, no other girl in our class – not even in the whole school – could lay claim to having seen Miss Roper's bare bum.

I turned, half expecting to be treated like Lot's wife. In those few seconds ... I did not glimpse Miss Roper's behind. She was not crouching low, but standing upright. She held her skirt up with one hand to reveal not pink cami-knickers, but sensible bottle-green directoires which were elasticated just above the knee. Her legs gave her the look of a heron: they were long but somehow ungainly. With her other hand she was pulling and tugging at something quite bulky which seemed to be stored in her drawers. I heard a faint sigh of relief as she brought forth a large potato-sack and began to shake it. Before she had straightened her skirt my eyes were fixed on the weather vane perched on top of the steeple.

Well, we staggered from the orchard about an hour later with a sackful of apples. They must have weighed a hundredweight. Miss Roper took the front of the bag and we girls took an end each. From time to time we would pause for rest on our way to our classroom. I was very surprised at the strength that Miss Roper managed to summon – it must have been sheer doggedness on all our parts that eventually got the fruit to its base.

'No, we will leave them at the front of the class, girls. Here, next to my desk. They are the basis of our history lesson next Monday afternoon.'

She sat at her desk and inhaled deeply in order to recover her breath pattern. The other girls excused themselves, she thanked them and asked them to pass on her greetings to their mothers.

Using the excuse of removing a pebble from my shoe, I lingered for a while. It was a rare opportunity of being alone with Miss Roper. I watched her examine her face in the powder-compact mirror; she dabbed at sweat bubbles (which had erupted on her nose and brow) with her powder-puff. It was impossible to guess what her complexion was like – I mean the real colour of her skin. I don't think anyone had ever seen it and, as we all remarked not unkindly, she laid her make-up on her face as though she were using a trowel.

After she had emphasized her eyebrows with two Rita Hayworth fine arc line drawings, she placed the pencil back in her purse and spoke to me as the catch clicked shut.

'I would not have guessed that it would be you, Janet. Such a small, worthless deceit. I would not have guessed that it would be you who would turn your gaze. Such a tiny betrayal of trust in order to satisfy your curiosity. Was it worth it?'

She had seen me, then. I felt so ashamed, I couldn't look her in the face. I began a babbling apology. 'I'm sorry, Miss Roper . . . really, I am . . . I know I let you down . . . I won't let you . . .' I began to cry – to sob in unforced contrition.

'Janet. Janet, my dear.' I can feel her hand on my shoulder now. 'There, there, there, there, shush your crying. Curiosity rarely kills a kitten – indeed, a kitten cannot grow without it. You are an intelligent girl. Intelligence should be used for questioning – particularly it should question isolated orders.'

I soon stopped crying; this immediate forgiveness was bliss to me. What's more, I had collected individual attention and praise – both rare commodities in my childhood. But if I had questioned Miss Roper's request what would I have said? And what could she have answered? ('No, I am not going to the toilet, I am retrieving a potato-sack which I have secreted in my drawers.') Poor Miss Roper, she must have itched violently.

'Off you go now, dear,' she commanded gently. I had almost reached the door when – 'Janet, Janet, dear', she called out as though the classroom were full of girls. I turned about only too keen to give her my whole attention. 'Why do you have that Dinkie-grip half-way down your face? It anchors your hair and causes it to cover half your brow. Why do you do it?'

I glared at her. She was well aware of my birth-mark – she herself had checked girls for making unkind remarks about it. My mother referred to it as my raspberry, my father called it a drop of spilled port wine. My only way of coping with it was to pretend it did not exist. Pretend it was not there – if I hid it with my hair then . . .

'Push your hair back, Janet – away from your face.'

I obeyed her as though it were all part of some bad dream – in a slow deliberate movement I exposed the scarlet insignia to her scrutiny.

She laughed lightly. 'My dear, how wonderful, how perfect. It is an exact replica of the map of India. Come closer.' I shuffled forward. 'Why, it's not more than an inch long – how decorative it looks etched there on your brow. Such a lovely brow, and those dark brown eyes – really, you are a very beautiful girl. A pity to hide such a face. If I had a distinctive mark like that, I would treat it as though it were a ruby brooch. I would wear it on some days, but not every day.'

She motioned me to bend forward. She took some pan-stick from her bag and rubbed some on my brow, then dabbed it with face powder. 'Look.' She held up her compact mirror for me – the mark was no longer visible. She smiled. 'Now, Janet, are you wearing the map of India today or discarding it?'

I clipped my hair firmly away from my brow. Miss Roper had made me feel beautiful and nobody had ever done that before. 'I'll leave it off for now, but wear it tomorrow.'

'There are times, Janet – there are times – when a declaration is the first step towards liberty.'

Not knowing what she meant by this, I just smiled and bade her good afternoon.

I do think my granddaughter might have told me she had gone vegetarian before I put the pork on her plate – just pushing it away to the side of her plate as though I were trying to poison her ... And what a waste. Fancy feeding a cat on roast pork. It's odd, so odd, all those years ago when meat was a once or twice-weekly luxury, I can't remember knowing a single vegetarian. I wonder if any of those five people on our history course were vegetarians? Miss Roper would have known such a detail had it existed. 'People To Remember' – that phrase summed up our history syllabus for a whole term. And which people were left imprinted on our minds? Not Lord Nelson, not Oliver Cromwell, not Sir Francis Drake, not ...

'Today, girls, I was to begin to tell you something of the life of Lord Nelson. In my notes here, it says he was a man of great courage. I would not argue with that – but history often edits a personality. Lord Nelson did cheat on his wife.

'Before I begin on Nelson's life, I'm going to describe someone else's life. Someone that you may even recognize. Someone who is alive – someone who is creating history – someone who is very brave indeed. I see that there are no women recommended to our memories on this syllabus. I shall have a word with Mrs Chaplin about that – such an omission prompts me to worry over our future roles in a free world. It is a woman that I am going to speak to you of now.'

Miss Roper surprised us by tying a headscarf around her head. On no other occasion had we ever seen her head covered. In a few deft movements she transformed the headscarf into a turban which enveloped her hair entirely. Her crowning glory was now covered with red and white polka dots.

Even nowadays, when we hear more regional voices on our radios, I'm still aware of the wide variety of accents that proliferate throughout the Midlands. Travel just ten miles north, south,

37

east or west from one town and it is as though you have distanced yourself from a whole culture.

We had never witnessed Miss Roper's imitative qualities before. There was no mimicry in her voice, yet we heard our tones, our modulation, our inflections – our parents' pronunciations. She had become one of us, our teacher had suddenly changed herself before our very eyes. Most of us felt very confused. What had all of this to do with history and people we should remember?

'When I wake up, I don't honestly know what time it is – and as I have the black-out curtains drawn I'm not even sure whether it is day or night. I never feel that I have slept long enough and once my eyes are open I keep them open because if I shut them I'd be in slumberland again. For the first few minutes I don't know whether I am on my arse or my elbows. It's not my work that bothers me, sometimes I think I'm happier at the factory than I am in my own home. I love earning. I mean earning for myself. Before this war there was never much paid work for women in this area. God knows, it was bad enough for our men – coal mines were never paved with gold for them that goes down them, nor their families.'

Here, Miss Roper paused and sat behind her desk and somehow managed to give her painted face that sad, weary, resigned expression that most of us had seen elsewhere. Then, instead of telling a story, she seemed to begin to deliver a message or speech. It might have been both. She wagged her right forefinger at all of us.

'I'll tell you all one thing, I'll tell you all one sure thing and that is that when this bloody war is over it will never be the same for us again. By that I mean me. I mean other women like me.' Miss Roper tapped her wedding-ring finger. 'Married or single we will not be put upon as we were before,' and then in gentler tones, 'but, oh God, it's not much of a life for the kids either. I leave this house at six of an evening. I'm picked up at Sankey's Corner by the factory bus – there's thirty-five other women on that bus and by the time we reach the factory gates in Darlaston there's no time for a cup of tea. We are all in our overalls and on that factory floor by a quarter past eight. And that's where we stay until half-past six the next morning. None of us talk much on the return home, there's so much noise from the machinery and it feels as though your brains have been blown out. Any noise is painful, even if it is the sound of your own voice.

'I get in the house by eight of a morning, get the kids ready for school – cups of tea and a bit of toast. As often as not they want to talk – tell me about what they have done at school or who is on at the pictures, complain about this and that and the other. I know I'm snappy with them – smack them too often – and feel sorry for it afterwards. Dear God, it's a relief when they've gone from under my feet. After they have left I have a bit of peace – a little time to myself is a luxury, I can tell you. I kick my shoes off by about nine in the morning and get myself down on the settee.

'I never remember going to sleep – it's as though once I've put my head down I've been hit on the crown with a hammer. I'm out. If my old man is on afternoon shift, this is how he finds me, my legs splayed out on the settee, the top of my overalls undone – and my teeth in a glass on the floor beside me. Not much romance in that.

'The kids are home just after four and I have to get their dinner ready before I'm off for work again. In this village alone, there are twenty or more women who live as I do – if you can call it living. On our factory shop floor there are a hundred and forty of us – and do you know? Do you know ... we have a man in charge of us. A foreman. Most of us women could do his job blindfolded – and him on three times our pay. We think things have to be better for our daughters. We can't love or care for them as we want to – we just hope they can understand why we lose our wick and get bad-tempered sometimes. It's not meant. I like to put a bit of lipstick on of a Sunday night – perhaps have a milk stout or two at the working men's club – working men?'

Miss Roper untied the knot of her turban, removed it slowly from her head and waved it in a reverential way as though it were a precious, silken flag, as though she were making some patriotic gesture. Then, with great care, she folded it and placed it on the desk before her.

She had this way of looking at all of us, her great blue eyes

39

scanning us all as we sat behind our desks. They spoke out as though she were uttering some prayer.

'Who am I, girls? Think carefully. Who am I? Raise your hand if you know who this very important person is. Without this person there would be no history lesson being held here today – and yet this person will not be recorded properly. Ah! A very good response. Very good indeed.'

Most of us had an arm raised and I think that everyone of us was hoping to be selected to provide the answer. I'm sure all of us were certain that we could give the correct reply. I noticed even the dullest girls in the class had their arms raised – on ordinary occasions these girls would only hold up their hands if they wanted to go to the lavatory.

'Now, girls, as there is such an excellent response to my question, I'm going to ask each of you in turn. I shall start at the back in the far corner. Tell me who you think this brave, noble person is – wait until I nod in your direction.' She began to nod.

'It's my mother, Miss Roper.'

'Do give us the full name, Pauline. State your mother's full name.'

'It's Dora Cartwright.'

'It's Ada Lena Statham, miss.'

'It's Esther Alice Bird – my mother, Miss Roper.'

'Sylvia Doreen Haycock of 37 Cecil Street – my mother.'

'It's Doris Jane Johnson – she's my mother.'

Miss Roper went all round the class. She did not miss one of us. When the exercise was complete she clapped her hands three times. This was usually one of her signs for asking for quiet but at this moment we were already quiet so that it was not a call for order.

'Girls, girls, I have to congratulate you all. Ten out of ten marks for the whole class. An excellent effort, cannot be bettered. Yes, girls, you have the answer – and remember your answer. Keep it locked in your hearts.' She picked up the history book from her desk and strode forward. She held the book high over her head so that her bracelets clattered downwards from her wrists.

'Your mothers, girls – your mothers do not fight single isolated battles at Trafalgar or the Nile. They fight a battle every day. They fight a battle on your behalf.' She lowered her head and spoke more quietly. 'And on mine.' She let her arm flop to her side, then turned and placed the book back on the desk.

'In later years, see to it that you tell your mothers' history because no one else will if you do not. If they are not recorded, that would be a great tragedy. Girls – how could we let your mothers know that we have been thinking about them this afternoon? Do any of you have any ideas or suggestions on this matter?'

These questions drew a complete blank from all of us. If any one of us had gone home and told our mother that she ought to be in a history book she would have thought we were lying or had become deranged. Miss Roper sat behind her desk and smiled – she didn't seem at all put out by our tepid response. I knew this was because she had one of her 'plans' or 'projects' with which she would inveigle us. Ensnare us. I was not entirely innocent with regard to her class management ploys.

'We will leave those questions for another day – I see we don't have a great deal of time left this afternoon. Oh dear, what do you think we should do with all these apples, girls?'

We were all hoping that we might eat them, but we knew now that this was not to be.

'I think we could place them in our church's Harvest Festival, Miss Roper.' Elsie Williams was of a pray-together stay-together bible-loving family who shook tambourines three times a week in a local chapel made of corrugated tin sheets.

'We could do that, Elsie . . . We could . . . It's a suggestion to dwell on for another time . . . not on this occasion.'

Obviously Miss Roper was not keen on the idea – neither were most of us – and she gave herself plenty of time for making up an excuse for rejecting it. I know I felt furious. I hadn't lugged all that fruit from the sanctity of one church for it to be placed in another one. Tambourines or not.

'This fruit is ready for eating and shouldn't be left lying about. The apples might easily bruise if they were tumbled over an altar. Time is short. I can see that I will have to help you all to come to

41

a decision. A plan has formulated in my mind but I shall need all your help to effect it successfully – it also has to be kept secret.

'It is very hard for over forty people to keep a secret – one careless word, one blabber-mouth could ruin everything. Careless words have been known to cost lives. Cup your hands behind your ears, girls: it will improve your natural hearing. I am going to speak very, very quietly in a loud whisper. I do not wish anyone outside this room to hear what I say. It's private information.'

Then, in hushed, confidential tones, we were drawn into her web of strategy and subterfuge. It was so exciting being special in this way – more delicious than the ripest, juiciest apple. Miss Roper made secrecy appetizing.

Early that evening Miss Roper led most of us out from the dark, narrow alley-way which ran down the side of the Star and Garter hotel and opened on to Sankey's Corner. This was the coach stop where all the mothers of our village were picked up for their evening's work. Miss Roper played Pied Piper just as the bus was pulling into the kerb.

On first sighting us, two of the women thought that there must be something wrong and called out in a nervous, querulous way.

'Nothing to worry over, nothing to worry over. Your daughters are just here for tonight, here to say goodnight to their mothers. Here to honour them.'

The bus driver leaned from his window to get a clearer view of things.

'We won't keep you for more than a few seconds, driver. I'm sure you will grant your beautiful passengers a little time.'

The man had probably never heard the word 'beautiful' applied to his cargo before – and we had never thought of our mothers in such terms. Yet Miss Roper meant what she said. I thought that some of the women might ridicule Miss Roper with all her 'airs and graces', but our mothers didn't see it that way. Miss Roper seemed to connect to parts of them which their harsh daily existence had repressed. They sat themselves on a low wall whose palings had been torn away to make shells or bombs or something to do with the war. They murmured just a few words to one another – and then they went quite still, quite silent, as Miss Roper began to place the apples into our hands.

'Give the fruit to your own mother, girls – or someone else's mother. Touch the hands and look into the eyes of these women and know that they are a bigger part of your history – and mine – than any of those names of the past that may flicker into our history books in school.' She spoke in a cool, level way so that none of it seemed declamatory.

My mother shook her head and kissed me – normally there was not much time for such tender statements between us. Some of the other women stroked their daughter's heads and whispered something to them and one mother called out, 'I'll not let you go, Peggy. I don't care how naughty you've been, I'll not let you be farmed out. It's not natural.'

'Shush . . . shush . . . Beryl . . . There'll be no evacuees from this village,' the other women affirmed.

As they climbed on to the coach, clutching the fruit, some of them called back to us and our teacher. 'Oh Roper, you are a case.' 'See that you do what Roper says.' 'Now straight home after you have said goodnight to Roper.'

We girls knew and Miss Roper knew that for our mothers to refer to one another by surname only was tantamount to declaring great friendship between women. Such a reference was only conferred after long-term and deep neighbourly trust and bonding. Our mothers pressed their faces to the window panes of the bus and waved to us as the coach drew away.

Miss Roper led us homewards, directing some girls down each side road as we trooped along the high road. There were just two of us left and we lived quite near to Miss Roper's house. She said goodnight to us at the top of our street. I delayed her with a question.

'Miss Roper . . . er . . . erm . . . do you really think that our mothers are beautiful?'

'Yes, I do.' The promptness and curt delivery of her reply was unexpected. 'Your mother's eyes, Janet – the eyes of your mother are larger and more appealing than the eyes of Jeanette Mac-Donald. And your mother's laugh, Irene, is more charming, more infectious than any confection of humour Judy Garland could offer. The women I have mentioned are stars of the screen.'

'Judy Garland is younger than my mother,' Irene innocently observed.

Miss Roper offered gentle correction. 'No, dear, they are of approximately the same age. One is made to look younger by work demands and one is made to look older – they both suffer for their occupations. Now, off you go – my father will be waiting for me and we have promised ourselves a visit to the cinema tonight.'

'What are you going to see, Miss Roper?' I sought to extract as much time with her as I possibly could.

'*The Hunchback of Notre Dame*.'

'Oh, oh, it's frightening, Miss Roper – there's a horrible-looking man in it who rings bells and . . .'

'There is a man who is disfigured, Janet. Disfigurement is not horrible – someone with perfect features could be horrible. Now off you go or I will miss the beginning of the picture show.'

Miss Roper's preoccupation with food did not end with apples and history lessons. She seemed intent on scavenging for anything that lived or grew within our environs. We picked wild damsons, blackberries and bilberries whilst they were in season and if someone's mother was ill, or if a father or child was not well, they would receive one of Miss Roper's 'protein' visits. I suspect her mode of entry was the same for every house.

'Ah, Mr Haycock, I'm sorry to disturb you at this hour. I see you are getting ready for work so I won't stay long. I hear Mrs Haycock is unwell?'

'Too true, Miss Roper – gone down like a skittle. The flu. She would insist on going to work when it started. Said it was only a bit of a cold – there is a stubborn side to her, you know. Now she's knocked down for six. Come in, come in. She's on the settee.' My father ushered Kay Roper through.

'I've brought you some fish, Mrs Haycock, it's most nourishing – just bake it in the oven. Janet, I'm sure you could do it.'

44

'But where have you got it from, Roper?' My mother spoke through coughs and snuffles. 'There's been no fish in the village or town for weeks – did your father bring it back with him?' My mother's question was peppered with sneezes.

Miss Roper had this way of motioning you with her hand, a kind of half-hearted beckon which seemed to indicate that you had a choice. Of course you didn't. I followed her into the kitchen. 'I'll just wash and fillet them, Janet.' Miss Roper placed the newspaper package near to the sink. 'If you watch me you can see how it is done. Do you have a sharp knife? The sharpest you have got.'

I watched her unwrap the package.

'There – don't they look appetizing?' She placed the three silvery fish on the draining board.

I remember studying them – their open eyes and open mouths looked as if they had just received some great electric shock. Or as if they had been horribly surprised or mortally astonished. It was at this moment that I recognized them – or recalled their species. I don't know why, but I attempted to ensnare Miss Roper. Force her to tell a lie.

'Did your father bring them back from the seaside, Miss Roper?'

'My father? The seaside?' She held the knife in her hand and seemed momentarily disconcerted by my queries. Startled even.

'The fish, Miss Roper – did your father bring them back with him?'

'Oh, no, oh no, dear. He has just returned from inspecting the lines at Crewe – no town could be much further from the sea than Crewe. It is at the heart of the rail network not at its perimeter. These fish did not come from the sea.' She looked at me as though she were aware of my minor intrigue. 'I believe you know the locale of this food, Janet.'

I nodded. 'They are roach, Miss Roper, they are freshwater fish. I have seen them before. I recognize them now.'

'Yes, caught early this morning by my neighbour, Mr Harper – apparently he landed them before it was barely light.' As she spoke I watched her sever the heads from the fish with clinical, determined precision. I wanted to look away when she slit their bellies and began a deft process of disembowelling. She placed them in a baking tray and added a little milk, a knob of margarine and some salt and pepper.

'Bake them for twenty-five to thirty minutes. The oven should be moderately hot, my dear. Serve them whenever your mother is ready for them.'

She had begun to wash her hands – I watched her pat them dry with a tea-towel. Then she took out some cream from her bag and massaged it into her hands. Out came the powder-compact, she inspected her face and dabbed a little powder on her nose. I have never known a woman who scrutinized her appearance more than Miss Roper. It must have been for her own pleasure and satisfaction as there was no man in her life.

'It is all ready for you, Mrs Haycock – all prepared. When you fancy it, Janet knows what to do. Now you must get plenty of rest, and do keep warm.'

Miss Roper had all but got to the door, but my mother's call delayed her.

'What kind of fish is it, Roper? I can't eat whiting – it disagrees with me for some reason.'

Miss Roper glanced back at my mother and smiled with the friendly type of condescension that adults often offer children. Then she gave one of her level gazes. Oh, that gaze said so much.

'No, it's not whiting, Mrs Haycock – it's . . . it's sea trout. A real delicacy.' She wagged her forefinger. 'And you are not to share it. We want you well. We want you well as quickly as possible. Don't we, Janet?'

'Yes, Miss Roper,' I replied and saw her to the door.

Not much less than an hour later my mother had eaten two of the fish and my father had polished off the other.

'Tasty. There were a lot of bones in it – but very tasty, I have to admit.' My mother gave her verdict.

'You heard what Roper said,' my father mildly rebuked her. 'It's a delicacy – sea trout is a delicacy. When will we be eating the like again? They've got to be rare – must cost a fortune – like eating gold dust.'

I couldn't dare tell him that this particular brand of gold dust swam about in the canals, the small rivers, and the pools of water left behind by derelict Jack-pits. They were as much a part of the place as we were – and as such, Miss Roper expected them to make their contribution to the general welfare. She was a woman of great sentiment but, as far as I could judge, she was not typically English in her regard for animals. Even humans she disliked she gave preference to over any other living creature.

No one was sentimental about rabbits, and wild rabbits had become scarce. They were hunted with nets, loop snares and red-eyed ferrets. It seems a miracle to me that they did not become extinct in our region. Without any doubt their numbers must have been seriously depleted.

Miss Roper declared that the eight rabbit hutches behind our day-room were kept there for our general science lessons – with special reference to biology and botany. She had organized a rota as to who was responsible for feeding, cleaning and pairing the animals.

'Girls, I must insist you do not give names to individual rabbits. I would prefer you not to get to know them in any special way. They are not pets. This does not mean that we should neglect them, far from it – remember the petting and spoiling of an animal could in itself be viewed as a type of neglect. These animals do not require human affection – only human care. With care, they will grow, breed and multiply.'

And that is what they did. We girls marvelled at the intensity of their love-making and their fecundity left us in no doubt about their fertility. Sadly they never had time to exhaust themselves. Few seemed to die of love – and yet the number never seemed to get out of control.

'The brown and white one with the pink eyes isn't here.'

'The buck – the big black one – seems to have escaped.'

'Floppy ears – the brown one with the white patches, it's gone.'

These comments or observations were muttered between ourselves but we knew very well that they hadn't just disappeared into a conjuror's hat. Nor had any of them escaped – those hutches were as fortified as Stafford jail. To this day rabbit stew holds no appeal for me.

One of the girls told us how she had seen Miss Roper grab a rabbit and lift it from the hutch: 'She was as cool as a cucumber, she stroked it first, calmed it down, and then she held it upside down by its back legs with one hand and then she used the side of her other hand as though it were a chopper. Thwack! Thwack! Thwack! Just three chops on the back of its neck and it was dead. She's so strong – Miss Roper's so strong.'

Roper's rabbits were known throughout the village. Vegetarianism was unknown and shortage of meat was not uncommon. Her method of increasing production was viewed with admiration – so much so that several households adopted it. Those that did not were often grateful recipients of our intensive farming. Miss Roper was not generally considered to be cruel or heartless in this matter – but brave.

4

'I'll just brush it a little at the back – lean forward a little, dear, would you? There that's better – you know, there are one or two little curls around the nape of your neck. We can't have you like anything but your best on Christmas Day, can we, Mrs Chaplin? Everyone should make an effort to look nice at Christmas time, don't you think?'

'No, I don't think. If I'd had a baby in a stable I'd have hardly looked nice with straw in my hair and cow-flop on the floor. I don't want to look nice. I'd like to look attractive, but I don't believe in miracles. Chocolate biscuits are nice – who wants to look like a chocolate biscuit?'

'Your daughter is calling in to see you this afternoon.'

'I'm not a Christmas tree – I don't respond to decoration – and a visit from my daughter is not a cause for jubilation. I do not like being the object of her dutiful nature. If the truth be told, we have come to dislike one another – it is a ridiculous assumption that we have to like people merely because we are related to them.'

'I'll hold a mirror up for you to see. There, doesn't that look better?'

'Lovely, dear. Yes, it looks lovely. Is Janet Haycock calling round today?'

'Did you want more than immediate family? It might be too much for you. I said I would let Mrs Haycock – er, Mrs Read, know if you could see her.'

'I want to see her – I want to see her very much indeed. I want to see her today. Charge your telephone call to my account.'

'Very well. You had better rest a little now. We don't want you exhausted and tired out before half-past six – we are having carols around the tree and you wouldn't want to miss the festivity, would you?'

'Are you telephoning Janet Haycock or do I have to dial 999?'

'As you wish, dear. What time do you want her to call? After lunch?'

'Yes, that will be excellent.'

I had better hide this tin of mince pies – Janet Haycock left them with me the last time she was here. I've only eaten one, and I won't touch another – I'll swear that pie settled down on my stomach like a depth-charge. Let's look in the mirror and see what that woman has done to me. Her presence is beginning to make me feel physically sick – her views, her grating voice, her cheap goody-goody outlook, her demeanour even, give me nausea. Brace myself . . . Let's look in the mirror.

I look at myself and the face I see doesn't seem to reflect me. There is some batty theory that you earn the face you end up with when you are old. I think it's nonsense. I don't believe I deserve – let alone have earned – the way that I look now. And that stupid bitch has made me look worse – brushing my hair up to hide my baldness. I look as though I've just had some mammoth-size electric shock, it's as though she had forced some high voltage up my arse. Plugged me in like an electric kettle. She's making a female Frankenstein's monster of me. I have to resort to this vulgarity in this place, it's the only way that I can organize my contempt for it. It keeps the rancour at bay – and rancour gives you real sickness of the mind. There are times when you have to let your feelings go . . . Now I'm smiling.' Let your feelings go' – I'm back with dear Kay once more. Let your feelings go.

It must have been some time in June. I know the day seemed unbearably hot, too hot to go outside – and inside, my room was stifling. I had left my study door open as the faintest whiff of fresh air seemed more important than privacy on that particular day.

The door remained open after morning assembly and I had

cause to leave it that way throughout the day. A great collective torpor seemed to have settled itself over the school. The heat affected us like some powerful tranquilizing drug, the girls and staff moved about slowly in listless fashion and there was little noise or trace of the usual hubbub connected with learning. These alien weather conditions had caused one of the girls to faint – the casualty was easily dealt with and a cure simply effected. The poor girl had on layers and layers of clothing – woollen vest, petticoat, blouse, jumper, cardigan, coat. I was surprised she hadn't expired completely. She had lain for an hour or so on the couch in my room and I had returned her to her class minus coat, jumper and cardigan. Her mother complained the next day that I had invited pneumonia into the family, and that she would hold me responsible if her daughter caught a chill.

Apart from all this, it was largely a day without incident, a day that we drifted through in a slow, deliberate, mechanical kind of way. Mrs Pickett proved to be an exception.

The heat seemed to agitate her metabolism and throughout the morning she behaved in a restless, forgetful, nervous way. She went from one task to another, never completing what she had intended to do. The poor woman looked flushed and fraught – she brought in bits of paper and placed them on my desk as though they were important missives yet they were only old stock receipts.

During lunch she barely ate anything. This was far from usual as Mrs Pickett's appetite could hold its own with a healthy working man. It wasn't until after lunch break was over that I recalled that Mrs Pickett's husband was home on leave from his RAF posting. This was the last day before he was to return to active duty. Perhaps this could be the reason for her hypertension? I wondered if she would be upset if I suggested that she went home. She was not the kind of woman who could easily share confidences with another woman. But then, nor for that matter was I.

The events of that afternoon caused me to regret my inaction. It was rare for teachers to visit the lavatory during teaching hours. I suppose one of the earliest things a teacher has to come to terms with is control of temper and control of bladder. Oh hell, I wouldn't even pass even those rudimentary requirements as I am now.

From my desk, the view into the corridor was unimpeded now that my door was ajar. The girls' cloakroom took up one side of the corridor and opposite were the stock room and staff toilet. I'll swear to it that Mrs Pickett went into that lavatory half a dozen times or more. She was in and out like a yo-yo.

After her third or fourth visit, I found myself feeling very sorry for her, as she seemed more distraught after each incarceration. I think that of all illnesses, diarrhoea must be about the most stressful for a teacher to contend with. If they are attempting to work throughout the illness (and most teachers did in my day), they have to give lying excuses to their class if they feel the needs of nature over-visiting them.

There are a limited number of excuses that can fool older girls on such occasions ... and my own gender can be unkind in delicate circumstances. For a teacher to have a bowel accident in the classroom ... Well ... I never knew it happen, but if it had done so, her status might have been irredeemably injured for years.

Before the afternoon session was over my pity for Mrs Pickett had turned into real worry. I became deeply concerned as I watched her fling her arms about in a wild abandoned kind of way. Also, I noticed that on two occasions she came out of the lavatory with her right hand clasped over her crotch. It also occurred to me that I could not hear the cistern flushing and I could only surmise that Mrs Pickett was neglecting to pull the chain after her. This was most unlike her, as her usual nature was fastidious to an irritating degree.

I was glad and relieved when the time came to ring the homebound bell. No one lingered about too much and I couldn't blame the teachers for handing in their keys earlier than usual. Some muttered that they would do their preparation at home, or come in early the next morning to get their rooms organized.

From the window I could see Kay Roper on the steps of her Nissen-hut classroom saying goodnight to her class. She always went through this ritual with her girls before they left her: she shook hands with each one and said something personal to every girl. One might have thought the girls might have become impatient by this lengthy farewell every night – but they never seemed to tire of it. In fact, if one or another had been engaged in an activity elsewhere, they would say, 'I have to go and say goodnight to Miss Roper, miss.' They said this in a quiet but boastful manner, as if it were something special for them. For them alone. Of course, it was. We all knew that Kay worked more diligently than any of us . . . We all knew that Kay got better results . . . And we all knew that Kay was highly individual and entirely without ambition. She received no jealous thoughts from her colleagues, rather the kind of respect that is given to actresses like Peggy Ashcroft and Edith Evans. Did those two women like one another?

I saw Kay wave to Janet – that child was always the last to leave. Stricken! Totally stricken in her worship of Kay. Kay dealt with this adoration in the same way she dealt with Christian belief: she pretended to be unaware of its existence no matter how many reminders she received.

There was a short piercing scream, followed by a thin whining noise – high-pitched, and somewhat unearthly. The reaction could have come from some wounded animal. It was not an animal that staggered through the entrance to my room – it was Mrs Pickett.

I moved quickly past her and shut the door before turning to face her. Although she was looking directly at me it didn't seem as if she were seeing me. From her open mouth came this horrible keening sound – then her hysteria seemed to break all boundaries and enter into madness.

She lifted up her skirt so that the edge of it reached the tip of her chin and stared out at nothing. One of her lisle stockings had been torn and was pulled down below the knee – her pink satin knickers did not appear to be stained in any way.

'Mrs Pickett, please – please try to calm yourself,' I attempted to remonstrate with her. 'Mrs Pickett, do sit down – sit down and tell me all about it. Please, my dear.' I cajoled and pleaded but got no coherent response. 'Mrs Pickett, lower you skirt.' I decided a firm approach might be of more use. 'Lower your skirt, Mrs Pickett, and sit down. Sit down now, I tell you.' This was an order.

It was not obeyed – far from it. There in broad daylight, with a bright afternoon sun still streaming through my study window, Mrs Pickett began to laugh and sob . . . and to my horror attempt to discard her knickers on my linoleum floor.

I restrained her as best I could, but soon realized that her flight into madness had given her extra strength. Just as I was intent on keeping her knickers on her, she seemed even more intent on getting them off. During the struggle, I noticed Kay Roper crossing the playground.

I called out to her, 'Kay, Kay, come to my room. Come at once. Hurry, hurry. I need help. Quickly, Kay, come quickly. Help me.'

Thinking back, this must have been the first time I had used her Christian name. I never addressed any other teacher in such an informal way – not ever again.

On entering the room Kay acted swiftly. She must have conjectured that Mrs Pickett and I were in the middle of some fearful quarrel that had deteriorated into a physical struggle. She went into action as though she had been trained in commando techniques rather than schoolteaching. In a matter of seconds, she had got behind Mrs Pickett and taken hold of her in a position that left the poor woman helpless. I believe the term is a wrestling reference – is it full-Nelson? Or half-Nelson? The hold was some kind of Nelson anyway – and it was most effective.

I immediately drew the curtains across the window as these events could hardly be expected to be shown on the silver screen let alone seen in a headmistress's study. Had they been witnessed I'm sure it could easily have ended Mrs Pickett's career. Mrs Pickett began to sob and, to my relief, utter a few words.

'Scrub this place . . . disinfect it . . . scrub this place clean. Scrub it with carbolic soap . . . Take them off me . . . take them off me.'

'Steady yourself – steady yourself, dear, then I can let you go. I don't want to hurt you – steady . . . steady.' Kay did not seem distressed in any way. She remained entirely unruffled apart from the bun on top of her head which seemed to have moved from its mooring.

'I got them from this place – not from my home. Never, never could I have brought them in – I got them from here. I shall sue. I got them from this building . . .' Mrs Pickett babbled on.

I was now quite convinced that Mrs Pickett had undergone some huge kind of mental breakdown. In her present state, it seemed that a committal would be inevitable. I decided it was best to take her ravings seriously.

'Got what, Mrs Pickett?' I asked. 'What have you got from us?'

'Insects!'

'Don't be silly – you are not yourself. Do lie down quietly until you feel better and I'll make you a nice cup of . . .'

She bawled out, 'I have insects. I have insects, I tell you. Take them off. Take them off me.'

She began to struggle again but Kay held her firmly. I suggested to Kay that it might be as well to telephone the police or the hospital – but Kay shook her head in dissent.

She spoke calmly to Mrs Pickett and talked to her as though she were addressing a rational human being.

'Where are they located, Mrs Pickett?' Kay asked.

'Located?' At last Mrs Pickett's voice bore some semblance of normality.

'The insects . . . In . . . er, in . . . er, in what region have they settled?'

Mrs Pickett began to cry steadily. Her head fell forward as though it were over-burdened with the weight of shame it carried, but she managed to quench the outflow of tears.

'At my front – in and around my knickers. That is where they are.'

She began crying again in a resigned, tragic way. I felt deeply sorry for her as I knew that mental affliction and pain could be more agonizing than physical.

'Lie on the couch, Mrs Pickett. Rest on the couch and we'll take them off. Just lie down for us.'

'Kay! Miss Roper – please. Do you think this is wise?' I asked.

Kay nodded. 'I think there may be every truth in what Mrs

Pickett has had to say. Now my dear,' she spoke to Mrs Pickett, 'are you going to lie quietly on the couch? Let us see if we can help you – I'm sure that we can.'

I watched as Kay released Mrs Pickett from her restraining hold and led her gently to the couch. Much to my astonishment she let herself be manoeuvred as though she were some docile bitch in a dog show. She lay prostrate on the couch and placed her hands at her side and stared intently up at the ceiling.

I felt the need for intervention when Kay lifted up her skirt and removed her shoes, but I remained transfixed by what was going on. I suppose I was fascinated by it all – or horrified – or both of these reactions. However, I could not repress a gasp of dismay and . . . 'Kay, do you think you should . . .' My voice seemed to leave me and I watched as Kay peeled off the pink knickers.

She held them between her thumb and forefinger and said, 'Such a pretty shade,' and then dropped them unceremoniously on to the rug.

She turned to me. 'My torch. My torch, it is in my handbag over there. Near your chair, that's it. Could you pass it to me?' She knelt down beside the couch as she spoke.

I had raised my eyebrows in a questioning manner but Kay ignored my silent enquiry and waited for me to do as I had been told. I passed the torch to her. She switched it on. I wanted to look away in a show of modesty but found myself riveted to what was being enacted before my eyes.

Kay switched on the torch and beamed its rays directly on the V-shaped mound of Mrs Pickett's pubic hairs. She peered at my deputy's most private parts, her eyes not more than an inch away from them. I felt tense and uncomfortable and could scarcely breathe. Mrs Pickett had stopped blubbering and the only sound coming from her was her breathing mechanism.

'Mmm . . . mmm . . . yes.' Kay spoke as though she were a doctor and continued to peer into the vaginal hair in a knowing professional way.

'Yes . . . yes, Mrs Pickett. It's just as I thought. Nothing to worry about. At least, nothing serious. Nothing that cannot be remedied in a few hours. There is quite a heavy degree of infestation . . . it must be most uncomfortable for you.'

'Infestation? Infestation?' Mrs Pickett called out in a thin lamenting tone but remained horizontal.

I said, 'Kay, it isn't right, it isn't right to feed a fantasy in such a manner, I feel I must ask you to . . .'

'Body lice. Body lice are no fantasy, Mrs Chaplin – if any feeding is being done it is they who are doing it. If you had experienced them – and I am glad you have not – you would realize that their presence has nothing at all to do with the imagination.'

As if to prove her point, she picked at something on Mrs Pickett's flesh, then motioned me forward and indicated that I should scrutinize her thumb-nail. I saw the minute creature scuttle across the red nail varnish – Kay crushed it with her other thumb-nail so that it made a cracking noise.

'Sometimes they are referred to as crab lice.' Kay's tone was medically nonchalant. 'They feed on human blood.'

'How ghastly.' Initally, this was all I could offer in response but I recovered myself. 'Shall I call a doctor?'

'Not necessary.' Kay rose to her feet, took a pace back and looked down on Mrs Pickett, who turned her eyes towards Kay in an appealing manner. Kay continued to look at her but spoke to me.

'In spite of their somewhat alarming appearance and foul habits, not to mention the intense irritation that their presence causes, these creatures are swiftly and easily removed. To pick them off one by one would be arduous indeed – and in any event I'm afraid they are very fertile and produce eggs at rapid intervals. In the words of the bible they do tend to increase and multiply.'

'Eggs? Eggs? What do you mean?' Mrs Pickett questioned in a thin hopeless voice without moving her position.

'Don't worry, my dear . . . It's just like head lice, they leave nits deposited in your hair – but these have a penchant for the pubic regions.'

Kay spoke in such a matter-of-fact way that she managed to modify my initial revulsion and present sense of recoil from what

57

lay spread-eagled in front of us. A degree of relief brought more tears from Mrs Pickett.

Kay offered more information. 'They never progress further than the eyebrows, hence their nomenclature.' She bent over Mrs Pickett. 'Let's look under your armpits.' She inspected first one and then the other . . . She nodded her head. 'Yes, yes, they have travelled. What an adventurous breed you have adopted, my dear. Truly British. Colonies everywhere.'

'Please, please, Miss Roper . . . how do I rid myself of them?' Mrs Pickett pleaded from the couch.

'It is miraculously fortunate . . . so fortunate . . . I just happen to have some ointment at home which will do the trick. Clear all of them in a matter of hours. If you can wait here for twenty minutes or so, I'll fetch it for you.'

'I'm so grateful – so beholden to you.'

If Mrs Pickett felt grateful towards Kay she conveyed no such feeling towards me. In Kay's absence she glared at me in a sullen, hostile way – rejected an offer of a cup of tea and slaughtered every attempt that I made to conduct some kind of light, polite conversation. We waited in an atmosphere of silent loathing.

On her return Kay produced a jar triumphantly from her handbag and held it aloft. 'This ointment will clear you up.' She read out the instructions. 'Apply to the affected parts. Leave for six hours, and repeat the application if necessary after bathing.'

'What is it called?' I asked, thinking that it was just as well to have a knowledge of such things.

'Blue unction. A romantic name for a medical cure, don't you think?'

Mrs Pickett raised herself into a sitting position and took the jar from Kay's hand. 'Er . . . I cannot apply it . . . I cannot put my hands near the horrible creatures. I shall vomit if I have to do this for myself. Miss Roper, could you? Could you assist me – rid me of this nightmare infection?'

Kay knelt beside the medical couch and retrieved the jar from Mrs Pickett's hand. Mrs Pickett lay flat. Kay unscrewed the top from the jar. I glanced at the ointment. It was indeed dark blue in colour and had an unpleasant odour that put me in mind of diesel fumes.

I suppose I ought to have turned away from this doctor-patient situation. After all, the areas of concern were intensely private. For some reason, I chose not to turn my back on the proceedings. I did not avert my eyes for a single second. I expected to feel nauseated by what Kay had to do in the course of duty but found that I was intrigued by her dexterity and skilful application to the task at hand. She seemed to find it easy and did it as though it was a usual everyday kind of thing. Like an idle trainee nurse, I watched and admired.

Kay talked as she applied the ointment. 'If you can just open your legs a little wider . . . that's better . . . I just have to be careful over this area on the edge of your clitoris . . . quite a cluster of nits in these shorter hairs, but I want to avoid making you feel uncomfortable . . . There. If you could turn over and kneel on the couch I can deal with the other parts more fully . . . There, that's better . . . Now on your back again . . . Raise your . . .'

Kay applied the ointment so deftly and with such lightness of touch that Mrs Pickett's occasional sighs seemed more close to relief and satisfaction than to embarrassment or discomfort. After Kay had declared the treatment complete, Mrs Pickett rose from the couch and coughed in a determined manner as if to find the true voice of her former self. She fastened her blouse buttons, clicked her suspenders into place and straightened her skirt. She was calm now – but I seem to remember she looked a little flushed, in much the same way that young women do if their dancing partners have been too attentive or too close during the last waltz. She thanked Kay in a formal manner and turned to me.

'I am going to sue you. I am going to sue you over this matter, Mrs Chaplin.'

'Sue me? Sue me?' I asked. Mrs Pickett never failed to surprise me.

'Yes, Mrs Chaplin. Sue you. I intend to seek damages in court from you over this matter. Would you deny that you are responsible for this building?'

'No, no. No, I would not – the responsibility is written into the contract of my employment.'

'And in that contract, Mrs Chaplin, in that very contract there is a contagion clause, is there not?'

'Why yes, yes, there is – and I thank God that so far I have never had cause to use it. A school closure is to be avoided in these difficult times.'

'No cause? No cause, Mrs Chaplin?' Mrs Pickett almost spat out her words.

'There have been no serious epidemics for years, and hygiene . . .' I was interrupted.

'Do you think that my present state of infection and distress came from the countryside all about us?' She continued with increasing venom and bitterness. 'Do you think it was a visitation from heaven? Was this plague of locusts that settled and mutiplied on my body sent by Him? Is that what you think?'

'Mrs Pickett, please, you are still upset, you are overwrought.'

'Overwrought or not, Mrs Chaplin, I shall not return to this building until it has been fumigated. I shall inform everyone – authorities, parents, teachers, members of our local council – of the appalling conditions which you are allowing to exist here. I should be shirking my duty if I did otherwise. I'm sorry if this disgraceful occurrence reflects on you – or on your lack of vigilance in health matters. As I have said, I shall look for reasonable compensation. I am afraid I shall have to speak out boldly and clearly. It would be irresponsible of me to remain silent.'

I was about to respond sharply to her absurd accusations but paused for reflection. Had Mrs Pickett contracted the crab lice in my building? What if other teachers or, God forbid, other girls had been infected? There were regular and routine inspections for head lice but this was an entirely different matter. Kay must have noted my perplexed expression for it was she who took up Mrs Pickett's challenge.

'I agree with you, Mrs Pickett – that is, I agree with you on the issue of speech. There are times when one must speak out and there are times when it is prudent to remain silent. In the past, I have regretted remaining silent when I should have spoken out and I have regretted speaking out when I should have remained silent.'

'Your exposition is too legal for me, Miss Roper.' Mrs Pickett spoke with false humility. 'What advice are you seeking to offer me?'

'I would never presume to do so much on a delicate matter of this kind. However, I do urge you to take the ointment home with you.'

'I was hoping it could be applied here – if a second application is necessary.'

'There is someone at your home who will have need of it.'

'My home? How dare you . . . how dare you imply that I have transported this vermin . . .'

'I am not implying it, Mrs Pickett, I am stating it. Crab lice cannot be caught from a building. They choose to live not near humans, but on them. Our blood is their nectar. I am stating a medical fact: these lice are transferred or passed on by bodily contact.'

'You're quite sure . . .?' Mrs Pickett spluttered in dismay.

'Certain. Absolutely certain. You must speak with your husband, Mrs Pickett. It is imperative for him also to apply the ointment.'

Mrs Pickett said, 'I shall divorce him.'

'But on what grounds, Mrs Pickett?' Kay's question sounded sincere.

'You are a single woman, Miss Roper, and some of the ways of men are probably unknown to you. Where else could my husband have brought this trouble into my life? Where else except from another woman?'

'It could have been a man,' Kay suggested.

'A man? A man, Miss Roper? I do assure you that Eric has never had any unnatural sexual inclinations.'

'Unnatural sexual inclinations cannot be unnatural to those that do them, otherwise they could not be done. But I was not indicating this . . . I'm sure your husband does not burden you with every strain, stress and discomfort that he has to put up with whilst he is away at war. Men at war are forced to sacrifice a great deal, Mrs Pickett. What we might consider ordinary privacy is often withheld from them by circumstance. There are occasions when two – three – or perhaps four men must sleep in close proximity. This is not always due to lack of space – it can be lack of warmth. Imagine sleeping alone in nigh-on freezing conditions?'

'Oh, I see . . .' said Mrs Pickett quickly.

'When does he receive his new posting?'

'The day after tomorrow.'

'Go home, Mrs Pickett. Pass on the ointment. Don't judge him unkindly – give him your understanding. This episode is just a secondary war wound – don't let it harm either of you, not in any way. Continue to offer him . . . continue to offer . . .'

'Offer him what?'

'Your body – he has a need of it.'

Mrs Pickett went into one of her little coughing bouts and patted her tight curls into position. This gesture was hardly necessary as Mrs Pickett's waves and curls were held fast and still by some setting lotion that would defy a March gale. I wondered if Eric touched her brittle coiffure as he made love to her and I wondered how she would respond to such attentions. Perhaps her responses were more adept than my own – perhaps she enjoyed that part of married life more than I did.

'I'm sorry for my behaviour. Please accept my full apologies, Mrs Chaplin. I'm sure you understood my distress in the exceptional circumstances – the war is on our back doorsteps when we least expect it, isn't it? So kind of you to accept all this with equanimity – so kind, so kind.' Mrs Pickett then looked at Kay fixedly with her small penetrating eyes. 'And thank you, Miss Roper, for enlightening me about matters of which I was entirely ignorant.' When she reached the study door she paused as she opened it and said, 'I'm not a worldly person,' then left.

Kay and I sat and looked at one another. I think we were both too relieved or even exhausted to speak. By this late time in the term I could no longer feel any sense of indignation or personal injury with regard to Mrs Pickett's carryings-on. Somehow, I had managed to anaesthetize my feelings against her flow of anger and bile. She professed to be a religious woman – yet she possessed no generosity of spirit. She seemed void of . . . of . . . I remember sighing deeply, audibly.

Kay began to laugh. First there were a few titters which she attempted to suppress by placing her long white fingers over her mouth. Suddenly, she seemed to give up all sense of decorum. In one second her hand fell helplessly to her side, her head jerked back as though someone were pulling her by the hair, she snorted and then she laughed loud and long.

As she laughed she rocked to and fro on her chair and screamed out in the ribald kind of way that some of the more common women in the village did. I imagined her mirth would subside quickly but every time it died down her eye seemed to catch something which started her off all over again.

'Miss Roper, Miss Roper, please.' I did feel the need for intervention as the day seemed to demand some degree of propriety. Kay rocked forward on her chair and I followed the direction of her gaze before she exploded into yet another raucous bout of belly-laughter.

Just a foot or so from my waste-paper basket lay a garment . . . a pink garment. Mrs Pickett might have laid claim to be unworldly but she certainly wasn't innocent enough to be abroad minus her drawers. What if she decided to travel upstairs on the bus? Someone might . . . as she climbed up the stairs they would see . . .

Kay and I laughed and laughed and laughed . . . and in between the laughter I used her Christian name several times. Oh, Kay . . . Kay, my dear . . . Dear Kay, . . . Oh . . . Kay.

'What's tickling you today, Mrs Chaplin?'

'Crab lice.'

'I beg your pardon?'

'Something nice. I said something nice.'

'Are you coming down for tea and biscuits? We have mid-morning guests.'

'Guests?'

'Yes, we have Mr Keating-Bransford and his wife with us.'

63

'Never heard of them.'

'He's the new mayor, Mrs Chaplin – a local dignitary.'

'Give them my seasonal greetings – I want to stay here. Here by the window. I want to look out on the street.'

'Just as you will, but it would be nice if you were with us.'

'The biscuits will be nice. I would prefer to be not nice and stay here by the window. I'm not a biscuit.'

Every time I exchange any words with that woman she looks at me as though I have inflicted some mortal injury on her. I wonder why she should resent the fact that I would prefer to look out on the street. She brings out an anger within me which I must have repressed for years. Why should a meeting with her special guest hold any curiosity for me?

Yet this street, this street and what goes on in it, is another matter. There is often real drama happening down there and I can interpret it how I will. Television seems to dictate the lives of some of the other inmates here. I have rejected it, I have gone back to that time when it did not exist. Old women like me use the streets outside their windows for viewing. My God, we are watchful creatures – and what's more we neither approve nor disapprove of what we see. We merely absorb the lives that come and go before us.

I wish I could avoid lunch today. I wonder if I will ever enjoy the pleasure of hunger again. I am thinking of that meal, that feast that came so unexpectedly. The invitation delivered as though I were some close relative who ate regularly with her sister.

'You will come to dinner tonight, won't you? My father is returning from Barrow-in-Furness – such a bleak place, he informs me. I have looked at the map and the town appears to be perched on a tiny strip of land, it looks like a geographical afterthought. You will come, won't you?'

Kay stood at the bus stop with me and waited for me to answer. For some reason, I hoped the bus would come round the corner that very moment so that I could leap on it and forego the invitation in a flurry of vague excuses.

I always sought a distance, a social distance, from my staff – and, yes, from the pupils too in some ways. I was mistaken in that I convinced myself that it was unfair to like some people or some children more than others. Consequently, I was often lonely.

'But Kay, I couldn't possibly impinge on your hospitality. In ordinary times, yes, but with the state of rationing as it is . . .'

'Ah, then I can dispel your qualms – an excess of meat has come our way. Not a great excess, but enough for a surplus. It cannot be stored. You have not met my dear father, and my neighbour – Mr Harper – will also be joining us. It's a refreshing change to do something impromptu. Don't give it any more thought – just come. Won't you?'

I did give it more thought. Had someone slaughtered a pig secretly? I hoped Kay wasn't involved in that kind of village subterfuge, yet the thought of well-done pork with crackling and apple sauce caused my mouth to water and my stomach to rumble. Even so, I was about to politely proffer an excuse when Janet Haycock came around the corner. She walked up to us and, instead of pausing briefly to offer a greeting and then be on her way, that little madam stopped.

'Good afternoon, Mrs Chaplin. Good afternoon, Miss Roper.'

I nodded and smiled, indicating that she should go about her business, but she refused to recognize my signals. She stood her ground and without being downright rude there was little I could do about it.

'Oh, Miss Roper,' she cooed, 'there's a lovely film showing at the Tivoli.'

'Ah, yes, Janet. I have already seen it. Not a new film but one well worth viewing for a second time. You liked the star of the film, did you?'

'Which one, Miss Roper? The man or the woman?'

'Janet, there was only one star. The woman, of course – you liked her?'

'Marlene Dietrich – oh yes, miss. She was so mysterious and somehow you felt she knew everything about China and she wasn't even Chinese – she was so much better dressed than anybody else in the film.'

'Mmm, mmm . . . Forgive me sighing, Janet – it's just that . . . it's just that I did not feel the film reflected life in China one little bit. It so happened that the train was travelling to Shanghai and Miss Dietrich was on it.'

'Yes, miss, and I couldn't fathom out what her work was. I mean, what did she do for a living?'

'Oh . . . er . . . er, I think . . . I think she was involved in one of the caring professions.'

'Well, she didn't look like a nurse and she smoked a lot of cigarettes.'

'Bette and Joan usually smoke too.' Kay looked ruminative. 'You see, an actress with a cigarette often leads us into her inner activity – the deeper recesses of her mind are exposed through tobacco smoke and the camera close-up.'

I interrupted at this point. I felt I had to as Janet Haycock had commandeered all of Kay's attention. At the time I would have scoffed if someone had accused me of resenting the presence of a star-struck schoolgirl but, on reflection, it was jealousy which prompted my intervention.

I said, 'I'd love to come to see you tonight, Kay. The change will do me good.' I turned and spoke to the gawping Janet. 'Now, dear, I see you have some shopping with you. I'm pleased you are helping your mother. Hurry home now, don't keep her waiting.'

'It's only candles, Mrs Chaplin.' Janet responded in a disconsolate, crestfallen kind of way and continued to hover around Kay like a moth around a flame.

'Off you go then, Janet.' My tone left her no choice.

At the corner of the road she turned slowly and waved her arm forlornly in farewell. I knew that she was now jealous of me – and, strange as it may seem, I returned the thought. I remember saying to Kay that I found it hard to imagine Marlene Dietrich playing a nurse. Kay informed me that Marlene's part in the film had been that of a high-class prostitute. At this point my bus arrived.

*

66

There's the bell – it's a summons to eat. My working life spent in schools has left me with a profound dislike of ringing bells. I want no bell tolling for me when I die – yet I suppose what you get is not your choice as far as death is concerned. I'm not in the least hungry . . . I'd rather recommence my meal with Kay. I was hungry that night . . . and what a menu. What a feast. A magical feast!

'I won't hear of you taking more bus rides. My father will pick you up. Around quarter-past six. At your home. Look forward to seeing you.' Kay shouted out this hurried but precise information as I clambered on to the bus. I sat down and contemplated the luxury of taking a bath when I got home. We were supposed to deny ourselves such fripperies but I wanted to enjoy anticipating the evening just in case the occasion did not come up to expectation.

Peter Roper certainly exceeded my expectations. His appearance reminded me that my husband was away at war, it reminded me that other men were attractive to me, it reminded me that a man in his fifties could still maintain great sexual appeal.

Kay's father must have been well over fifty although one could never have guessed this. He looked more like a man in his early forties but this was a ridiculous conjecture: if that had been the case, he would have achieved Kay's paternity in his early teens and this was something too messy to consider.

'Mrs Chaplin? I'm Peter Roper, Kay's father. Ah, I see you are ready. Kay said that you were always punctual.'

He was a tall man. I suppose Kay's stature was partly inherited from him, but here any resemblance ended – yet he too had looks which commanded attention. The slightly curling dark auburn hair showed no flecks of grey and by the standards of the day it was grown quite long; small curls nestled about the tops of his ears and crept over the back of his shirt collar. A receding hair-line added further dimension to a wide brow; thick auburn eyebrows that met over the bridge of a Roman nose framed two light brown eyes. His complexion was pale – almost white, void of colour. And the lips – the lips were full and sensual. He wore an open-necked white shirt and grey flannel trousers. Adorning the pale skin where his shirt button was undone were the spring-coil auburn hairs of his manhood.

The Austin Seven motor car must have been regarded with something close to awe by the rest of the village as no one else owned a vehicle. Bread and milk were still delivered by horse and cart and the only regular road travellers were munition workers in their coaches and the poor wretches who succumbed to diphtheria and ambulances.

I felt like the Queen of Sheba sitting beside this handsome man in his car. I can see it now. We were approaching a hump-backed bridge which spanned the canal. He drew into the side and laid his hand on my shoulder, all in the most relaxed fashion as though he had known me for years, not minutes. He pointed through his near window.

'Look. A single heron. Poor thing – no one wants him.'

The bird stood in the shallows. It looked odd, unreal and eerily still. As if to dispel my presentiments it began to tread rapidly through the water before leaving the canal-side and taking to the air.

'Beautiful, beautiful,' he murmured appreciatively.

'It is, it is,' I agreed with him, yet I was not referring to the heron but to the dark auburn hair that curled over the top of his ears – and I silently regretted that both his hands were now returned to their place on either side of the driving wheel.

Most of the villagers in Padmore were dependent for their livelihood on the numerous local collieries dotted about their lovely rural surroundings. Dependency did not stop at salary source: shelter was also provided by the collieries and, without exception, the housing was just as mean as working conditions down the mines.

The network of village streets branching cobweb-like from the main town road consisted of row upon row of houses which were grim in terms of minimal comfort and unrelenting uniformity. Most of those colliery houses had two rooms upstairs, two rooms downstairs and a back kitchen. In some cases, back kitchens were shared between two families. Lavatories were usually situated outside, adjacent to the coal-house – some, built like a postscript, were placed at the bottom of the gardens. None of these homes possessed a bathroom. Although most of the families managed to maintain a high degree of cleanliness about their homes, we were aware (particularly during hot days in morning assembly) that some of our girls were quite without the niceties that prevent natural odour from becoming . . . well . . . sickening to anyone else.

Kay lived under a roof that was not dependent on the miserly patronage of the pit owners. Her tiny cul-de-sac was at the southern end of the village, within easy walking distance of my school. Originally, the three houses must have been built by someone with an interest in literature as their names were carved out of stone above the doorway entrances. They were called 'Pickwick', 'Nickleby' and 'Copperfield'. Kay resided in 'Copperfield' which was the end house of this unassuming project. The road itself was full of holes and rubble; it was called Dickens Close.

Kay's next-door neighbour was also new to the village. Young Patrick Harper lived with his widowed mother. I think they had originated from the south of England. She was a thin, pathetic-looking woman of a highly nervous disposition, who rarely spoke to anyone in the village: her acknowledgement of greeting was never more than a weak smile or a faint nod of the head.

I never knew the name of the woman who lived in the other house. She lived alone and displayed a sign in her window declaring that she was an agent for a corsetry company. Apparently, this was her sole income and she seemed to manage well enough on it. I never imagined that this would have been a lucrative enough occupation to keep a person and run a household. I recall Kay's words – she used her dreamy voice.

'Oh, yes, she is really quite busy, it's a demanding trade. There are at least three or four callers every day – including Sunday. I suppose her comfortable matron-like appearance exudes a homeliness which gives her customers sufficient confidence to make a call. You know, Ivy, it is amazing the number of men who require such support – either for their weak backs or their bulging stomachs or both. On Saturday three members of our armed forces called on her, all upright young men in their first flush of manhood. It's clear she must be something of an expert in her field – she must be, as her ingenuity has obviously been noted by more than a parochial clientele. I believe some of the women in the village refer to her as "the sergeant-major's mother". Such a kind and deserved description – she plans to retire to Cardiff in Wales when the war is over.'

Kay's house was unusual to our area in that it had three floors. The downstairs consisted of one huge room that was both lounge and dining room. She greeted us warmly and ushered us into the lounge-cum-dining room. I shall never forget my first view of that room.

I'm sure Kay noted my surprise even though I sought not to register it. The walls were white and void of picture rails, the floor was carpet-less and still had its original 'Mansion-polished' red-stone covering. There were four home-made rag rugs (similar to the ones which were found in most of the village dwellings); one was placed near to the hearth, another in front of the piano near the garden window, and two lay in close proximity to the large, round dining table. Apart from the six dining chairs and a faded red sofa, there was no other furniture in the room. A round Echo radio set stood on the floor and there were three vases displaying white, pink and blue lupins placed on top of the piano.

There were no curtains in place about the windows, no net either – only rolled-up black-out blinds. Two enormous maps of Europe and North Africa were affixed to one wall and the wall space above the mantelpiece was covered in photographs of film stars. I noticed that no male visage smiled out from this collage. Peter·Roper sat next to me on the sofa. I was glad of this male presence among so many women. After the initial aesthetic shock, I saw that this room achieved a great deal of comfort and quiet appeal with the minimum of effort. Kay introduced me to Patrick Harper, who completed our dinner company.

Patrick Harper was a tall, slenderly built young man who hunched his shoulders forward when he stood, almost as if to apologize for his height. His ash-blond hair was cropped short and parted down the centre; his parting so sharply defined his scalp that he looked as though he were carrying a white scar through the middle of his head. Pale brown eyes, blinking behind nondescript, hardly visible eyebrows and eyelashes, added nothing to a face which lacked normal animation. His complexion, like that of most coal-miners, was pale and white – but his lips were full and on the rare occasions when he smiled he became almost attractive. As far as conversation went, he seemed very reticent and would agree with everything that Kay said as if he were listening to some oracle.

Whenever Peter Roper addressed his daughter it was never without endearment. It was 'dear Kay' or 'dearest Kay' or 'Kay dearest'. This was not a shallow or artificial posture of affection – I believe he was utterly devoted to her.

'Dear Kay, shall we bring in the banquet? If our guests would kindly take their seats at the table? There are two bottles of Mackeson's milk stout, one for you, Kay – and one for Mrs Chaplin.'

I was about to decline this offer of alcohol. I had never tasted the drink but I knew it was a favourite choice of miners' wives.

'You do like a bottle of Mackeson, Ivy?'

'Now and again,' I answered lamely. I didn't find the dark-coloured liquid inviting but was so taken aback by hearing my first name . . . 'I think I will try a little as it is a special occasion.'

The meal was indeed a banquet, the centre-piece of which was a large tureen of jugged venison. This was complemented by fresh garden produce – potatoes, carrots, and peas. The amount of meat per person would have exhausted our ration books for a month.

'A solitary stag was hit by one of our goods trains – he must have been rejected by the rest of the herd. His death was quick by all accounts. I am sure he wouldn't feel grieved if he knew how well his presence was appreciated here.'

Peter Roper gave us all the most generous of helpings and I'm afraid I felt no guilt or qualms about swallowing the poor creature. It was a common type of accident during those years –

the pheasant hit by a car, the partridges that had flown into some telegraph wires, the wild duck that had been injured by a barge – they found their way on to our tables. Sad accidents all of them.

Patrick Harper pronounced the meal to be delicious and I heartily agreed with him. Kay said that cooking the venison in cider had made all the difference. What with a pint bottle of dark brown stout and venison cooked in cider, I felt relaxed and vaguely carefree by the end of the meal. Darkness was drawing near and Kay pulled down the black-out blinds and lit two or three candles.

Peter urged her to play a song or two for us. What assurance – what confidence. I can see her now, sitting at the piano in the glow of the candlelight . . . Her fingers sounded out a few chords before she commenced. She played a song called 'I'll Get By' and, to my surprise, sang an accompaniment. Her voice was low and husky, not much different from Alice Faye's; she seemed to caress the words as she sang them and made the lyrics so deeply personal, her interpretation made them seem much more profound than they really were.

Peter Roper and Patrick Harper appeared wholly enthralled, captivated, their eyes fixed on Kay at the piano, their expressions rapturous. Kay suggested to her father that I might wish to dance. Of course, I let myself be persuaded to take the floor. He waltzed me slowly, slowly over the tiles of the floor to the strains of 'Falling in Love Again'. It was so romantic being held in this way and I thought of my husband away on naval duties. He too was a handsome man . . . I had thought in my ignorance that marriage was a continuing domestic romance, yet there were parts of my marriage which at that time I dreaded. I was happier and more relaxed with a man on the dance floor than I was with one in a bed.

Afterwards, we sat and finished our drinks and both Peter and Patrick entreated Kay for one more song. I joined in with the chorus of pleading as the thought of the evening's end and a return to my lonely bungalow filled me with dismay.

'I'll sing just one more.' Kay waved a long, thin, white arm which cast shadows on the wall from the candlelight. 'This song is for Ivy, specially for her.'

She pulled the chair closer to the piano and looked about in a professional manner – we were no longer sitting in her lounge, we were in a night-club, an intimate, secret rendezvous . . . and she? She was the star performer.

She raised both arms and slowly stretched them high above her head. Then – very slowly – she lowered her hands and began to remove the hair-pins from her hair.

One by one she placed them on top of the piano, then she freed the tresses from the plaits so that her thick, black hair cascaded down her cheeks and came to rest on her shoulders. She pushed back some errant locks that had fallen partly over one side of her face. She looked directly at me – and I felt her reading my mind.

'This song is for you,' she said.

When she began to sing I forgot the rest of the audience; they no longer mattered. My own response filled my eyes with tears and my heart with longing. She sang.

'If I were a blackbird, I'd whistle and sing
And follow the ship that my true love sails in,
And on the top riggings, I'd there build my nest
And pillow my head on his lily-white breast.'

'You look beautiful, Kay,' Patrick Harper murmured and then cleared his throat as though embarrassed by the magnetism which had drawn out this admission from him.

'Oh, it's the candlelight, it's so very flattering. I hope that . . . I hope that . . . that . . .'

'Yes, Kay?' her father enquired.

'I hope . . . I hope . . .'

'What do you hope for, Kay?' he persisted.

'I hope that when this terrible war is over – I hope that when the gangrene of Fascism has been cut from us – I hope that we can all be with who we want to be with.'

'And who will you want to be with? Do you know?'

'Yes, I do.'

73

'Who?'

'You, Father. You,' she replied, and then began to plait her hair.

'And on the top riggings, I'd there build my nest
And pillow my head on his lily-white breast.'

'I'm sorry to interrupt your singing, Mrs Chaplin, but lunch is ready and on the table. The decorations look lovely and I'm sure you will be able to sing your carol after the meal. I haven't heard that one before. Is it one of the more modern ones? I'm afraid I'm a bit of a traditionalist myself.'

'It's not a carol. It's a love song.'

'Ah, I thought you were singing something seasonal.'

'Love songs or songs of love can be sung all the year round. They have no season.'

'I dare say you have got up quite an appetite – there's a marvellous lunch waiting for you.'

'What's on the menu?'

'Why? Just what you would expect for a Christmas lunch. You tell me what you would expect and I'll bet we have it.'

'I would like a pint bottle of Mackeson stout, roast potatoes, tender baby carrots, roast parsnips and fresh garden peas, and jugged venison that has been steeped in cider before cooking. Followed by three, large, scarlet, juicy Victoria plums. Have you any of those things?'

'Ahem! The roast potatoes – yes. Take my arm, dear – yes, steady yourself first. Now – off we go . . . Did you sing that song to your husband?'

'No, he never heard it. It was sung to me by someone else.'

'A childhood sweetheart, I suppose?'

'Patrick Harper sang it to me and he was not my sweetheart. Not at any time.'

If I told this woman only half the truth about any number of things she'd probably have to admit herself to hospital for shock. She'd think it was unnatural for a woman to sing a song of love to another woman. I noticed that when Patrick Harper stood close to Kay Roper the front of his trousers became contorted and stretched by the urgency of his erection . . . He must have desired her a great deal.

5

I wonder how many other people are spending their Christmas Day afternoon sitting in a greenhouse. Now that I think on it, I'm sure there will be quite a few and I hope it is as pleasant for them as it is for me. Our garden centre boasts three greenhouses; we call this one 'Exotico' as we grow orchids here. The temperature and humidity place me in a tropical jungle but my view is of English evergreens – small holly shrubs, variegated ivy, and miniature conifers. I never tire of the garden or of its plants – but in this grey, cold winter light it is the birds that have my attention.

I have hung clusters of peanuts on the naked branches of the high buddleia bush – it can't be much more than three yards away from me, yet my presence behind this glass seems to be of no consequence to the birds. Perhaps they have mistaken me for one of those grisly garden gnomes which sell so well. As far as the birds are concerned, I'll be a giant – I'm over six foot two in my stockinged feet. I've always thought of my long legs as an aberration. I am grateful they have plenty of hair coating them and that they are free of varicose veins – am I the only man who enjoyed having his legs stroked by a woman? Shouldn't it be the other way around? There are no rules to such things.

The birds demonstrate this point. In less than an hour I have observed sparrows, blue tits, blackbirds, a robin, a wren, coal tits, bad-tempered goldfinches, thrushes – all taking their Christmas lunch – but it is the starlings that have caught my attention. At least, one of them has. It is pure white and I'm wondering if it feels different. It behaves the same as the rest of the flock: perhaps it is the case that one feels different only when one is treated differently. So much for an albinotic starling.

I ought to get back into the house. My brother-in-law and his wife are in there playing backgammon – arguing over pennies. I do hope the game drags on . . . I would rather be here. I didn't want guests. Alfred is a decent if uncomprehending man.

His telephone call . . . 'I thought the wife and I might pop over this afternoon, Patrick. It being Christmas.'

'Oh, I'm not out of sorts, Alfred – there's no need to make a duty out of it.'

'It's not a duty, it's Christmas. A time for families . . . and you are on your own.' He constantly reminds me of my widower existence – is this something he fears? 'Look, Patrick, we'll be over after lunch – we'll see our Betty and her husband and kids first and then make our way over to you. After all, we are all you've got, aren't we?'

I never answered his question. I have never felt part of a family. Never had a father – not one I knew, anyway. My mother invented the idea of him; like most snobs she deceived herself with enormous success.

Although I have to pay homage to her for bringing me here – there is no other place I would rather be at this time. I doubt if she would recognize Padmore now. It was an enclosed little mining village that fed its populace to four or five pits when she came here. Those double-fronted, twin-garaged houses, where the well-heeled business executives of Wolverhampton, Walsall and Birmingham drain their gin and tonics, were once row after row of colliery homes. The leisure centre complex was once Number Five pit, and the plastic ski-run was originally a slag heap. There are no pits and no miners here now, the working men's clubs have gone and another pit site is a supermarket. There is a wine bar and a chemist in the village. The other shops are gone. So is Kay Roper . . . Kay Roper . . . what a woman. She was the first orchid this village ever knew . . . Seems not so long ago. And the dog . . . an alsatian, I never liked the breed. My brother-in-law said it belonged to . . . I forget who it belonged to . . . Kay . . . Kay . . .

*

77

We did not see them move in. I was on afternoon shift at the pit and my mother was out shopping. We had only been in the house a couple of months or so and I spent most of my free time digging and preparing our vast garden. I was burning squitch and dead leaves and any manner of rubbish when I heard her voice call out to me – it was a husky, inviting voice.

'Hello, hello there. I don't want to drag you from your work.'

I looked up to see her calling from her land which was adjacent to mine.

'I'm Kay. Kay Roper. I have moved into next door. My father and I have taken the house.'

I stared at her and her looks stultified any response from me. I suppose it must have been mid-August or thereabouts. I know that it was warm because most of my shirt was wide open – the nation was more modest about things like that then and in a state of shyness I clutched the shirt front together with my hand, as if to hide the hairs and perspiration on my chest from her.

I ought to have introduced myself, given my name and mentioned my occupation. All I did was say 'Oh!' and continue staring at her. She looked like what I imagined a glamorous artist should look like. Was she working with ENSA or appearing in 'Workers' Playtime'? It was satisfying to me to meet a woman almost as tall as myself.

At this time, when I was not quite twenty-one, I tended to think of all women in terms of sexual coupling. I rarely had a chance for discourse with the opposite sex save for my mother – and she seemed to loathe the members of her own gender. Within the village she liked no one over-much and wanted little social contact with anybody.

Kay, in her pale yellow dress, her purple chiffon scarf trailing over shoulders and bosom, her long legs, her studio make-up face and fluting speech, instantly captivated me. I stood and looked at my new neighbour who seemed to decide that if I would not reveal anything about myself she would keep me there until I did. No, that is not fair. All she did was talk through the unbearable shyness which had come over me like a tidal wave. I made no

78

excuses to escape from my pain. I was quite ready, even at this early stage, to drown in her presence.

'My father is a technical engineer on the railways – it means he has to do a great deal of travelling. He is away from home a lot so we decided on this spot. We wanted to reside somewhere near the centre of England – then no journey could be too great or too far. So you see? This is ideal for us. This is it, and we are here.'

'My name is Patrick.' Thank God. I had managed to speak.

'Such a lovely name, the name of a saint. The patron saint of Ireland. Some believe that he banished snakes from that beautiful country. If he did, it seems a sad loss. I'd gladly welcome a few non-venomous snakes into my garden but I could not cope with a saint. A saint would cause me more suffering than a viper. Are you a saint or a serpent, Patrick?' She laughed as she said this but her deep blue eyes never left my face.

'Neither, I'm neither of those things,' I replied. 'There are several churches here, at least four in the village and over a dozen in Batsford. I think most denominations are represented.'

'Really? Oh really? My patron saint must be St Jude – he's the heavenly representative for hopeless cases, you know.' Kay offered no other religious interests, but asked, 'Are there any cinemas? I tend to worship in an unconventional kind of way.'

'There's just one in the village – it's known locally as "the bug and flea-hole" – but it has three films on every week. In Batsford there are three picture-houses so you have plenty of choice – miles of celluloid in one week.'

She clasped her hands together and did nothing to disguise her delight. 'What is showing locally this week?'

'Deanna Durbin – it's called *Can't Help Singing!*'

'Sometimes I wish she could help it. Such a cheerful, dreary performer, such limited facial expression – it's like watching an animated singing doll. Are you from these parts, Patrick . . . er . . .?'

'Harper. No, we haven't been here long – just over two months. There's my mother and me in the house, that's all.'

I was relieved she did not ask after my father so I didn't ask to hear about her mother; we both chose not to mention our missing relatives. She turned slowly and looked all about her and I studied her neck, the dark hair piled high about the top of her head.

'Tell me, Mr Harper – do tell me . . . Is all this . . .' She stretched out her arm in a semicircular movement, a slow expansive gesture, 'is all this land part of my garden? It is quite overwhelming. Is it all ours?'

'Well, the trenches separate the three fields. The field you are standing in is your garden and this field is mine. I must admit it's a large slice of land. A bit daunting – I've never lived in a place with a garden before, it will need a lot of maintaining. Yet I'm looking forward to the prospect of growing things.'

'We must face the challenge, Mr Harper. I shall till the soil alongside you. We'll dig for victory.'

'We could produce enough vegetables to feed us throughout the year, we could be entirely self-sufficient,' I observed. 'You will have more time in the day than I have, won't you?'

'No, Mr Harper. I am a teacher, Mr Harper, my days will not be my own. I will do my gardening in snatches of time the same as you. I begin at the local girls' secondary school in September – all the schools apart from the infants' school are single sex. I think it is a pity, don't you?'

'I don't know,' I replied truthfully.

'Don't you think the sexes have a need to mingle, Mr Harper?' I'm sure she noticed my confusion, saw the blood rush to my head. 'And your work? Your work here?'

'I am a coal-miner – a Bevin Boy.'

'How wonderful – how marvellous of you to enter the war in such a way. However, I would suggest, and I do this with the utmost respect, I would suggest, Mr Harper that you are not a boy . . . It is my belief that you are a man – a fact few would doubt. We will speak again.'

She turned and retraced her way down the garden path, her chiffon scarf floating in the mild breeze as if it had an independent life of its own away from her. Before she reached the back door she called to me again – I'm sure she knew that I had been watching her every step.

'Mr Harper? The tree at the very bottom of the garden? Is it your tree or mine?'

'The roots belong to you. It is your tree.'

'What kind of tree is it?'

'It's a plum tree. It bears red Victoria plums.'

'Are they good?' she asked.

'Luscious! Luscious!' I shouted to the back of her head.

I still find it difficult to think of my mother with any affection – or indeed grudging admiration. There were none of the usual manifestations of maternal love. I still wonder if she ever liked me. I believe she regarded my birth as a mishap, the result of which was me. In her terms, she had to live and manage as best as she was able. At this time, she appeared more elderly than she was – and people would often mistakenly refer to her as my grandmother. When I was a child she informed me that my father had been killed in a car accident and that he had been a gentleman – a real gentleman – with a great future.

I had been brought up in a small ground-floor flat in Croydon. She seemed to be reasonably well off for a widow and I never knew of her taking up any paid employment of any kind. I had left school at fourteen and longed for some kind of work – physical labour, work which would reveal a result. I wanted to be free from all kinds of constrictions. Instead, she insisted I take up a job as a ledger-clerk – 'I couldn't be seen walking down the street unless you were in a collar-and-tie job. You a labourer – a common labourer – I swear it would be the death of me.'

The war changed everything. My birth certificate had to be produced on my application for a Bevin Boy placement, I would have been happy to take on a non-combative armed forces posting, but the officers assured me they were in more dire need of men to dig coal than to carry stretchers or roll bandages. My mother was happy enough to go along with this edict. She did not wish to be left alone.

'You were single when I was born. You have not been married?'

'Your father was a gentleman – from a very good family. The right sort of background.'

'Why didn't he marry you, then, if he was so perfect?'

'Not possible.'

'He was married already.'

'Yes.'

'How did you meet him?'

'I worked for him – I worked in his house . . .'

By questioning in this way, I discovered as much as I wanted to about my background. I wasn't shocked or put out by learning that I was born the other side of the blanket. To this day, I can never understand why the word 'bastard' is used as a term of abuse.

My mother had clawed her way up the ladder of domestic service and by the time she was forty she had achieved the dizzying height of housekeeper to a wealthy, retired banker in Reigate. Two months before her forty-third birthday, she gave birth to me.

'He stood by me,' she said flatly.

She meant that she was sent away and placed in receipt of a small annuity as long as she and I remained anonymous. I used to try to imagine how my conception had taken place. Had this 'gentleman' regularly crept into my mother's bed in the early hours of the morning? Had he taken her just once – in some mad abandoned passion across the kitchen table late at night? Had he wooed her and made false promises? Had he ever declared love? It's quite impossible to imagine that one's parents fuck . . . and if you have just one parent, and that one parent looks like an elderly woman, then birth does seem like a miracle. Light years away from conception.

Initially, when we moved here, my mother was overjoyed that we could buy a whole house for so little money – ownership of a house carried more prestige than that of a poky flat in Croydon. My earnings plus our fuel allowance improved our finances to quite a degree. After a few weeks she spoke of her distaste for the village, and by the time Kay Roper and her father arrived, she had concluded that she detested the place and all the people in it.

The sight of the men blackened with pit-grime nauseated her;

she thought that all the women were common. 'Dress like gypsies!' She herself was never out of matching shades. Dark browns, greys, fawns – sensible unprovocative tones.

I love to see a woman in bright colours, I love to be dazzled . . . My mother regarded all such display or decoration as the first step towards prostitution and loose living.

Fortunately, the people of the village viewed my mother's 'stand-offish' attitudes and social reticence as an indication of innate shyness. This accepted point of view was way off the mark. My mother's withdrawn behaviour was based in deep hostility and as far as she was concerned it was 'us' and 'them'. She maintained this war-like stance until her death.

She did meet one or two women in the main town of Batsford. I never knew them, but I do know she let it be known that I was a clerk at the colliery: she never actually admitted that I worked down the pit. Also, to quote her, we lived 'on the edge of the countryside'. She would not own to being a resident of Padmore.

Of course, she had watched me talking to Kay. I had seen the net curtain fall back into place as I made my way back down the garden path.

'She seemed to have a lot to say for herself. I hope you didn't tell her all our business.'

'What business? Are you thinking of opening a shop?'

'Mind your own business and you will hear no lies. I saw her husband yesterday. I nodded to him. I didn't speak. I hate pushiness.'

'She's not married.'

'Not married?' The sense of outrage my mother seemed to plant into these two words makes me smile now. Her hypocrisy didn't amuse me then.

'He's her father. Why do you always think badly of people?'

'She's dressed up as though she were going to a carnival, I'll swear she's tipped a pot of paint over her face. I was hoping a better class of person might move in there.'

'She's a teacher.'

'A teacher, a teacher? What of . . . tap-dancing?'

'No. A secondary school teacher.'

'Don't snap at me, young man. I wonder what this country is coming to . . . what with teachers getting themselves up like tarts.'

'I don't think she looks like a tart.'

'I hope to goodness you're not going to chase after her. You don't want to make a fool of yourself. I think she might have acne.'

'Acne . . . what do you mean?'

'She must have acne. That's why she covers her face with all that muck. No woman in her right mind would want to look like that. I'd never step out from the front door painted up like that.'

For my part, even from this first meeting, I had already decided to make a fool of myself by chasing after Kay. I inhaled deeply when I returned to my work in the garden. Not to take in fresh air, but in the forlorn hope of getting a whiff of her perfume.

At this time my sexual experience was limited to masturbation but my knowledge of such matters had greatly increased since working down the pit. Most of my workmates spoke in broad Midlands accents and initially it was hard to decipher what they said. Almost like listening to a foreign language – almost like being in a foreign culture – but the rigours of grafting for coal were so harsh that these barriers were soon overcome.

Even now, miners will grieve for other miners who are maimed or killed at work – their respect for one another seems to overcome international boundaries. Once, I watched some of my workmates contribute a half-crown each towards a disaster fund for miners in India. I think the solidarity among them is more emotional than political.

My work was to feed the conveyor belt and I toiled in tandem with a local man who was just six months older than me. He was married to a local girl and was the father of a one-year-old son. Towards the end of the shift he would talk about the romantic side of his marriage in the most tender, crude, graphic manner.

'My missus has got a lovely cunt. Bloody lovely it is. When I get my hand capped over that little nest, I know I'm home. And I'm glad of it, I can tell you – after eight hours down this shit-hole. You don't know what you are missing being single, Patrick.

I'm more attached to my missus now than ever I was when we were courting. I am – and that's a fact.

'Last night we got back home from the club around about nine o'clock. She wanted to get home early to put our boy to bed. I'd not stayed on without her but had bought a couple of bottles of beer to bring home with us. I banked up the fire while she was putting the lad between the sheets. By the time she came down the flames were blazing and there was a good record programme playing on the wireless. I'd poured myself a drink and switched the light off as I like to watch the roar of a good fire. I never heard her come down – I must have been half asleep in the chair.

'It was lovely coming back to my senses so slowly – feeling her hand stroking the back of my neck. She weren't saying anything – me and her don't have to say a lot to one another. Never did. Known each other since we were twelve or less. Course, in no time I was wide awake – well roused, I tell you. I had a hard-on right up to my neck-hole and I hadn't even touched her. Troise and his Mandoliers were playing on the wireless.

'I started stroking her arse, then she knelt down by the side of me and I unbuttoned the top of her frock . . . I tell you honestly . . . I laugh with pleasure now just thinking on it . . . we undressed one another . . . and then lay naked on the rug in front of the fire.

' "It can't be all work – it can't be all work and no fun, can it Jack?" she asked me.

' "No it can't duck," I whispered. I had my hand on her nest and played in and out with my fingers on the lips of her cunt. She had her hand on my prick while we kissed and canoodled and I had her cunt all wet . . . and . . . oh . . . it were lovely . . . and she said, "Slowly, Jack . . . slowly . . ." as I went inside her. We both managed to come at the same time and I thought her moans might wake the baby – we called out together . . . You make funny sounds when you are coupling, you know.

'I don't see how some men can enjoy such things unless their women do – I'd want no part in it if she weren't interested. Afterwards, we lay there on the rug and watched the fire die down – and her head was in the crook of my arm and even after it was all over I told her I loved her. And do now. It's not just a case of

85

good fucking between me and my missus – when we first married I said I didn't want a skivvy or a servant. I wanted a wife – well, I've got a bloody good wife and friend all rolled into one.'

Now some men in this village, I won't name them, don't deserve marriage. There's a man just four doors down from me – works at Number Two pit. His poor missus is forever showing the marks of his bullying. One week it's a black eye, another a sprained wrist and just before we had that last bit of snow her top lip was swollen up like a barrage balloon. Oh, I've no time for such people as him. My mother says his wife's made her bed and she must lie on it. That's fuckin' squitch – rubbish. That woman didn't get married to be knocked about. Dear Christ – they'd have you up in court if you treated a dog like that let alone your missus. I'll bet he gives his dog more affection than her. She, poor woman, always says she's bumped into a door, or tripped on the pavement – it's as though she feels ashamed for what her shit of a husband has done to her. It's not right.

'You'll be good to your missus when you marry, won't you, Patrick?'

'I will, I will,' I affirmed readily, 'although I haven't met one yet.'

'Not courting?'

'Chance would be a fine thing.'

'Ah, it'll come. It'll come, don't worry.'

In spite of Jack's reassurance, I seriously wondered if I would ever get to know a woman. For some reason, I didn't count my mother in this category. Unfair of me, I suppose – but that is how it was. Somehow she never talked to me about anything much beyond the efficiency of our Ideal boiler and the importance of saving any odd bits of string. She also saved tissue paper which covered oranges and the like – but never mentioned that this was for wiping our arses.

Sex was never mentioned apart from her perpetrating the idea that all young women in the village were crazy for it. Once, as we were returning from a shopping trip, she saw a used condom caught up in the privet bushes in the cul-de-sac near our house.

'Patrick, don't look. Don't look at it. Don't touch it, whatever you do, you could catch something from it. Please don't ask me what it is.'

'I won't, I won't ask you anything. I have no need. I know what it is. I know what it's for, too. You get them at the barber's shop.'

I wanted her to recognize that I was not a child, but a man. Yet I knew that for me to achieve any kind of maturity or adult understanding constituted a terrible threat to her security. Her control over me was based on any number of doom-laden gifts that the world was waiting to grant me, and her mortality was a constant source of blackmail.

'You will be the death of me one of these days as sure as there is a God above,' or 'It will be an early grave for me worrying over you.' Her vulnerability to sudden illness could be set off by a chance remark; after my reference to the French letter (the word 'condom' was unknown to us) she took to her bed with a sick headache for the rest of the day.

Jack Edwards, the workmate who was responsible for my sex education, showed me a photograph of his older brother who was serving in the Tank Corps in North Africa. There was nothing unusual about his brother's appearance: he sat in his khaki battledress with a beret tilted jauntily on his head. He smiled out at the camera and held a bren-gun across his knees. Over the barrel of the gun hung a condom.

Jack said, 'Oh, that's there to keep the sand out. I'll bet our Frank could put it to better use on his prick. As for me, I'd rather fuck somebody than shoot them any day of the week – but careless fucking holds no joy for me. I've heard lads tell tales of things they've done with prostitutes – I take all that stuff with a pinch of salt – most of them are lying or fabricating. I never join in. I wouldn't fancy it without love. It never enters my head, not even if I watch Rita Hayworth.'

I think it was close to this time that my passion – no, obsession would be nearer the truth – with Kay began. I recollect I went to the pictures that night, the night after I had talked with Kay in the back garden. I got myself there without even checking on what was being shown, I just went to get out of the house and avoid yet another evening sitting next to the wireless. *Song of the Islands*, that was the name of the film.

It was a musical set in Hawaii and it starred Betty Grable, I don't remember a single tune, I suspect there wasn't much of a story to it all – if there was, I missed it. I do remember Betty in a flowered sarong and the appreciative whistles that came from lads and men in the audience. Through the haze of smoke I admired Betty's body but it was Kay's face that smiled out at me. Soon it was Kay's image that danced in the flowered sarong . . . the bare sanded legs, the long white arms, the purplish lipstick, the rouge and the arched eyebrows. The Technicolor features of her face were indelibly imprinted on my mind. I could see little else.

When I look about this village now, it's hard to envisage just what it was like in those days. These detached or semi-detached houses with their weed-free lawns, their mock Georgian façades, their redundant coach lamps fixed by the side of their doors, their external show . . . their debts . . . none of it existed then.

I could see fields, hedges and brooks from this very garden – now there are tight private housing estates and a massive oblong-shaped shoe-box of a building that is a supermarket. There is no industry here; it has become a posh suburb to the main town, and has no separate identity. Most of the retired mining community left behind are housed in a council estate that was once marshes and the prisoner-of-war camp. In some respects, the present populace mirrors the existence of previous inhabitants – most are imprisoned by poverty and at least half of them eke out their lives on social security payments. Prisoners-of-peace live there now.

I don't have to close my eyes to visualize the young man that was me. Tall, awkward, unable or too shy to ask a partner for a dance – sitting and watching other men whirl their girlfriends about the ballroom floor. How many waltzes or quicksteps or foxtrots or tangos did I witness? When I did manage to co-opt a girl on to the dance floor it felt as though I were dancing with a dwarf.

Surely Kay would dance with me? With her, I wouldn't have to stoop my shoulders and my knees wouldn't seem to get in the way of everything as they usually did – and I could rest a hand on the curve of her spine just above her lovely buttocks.

'Have you ever thought of going to the dance at the Co-op Hall? There's one every Friday night. I'll be glad to take you – more than glad.'

'Thank you, thank you, Mr Harper. How very kind of you to ask me – but I'm afraid my father and I have set our hearts on going to see the new Joan Crawford film on that day. He prefers her to Bette – I can't say I applaud his . . .'

There was a surprising consolation – she agreed to accompany me on a fishing trip the following Sunday.

'Well, Patrick, we had best be leaving you now. We promised to get over to our Betty's place – her daughter is bringing over the new baby. We are grandparents now, you know. Time is catching up on all of us. If you want to pop over for Boxing Day, just give us a ring. Do you think it will be worth our while opening up the centre for three or four days before New Year?'

'I do, I do. We did very well with potted plants and cut flowers last year.' I answer his question, yet my thoughts still remain with Kay. 'And a lot of people seem to die at Christmas time, orders for sprays and wreaths always increase.'

'Yes, you're right, Patrick. I wonder why it is?'

'Perhaps they get over-excited, some of them eat so much they must come near to combustion. Or perhaps lonely hearts become even lonelier and expire with gratitude. Who is to know? There are more murders over Christmas than at any other period in the year too – families go to war with one another. Too many presents, too much food, too much drink – it's a time when jealousies blossom.'

'It's very sad about Kay Roper. I thought you might have been upset by the news. She was good to you and our Evelyn. No, I'll speak the truth, I knew you would be upset, that's why me and the missus weren't going to mention it.'

I look at my brother-in-law and his wife. Decent enough people

– I see their anxious expressions which purvey a genuine concern for me – but . . . but chart out an inventory for them and theirs.

I reply, 'And now you have mentioned it.'

'Have you thought of what is going to happen to her share of the business . . .?'

'No, I haven't.'

'Did you ever have the keys to Kay's house? Being such close neighbours for all these years, I would have thought that you . . .'

'No.' I shake my head. 'I never had the keys to Kay's house.'

'Does she have any relatives? Has anyone been in touch with you? Have they traced the dog owner?'

I look away from him and stare emptily out through the bow windows. I see the potted cyclamens – row on row of them. They have sold well this year – white, pink, deep red and . . . and purple. All the colours are there – very bold – but they are fragile flowers, all show and no guts. Not like Kay . . . not like Kay . . . What a Sunday that was – I was so proud to be walking through the village with her at my side.

'It's too painful to talk about at present?' My brother-in-law breaks my reverie.

'Yes it is,' I mutter.

'Well, we'll be off then. Don't forget to telephone us if you feel the need of company.'

'We do understand, Patrick, we do understand.' His wife murmurs sympathy as I close the door behind them.

I'm so relieved to have this place to myself again. Their visit was well intentioned but raw in its lack of comprehension. How could anyone understand a passion – a passion so full of bewilderment? I never fully understood it myself. Perhaps it's mystery that's at the source of all worship. Was my worship of her any more far-fetched than bread becoming bones or wine changing into blood? I have to dwell on it. That's not me, I'm quoting her.

'I have to dwell on the past in order to give the present any meaning – my presence – my meaning.' She said that, Kay said that.

*

90

She insisted on carrying my fishing rods as well as holding on to the shopping basket where our fish-paste sandwiches nestled in their grease-proof paper alongside three apples. I had told my mother I wouldn't be back in time for tea.

'Starve then,' had been her retort.

It was early October but the day had no chill in the air. Kay had her cardigan balanced about her shoulders as if it were a cape. In those days a walk of ten or maybe fifteen minutes would plant you outside the village into open countryside. It took us longer as Kay seemed to know everyone who we saw in the street; if they were on the other side of the road she would wave and they would cross the road to exchange words with her. Unlike my mother, Kay adored the mining families . . . and . . . and it seemed to me as if they regarded her as some kind of exotic property which belonged to them. I resented anyone who paid attention to her but still got satisfaction from being in the aura of her social limelight.

I was overjoyed to see my workmate Jack Edwards approaching us, accompanied by a woman pushing a push-chair. At last, here was someone who I could introduce to Kay, a reversal of the social round that had gone before.

'Hello, Patrick. Off fishing, then?' Jack didn't wait for me to answer as his question was put as fact. He gestured to his wife, who stood smiling at his side. 'This is my missus – and here – here in the push-chair is our lad. He's George.'

'It's a lovely day for the time of the year, Miss Roper – we thought we'd take George out for the air . . . My mother was ever so grateful to you for helping her with the forms. She's no scholar and worries like mad every time she gets an official-looking envelope.'

'Do you know Miss Roper?' I addressed my question to the two of them.

'Everybody knows Miss Roper.' Jack's wife smiled and picked up George from his push-chair and held him forward for Kay's approval. 'Say hello to Miss Roper, George. Go on – say hello.'

'Hello George, hello George . . .' Kay clucked and tickled the child's chin until he grinned. 'Cheeky boy . . . cheeky boy.'

When they said cheerio, Jack tipped his cap to Kay – not in a sycophantic or servile manner, but with the utmost respect. Some minutes later, we had reached the edge of the last row of houses and I felt excited in realizing that once we had crossed the common I would have Kay all to myself. As we turned the corner and stepped off the grass verge there was a cry for attention.

'Miss Roper! Miss Roper!'

'It's one of my girls – one of my pupils.' Kay held her hand over her eyebrows like some captain on the prow of his ship who has sighted land. 'It's Janet, Janet Haycock, such a dear girl . . . Goodness, it's time she wore a bra.'

The girl, dressed in a green and white checked dress, grubby white ankle socks and black plimsolls, panted to regain her breath when she reached us.

'My mum says . . .' she gasped, 'my mum says . . . that I can come with you.'

Kay introduced us. The girl responded politely and said that she was pleased to meet me. All I could do was nod; I felt too choked with disappointment to speak. Kay chatted away as we crossed the common. For the most part she sounded like one of those boring country diary bits in the newspaper or on the wireless – autumn is red, ochre, brown and gold, all that kind of thing. Janet Haycock never took her eyes off her all the time she was speaking – it was as if every word Kay spoke was a verse from the bible. For my part, I think I must have sulked all the way to the canal bank.

This was a working canal then and one or two barges were moored along the towpath. We walked past the barges and came to a section where a disused water basin or canal harbour spilled itself away from the main water course. I stopped and moved my tackle from my shoulders on to the grassy bank.

'Is this where we are sitting, Mr Harper?' Kay asked.

'Yes. I'll fish for a few gudgeon first. Live bait. Then I'll cast a pike-line into the basin over there. You and Janet can take turns to keep an eye on the pike-line if you like. Just watch the three corks – if one starts to bob or go under, give me a call straight away.'

Like most anglers, I took great care over the methodical unpacking of my fishing tackle – there is always a right place for everything. Janet Haycock's attention was drawn away from this activity by Kay who enthused about the wild flora all about us. I wanted to quibble with Kay and tell her to stop being a 'teacher' when she was away from work. Yet, before my rods were assembled, I too paused to listen to her gentle didacticism and observations. It became clear to me that she was not showing off her knowledge but sharing her sense of wonder, which was entirely genuine.

'... and from the look of this canal bank we could say that early October was a bluish time of the year. It demonstrates that nature can deal attractively with opposites as well as harmonious shades. See how the purple, lilac, pink and blue combine to give the tufted vetch its blossom. These colours we can see again in the Michaelmas daisies, campion and speedwell. I think the shades of colour are more defined because the hedgerows have lost most of their foliage . . . You see the berries? The hawthorn fruit has come into being – bird fodder.'

Then she directed her attention towards me, fixing me with her deep blue eyes and invitingly painted red mouth. She drew responses from me gently and slashed away my truculence and crippling shyness. Cleverly, she placed me in charge of our afternoon's leisure so that I was obliged to make our outing informed as well as pleasurable.

I explained the functions of the keep-net as I secured its rope to the bank; I talked about different kinds of floats, different sizes of hooks, and different types of bait.

'These are maggots.' For a few seconds I let them stare as the fly larvae writhed around cupped in the palm of my hand. 'They are good for roach, bream, tench, or perch or gudgeon . . . an all-purpose bait, really.'

Kay and Janet stared in fascinated horror at the mass of creamy white grubs wriggling and writhing within the bait tin.

'They seem to be in a frenzy or some sort of ecstasy. Do you think they are capable of anticipating their fate? What unrelaxed creatures they are – I suppose frenzy and ecstasy are harmonious too.' Kay held out her palm and I sprinkled a few on to her skin.

'Why?' she exclaimed. 'I cannot . . . I cannot prevent them from burrowing through the spaces between my fingers no matter how tightly I keep them closed. Such determination and persistence deserve a reward.'

Janet Haycock denied herself the experience and looked away when I impaled a maggot on to the hook. Kay watched the operation carefully and noted the role of the barb in securing both the bait and its future prey.

I cast into the centre of the canal so that my line could catch the drift and hoped the gudgeon might be feeding. I allowed Kay to toss a few maggots about my float and explained that this ought to attract some fish to our area. I had expected the two females to chatter but they remained quite still and silent. Janet looked about her a great deal, not in a restless way, more as if she was giving herself a rerun of what Kay had said before.

For her part, Kay never took her eyes away from the water. They centred on the red tip of the float and the ripples surrounding it. I've never seen a match-fisherman concentrating as intently as she was. I had to catch a fish – this could not be a day when we only contemplated the joy of the sport rather than partaking of it.

'Oh . . . oh . . . oh, Mr Harper . . .' Kay whispered as the float lurched and then began a series of bobs in the water. 'Oh, he's taken it . . .' Kay could not contain her excitement as I struck when the red tip of the float dived down. Both women watched me land a four-inch gudgeon. Kay continued watching as I prised the hook from the fish's lip. Janet's gaze returned to the hedgerows.

'The purple and the blue . . . they are in the scales of the fish too.' Kay took it from me and let it flop into the keep-net. She placed her hand near her nose and sniffed. 'They have a very strong odour for a small fish, Mr Harper.'

'That's what the pike like about them.'

'Their smell? Their colour?'

'Both. And their taste.'

94

I felt myself blush after this short exchange and applied myself more determinedly to catching more unsuspecting gudgeon. The thought of colour, smell and taste in Kay's presence had given me an uncomfortable erection – such was the state of my enchantment with her.

In twenty minutes or half an hour, I'd added half a dozen or more gudgeon to the keep-net. They are greedy little fish if you find them at the right moment. Kay loved the excitement of the catch ... the silent waiting ... the anticipation ... the fatal attraction of the fish to the bait ... and the strike. She seemed euphoric over the success of our haul and I suggested that this was as good a time as any to take a break and have our meal. Before we began the meal I cast the pike-line into the basin and fished at a deeper level for large roach or perch where we were sitting.

Kay washed her hands in the canal water, dried them on the edge of her skirt, took scent from her handbag and dabbed it generously about her. She also took out her powder-compact and eyed her reflection in its mirror. Lipstick, powder and rouge were generously applied to her face, which appeared to have no need of them.

'There are plenty of sandwiches here and an apple for each of us.' Kay spread the food out before us on the towel as she spoke. I realized then that Janet Haycock's presence was no accident – no off-the-cuff invitation – but planned. Yet I could no longer feel angry, and I had grudgingly come to like this wide-browed, mean-faced girl ... there was something brave about the way she exposed her red birth-mark. After all, it was only another colour.

'My mother gave us some pie.' Janet revealed her contribution from its newspaper wrapping and placed it on the towel. I took out a large bottle of Vimto from my haversack and handed it to Kay.

In those war years, the weather, like our pleasure or sadness, always seemed to be a matter of extremes. In winter, we spent weeks of snow-bound discomfort, in summer we sweated but worked even harder, and in autumn – particularly this autumn – we absorbed its glow.

I recall looking over at the two women who sat opposite me and thinking how lucky I was to be in such charming company. No, it's not just recall: the pieces are set in my mind like a series of photographs or oil paintings. Janet's slow smile and the beautiful cow-like manner in which she chewed on each bite of her sandwich – and the way Kay used her fingers even when she was not eating or gesticulating, sort of feeling the air, the way young infants perform during their first few months.

Kay said, 'There are times since I have been here in Padmore . . . there are times when I have experienced such moments of happiness, I feel guilt that such bliss could come to me in a period of war.'

'Are you happy now, Miss Roper? Is this one of those times?' Janet asked.

Before Kay had time to give this question any thought, I asked her another one. 'And do you feel guilty?'

Kay laughed lightly and asked for another sandwich and a spot more Vimto, then she said, 'The questions are too big – too complex for me . . . Can you answer them, Mr Harper?'

I wanted to answer them without speech. I wanted to take her in my arms, hold her close to my body, pass my hands all about her, enter her and whisper a torrent of endearments and worship into her ear. Instead I shook my head, an act of cowardice that I still regret.

I addressed Janet. 'I suppose you will be leaving school soon?'

'I'll be leaving my present school next July but I won't be going to work.' Janet registered a sideways glance towards Kay Roper as she spoke.

'You are not getting married?' I asked, knowing that many girls married soon after they left school. It was not unusual for girls to leave school in July and marry in the following August. Some managed to give birth to their first child by Christmas. Janet must have read my thoughts.

'I don't intend getting pregnant, Mr Harper, if that's what you were asking.'

Kay saved me from further embarrassment. 'Janet is leaving us for Trentfield High School for Girls. She has been awarded a scholarship. There are a few places given for talent rather than money, and she is to take up a PGT place next September.'

'A PGT place?' I was genuinely perplexed. Was this some young women's auxiliary force?

'A Poor Girls' Trust ... Janet's award is decorated by the patronage of its donors – it should, of course, be called a PGR.'

'A PGR?' Janet enquired.

'A Poor Girls' Right. It is your right. It is your right to attend that school, Janet – always remember that. They are giving you nothing that is not your rightful due.'

This short display of Kay's anger thrilled me and I observed its effect upon Janet. She pushed the dark brown tresses of hair away from her brow and looked out towards some point well beyond the other side of the canal.

'I must tell my mum and dad that – it's my right ... it's my right ...' She gave us another one of her slow satisfied smiles. 'Let's eat the bilberry pie.'

Never since that time has anything matched the taste of that pie. The fruit was strange to me. I had never heard of such berries, let alone eaten them in a pie. We asked Janet to pass on our thanks and pleasure to her mother as we finished off every morsel of this delicacy. I owned up that I had never eaten it before and made clear my ignorance in its cultivation.

'Oh, bilberries are not cultivated – they are wild. Their habitat needs a wilderness. They grow on the edges of the heath and chase-land that border the pine forests. People here have picked them for years ... long before this war ... long before the last. They have been gleaned for centuries. A true local delicacy.'

Kay looked down at her fingertips after she had completed her discourse. It was as though she had suddenly seen her hands changed into some other form of growth. First she looked at Janet and then turned her full attention on me. She gazed at me as if she were about to devour the features of my face, then shyness came over me and I made a movement as if to stand, a move to break this silent communion.

'We too have entered the month – your lips and the area below your bottom lip have turned purple or blue – or both of those colours. Look at your hands, they have taken on the hue of the season. We are stained by it. Nature has left its mark on us.' Kay laughed at her own observations.

I said, 'We look like heart patients.'

Janet asked, 'What *does* a broken heart mean, Miss Roper? How can you *break* a heart? I've heard it said and sung, but how is it possible?'

I expected Kay to explain the workings of the human body, the correlation between emotional injury and physical suffering, how one can lead to the other. She began to fold the towel and collect together our apple cores. I thought she was going to ignore the question in the usual way that adults avoid telling the truth to adolescents . . . and then she said, 'A heart cannot be broken by the loss of a loved one, it can only be broken by betrayal. Things are not often as drastic as that. Some hearts harden to protect themselves.'

Was this an early code warning for me? I'll never know. We began our second angling session and Kay assisted whilst I withdrew a gudgeon from the keep-net and threaded it on to the pike-line.

'This is live bait. This is what the big pike loves to feed on and . . .' I explained the reasoning behind the impaling of the silvery fish.

Kay watched everything I did as though she were a theatre-nurse helping in some problematic hospital operation. Janet had turned her face away and it seemed as if she did not wish to hear what I had to say nor witness the sacrifice I had prepared.

Kay accompanied me as I walked along the towpath to the edge of the basin – she would watch the pike-float for the first half-hour, then Janet could take a turn. I pointed to the corks. 'If the first cork begins to bob give me a call. I'll take the rod and give you the landing-net. If I hook a fish do you think you can handle the net when I bring him into the shallows?'

'Yes, of course.'

'Have you fished before? Do you know how?'

'Instinct. I know by instinct, Mr Harper.'

'I'd prefer you to call me Patrick. Would you?' This was an appeal from the heart on my part.

'I will always be Miss Roper to you – and you will always be Mr Harper to me. Do not take offence, I beg of you, it has nothing to do with rules or regulations concerning our friendship. It is . . . it is just that I enjoy my single status and I enjoy being reminded of it by the use of the word "Miss". That's not a lot to ask of you, Mr Harper, is it?'

'You can ask of me what you like. Miss Roper it will always be, then.'

'Thank you. Thank you, Mr Harper.' This was addressed from her heart.

On returning to our central position I changed the depth of my line. There was no need of any more gudgeon and I hoped that by fishing deeper I might come across some large roach or maybe even a chub or two. Janet Haycock seemed little interested and sat quietly reading a magazine called *Silver Star Weekly*. I cast out my line and placed the rod in its rest.

'I'll bet there are no other teachers in your school as glamorous as Miss Roper. It's a good job it's not a mixed school.'

Even as I spoke, I knew that I sounded crude – but I had never had much opportunity for talking with girls or women. I knew I'd spoken with Janet as though she were a miner or a fellow Bevin Boy.

She placed the magazine on the grass verge and answered me in a civil but cold manner. Her face remained expressionless.

'There are no teachers who work as hard as Miss Roper. There are no teachers who care for us in the way that Miss Roper does. What she chooses to look like is her own business. My mum and dad think she is lovely – and so do I.'

'Do you want to look like her when you are older?'

'No, I want to look like me.'

'I suppose you will miss her when you start at your new school?'

'I shan't. I shan't because I'll always see her. She is not just my teacher . . . she is . . . she is my friend.'

'Do you think that she will ever marry?'

'I don't know. My dad says not, he says she belongs to the

village, he says she's like a budgerigar hen that will never go broody, he says that she's got too much spirit for any man to control.' She picked up her magazine and casually flicked through the pages before adding, 'She belongs to us, Mr Harper. All of us.'

We pursued no further talk concerning Kay. We chatted on a bit about the pit. How terrible it was for men working at the coalface, how all Janet's uncles were coal-cutters, and of the deaths of two of them during a roof collapse.

I had not thought too much about my work. In wartime what I was doing was a civic obligation. I merely felt grateful that I wasn't working at the coal-face. My height and inexperience spared me from the hazards of working hour after hour on my knees in stench, dust and darkness, nor did I have to consider the fragility of the pit-props which held up great seams of coal. This black gold was unselective and mercurial as to whom it chose to fall on. A fall of coal was not so different from an air-raid, only there was less warning entailed.

It suited me better feeding the conveyor belt. I liked my working companions – even so, each time I entered that cage ready for descent into what seemed like the bowels of the earth, I experienced a measure of trepidation. The descent was always alarmingly swift, and by the time it reached the pit bottom I felt I had left my stomach behind at the top.

'You won't stay down the pit when the war is over, will you, Mr Harper?'

'No, no. I don't think so, Janet.'

'What will you do? What other work will you do?'

'I don't know. I think I'd like to work outside. In the daylight. Perhaps I'll clean windows like George Formby. What about you?'

'All I know . . . all I know is that I don't want to live a life like my mother – or any of my aunties. That's all I know. Neither of us seems to have as much choice as there is in a packet of liquorice allsorts, do we, Mr Harper?'

Janet smiled again and indicated Kay Roper's approach with a movement of her hand. 'Time to change partners,' she said. 'It's like an excuse-me quickstep.'

'Oh, I'm no dancer. My legs always take on a life of their own once I put them on a dance floor. They don't seem to go where I'd wish them to go.'

'Try the Palais Glide. Link arms with three or four people . . . Here's Miss Roper. I'll take over her position.'

I watched them exchange a few words with one another as their paths crossed on the towpath. Kay was pointing to a forlorn-looking pool of water some distance from the canal and not more than a field or two away from the lane. A minute or so later she reached me, sat down and displayed her sanded knees and supported her body with one of her long white arms.

'The pike seem to have lost their appetite or gone on hunger strike, not a single movement from the corks. How has the sport fared here? Are the gudgeon proving to be as greedy as ever?'

'I'm not fishing for them; we have enough for our needs. I've lowered the bait. As a rule, the deeper you fish the larger the catch, but – and it is a big "but" – you need some luck. I was hoping for a few large roach or bream. It seems they've all gone off their feed.' I sought to change the subject. 'Janet worships you.'

'I cannot accept your observation, Mr Harper.'

'She does. I've just listened to a litany of your skills and attributes.'

'Janet is too intelligent a girl to worship an idol, whether it was alive or dead. I will grant that she is devoted to me . . . in the same way that Judy Garland is devoted to Mickey Rooney or her pet dog. You must have seen them on the screen? I would not call that worship.'

I laughed and said, 'I don't think you resemble Mickey Rooney.'

'I'm truly glad to hear you say so.' Kay offered this in a serious manner as though it were not part of a jest.

I thought, now is the time . . . now is the time for a declaration – a time for confidences. Once I had started speaking I knew that if I stopped, I would be unable to continue again and my shyness would prevent me from ever letting her know – letting her know anything.

'I was wondering, Miss Roper . . . Miss Roper, I was wondering, no, hoping, you might like to come out with me sometime. Perhaps to the pictures? You like the pictures. To a dance? Although I must admit I dance like a duck in a thunderstorm. Or perhaps we could go walking together? I was wondering if you would like to go out with me? I've never asked a girl such a question before, you see – I so very badly want to be very close to you. I hope you don't think I'm being too brazen about this. If the idea appeals to you, I can't tell you how happy it will make me feel . . . and . . . and . . .' I took my eyes away from the float and somehow mustered up the courage to face her, to look at her.

And I swear, I swear on it, I saw not only affection in her eyes but . . . but gratitude. I wanted to reach over to her, there and then in the broad daylight, and hold her to me. Yet I remained frozen where I stood – as though rooted in the banks of the canal like some unyielding marsh plant. At last, after what seemed a bloody lifetime, she spoke. She spoke in a tender, quiet, but measured way. She did not avert her eyes – it was me who lowered mine like some demure maiden. I gazed blindly at the tufted vetch and Michaelmas daisies.

'Mr Harper – oh, Mr Harper, thank you so much for saying so many beautiful things. I'll always, always remember them. I would never wish to make you unhappy . . . and I will go to the cinema with you from time to time. It's a privilege to have the friendship and companionship of a man who is as decent as you are. I offer you friendship with all my heart. I cannot offer more. No closer proximity than that. Not now, not ever, so do not hold out any hope of it. Do not think of me in terms of courtship or romance; I can never be persuaded into it. Not with you, or anyone.' She paused here, as people sometimes do if they are making a rehearsed statement.

I don't know whether it was the wilfulness of a first passion or the blind hopes that unrequited lovers always hold in reserve – but I refused to accept the gist of her words. Or was it that I enjoyed pursuing something I knew was beyond my reach?

She continued, 'Please, please, Mr Harper, do not suppose it is because I think you are unattractive. Far from it – you are one of the most beautiful men I have ever met.'

'I've never heard the word "beautiful" applied to a man,' I muttered grudgingly. 'To a woman – yes, but not to a man.'

Her retort was quick and sharp in delivery. 'I am not responsible for the limitations of your experience, Mr Harper. I do assure you – some men are beautiful. I can appreciate them only in an aesthetic sense; my life is devoted to my father. If I ever allowed a progression of feeling towards another man, it . . . it would not be right.'

She drew attention to a flock of noisy starlings who were extending their proprietorial rights to all the hawthorn bushes on the other side of the canal bank. The sparrows and three or four blackbirds seemed to have taken flight from this feathered army of occupation. Kay's gesture indicated that the talk on human nature, our nature, the two of us, was closed.

The fish had gone off their feeding. My float remained erect and still. There wasn't even a ripple on the surface of the water; everything was quiet and calm and the starlings had stopped their chattering. The somnolence all about us seemed to have affected Kay. I glanced covertly and enjoyed the kingfisher blue of her eyelids.

'Got it!' My float began to lurch and wobble before plummeting into the depths of the canal. I struck hard on my rod and realized immediately that I had hooked a decent-sized fish. Kay needed no apprenticeship: she slid the landing-net carefully under the fish, allowing me to bring it on to the shore without any line breakage.

'Oh, it's huge. What a beautiful colour. Surely, it must be big enough to eat.' Kay stared intently at the fish as it flopped about helplessly in the landing-net.

'It's a tench,' I informed her as I prised the hook from its upper lip.

'I've never tasted it,' said Kay.

'You wouldn't have. They are not much good for eating. They love the canal bottom. Mud lovers. They have a sluggish, unpleasant taste – you would only choose to eat one if you were starving.'

As I wiped the fish slime from my hands it occurred to me that, in one way, Kay and my mother were alike. They both enjoyed rationing. Every night my mother would count and check our coupons and talk endlessly about the things we couldn't have: 'I prefer egg-powder to eggs – hen's mess.' I think my mother liked a narrow horizon, a limited choice of things.

As for Kay, I imagine she thought of the war years as a permanent period of siege. In this sense, shortage of food could be complemented by considering anything that moved or grew as an edible proposition. Survival excited her.

I had recast my line, and sport and conversation seemed to lapse. I could think of little I wanted to say; I felt I'd already said far too much. After what had been said before, whatever followed would sound trite. Kay destroyed this theory as though she were dropping an incendiary bomb.

'I hope I've not upset you, Mr Harper. I wouldn't want to do that. It is true, I can never love you . . . but that does not mean . . . that does not mean . . . that as of a moment in time . . . I might not . . . I might not desire you.'

I couldn't answer her. Her statement caused my prick to rise up as erect as the float . . . I was so alive. There was a shout. A scream. Another shout.

'Come quickly! Come quickly! Mr Harper, Miss Roper, come quickly. Come. Come over here.'

We ran along the towpath in answer to Janet Haycock's appeal. She stood waving her arms like a windmill and urging us to make haste.

When we reached her she acted as though she had been struck dumb but managed to point to the corks which were rising and disappearing in the water and careering all about the canal basin.

'It's a pike, a big one. I've hooked it.'

The two women watched me take the strain on the rod.

'Thrilling, it's so thrilling.' Kay murmured encouragement.

'Get the landing-net,' I ordered.

Kay was off like a rocket, retracing our steps. I played the fish in the water: I needed to tire it before bringing it into the shore. By the time Kay returned, I had begun to reel it in. She entered all the drama of the catch – but Janet distanced herself a little from us as the fish began to thrash about in the shallows. Kay lowered the landing-net and lifted the fish on to the bank.

'My God, it's heavy,' she declared.

The creature lay there on the bank, all sixteen pounds of it, opening and closing its vicious bill-like jaws. Kay made some biological remark about the way its teeth turned inwards. I warned her not to get her hand near to the mouth. I slaughtered the creature by delivering two or three heavy blows to its head with a large stone. Kay stood near me and watched unemotionally as I gouged my hooks from the gaping throat.

'What a feast he'll make, what a feast. In Tudor times, fish like this often made up the centre-piece of a banquet. Janet, do come and . . .' I followed Kay's look of concern and saw that Janet had fainted.

Kay sat behind her and lifted her shoulders from the ground so that Janet's head rested close to Kay's bosom. Kay patted her cheek lightly. I saw Janet's eyes flutter and eventually open. She had gone quite pale, but it seemed to me that her recovery was more protracted than it need have been. She smiled coyly and murmured a vague kind of apology.

I can see that look of Janet's even now. It said, 'I'm where you want to be. It's me who is lying in Kay's arms.' For the rest of the day there was an air of dreamy triumph about the girl.

On our journey home, Kay was full of culinary enthusiasm in anticipation of preparing the pike for a dinner. She spoke rapidly and I noticed how she licked her top lip when she paused – as if to savour or relish her own preparation.

'It should feed four or five. I wonder if you would care to join us, Mr Harper?'

I nodded. I didn't owe too much for the idea of eating the creature, but I'd have put up with anything just to be in her company.

'First, I shall make a stuffing. Stale breadcrumbs, some chopped parsley, a chopped onion, pepper, salt, and a little margarine mixed in milk should be just right. Then I shall stuff the pike.'

'How do you do that, Miss Roper? Do you have to chop the fish's head off first?' Janet enquired nervously.

'No, no, my dear – I shall place a large apple in its jaws. It will bake there. No, the baking of a fish – a large fish such as this – has something of a fairy-tale quality to it.'

'Really? It won't change into something else, will it?' Janet asked incredulously.

'Of course not. First you split open the stomach, then clean the fish thoroughly and pack in the stuffing. And finally, you sew it all up again with needle and thread and, presto, it's ready for the oven.'

'It sounds more like a horror story to me – hardly suitable for children.' I spoke lightly and looked at Janet and laughed.

'Fairy-tales are full of horror, Mr Harper – but the other ingredients offer hope and wonderment.' She sighed and added, 'I doubt if there was ever a prince who was both handsome and good.' She drew our attention to a pond just a field or two away from the lane.

'Is that it? Is that the place you pointed out to me from the canal bank, Janet?'

'Yes, that's it. That's the Dog and Cat,' said Janet.

'My mates at the pit never fish there. I've been warned to keep away from it, it's not a place to bide time near. I suppose it's stagnant.'

We stopped to look at the pool. A light mist had begun to gather over its surface – and in a strange, unspoken, collective agreement we made our way through a gap in the hedgerow and walked towards the perimeters of the water.

'I wonder why they call it the Dog and Cat?' I asked an open question.

'We know, Miss Roper and I know,' said Janet.

Neither shared their knowledge with me and we continued walking in silence until we reached the water's edge.

I pointed to a clear stretch of water between green algae and tall bulrushes. 'Look, there's life here. There's life.'

'What are they? They are too big for newts.' Janet sounded both shocked and captivated.

'Newts are what they are – great-crested newts. I've only ever seen them in books before now. Never like this. Never so many of them. It's as though they have inhabited this lost world for safety. They are protected here by a taboo of which they are entirely ignorant.' Kay held my arm as she spoke as if this were a natural thing to do.

I studied the newts as if I were under some kind of spell. One of the creatures – it must have been six or seven inches long – glided towards us, innocent and intrepid. It seemed to hang in the water so that we could see it display its lovely spotted belly and many-coloured, long, serrated tail.

'The pool can't be lifeless and it's not stagnant. There ought to be fish in it. I'll try it out,' I said.

'No, no, leave the place alone.' This was a gentle order from Kay.

'But why?' I asked.

It was Janet who answered. I think she answered not just for herself or Kay, but for the whole village.

'This is a pool of death, Mr Harper. It's a watery grave if ever there was one. When my mother was a girl of my age, they found here the body of a young woman.'

'Poor thing, had she drowned herself?'

'No, she'd been murdered. Not just murdered. Cut up. Cut up in little pieces. A sack was found with an arm in it, another with a foot, another with part of a leg . . . and finally they found one with a head in it.'

'How terrible, who on earth had done . . .'

'It was her husband – his name was Gantlin. He was a very jealous man and he'd imagined that his wife had been carrying on with someone else – but she hadn't. All the village said she was true to him. It made no difference what they said, he'd got this idea into his head and nothing or no one could make him see right. He strangled his own wife with a clothes-line . . . and then threw her . . . bit by bit . . . piece by piece . . . into this pond.'

'Was he brought to trial?'

'He gave himself up and he was hung at Stafford prison. He

never said he was sorry or anything like that and he smiled when the judge said he was for the rope.'

We began to make our way back and Kay placed herself between Janet and me, linking arms with us both. We were glad of one another's company as the atmosphere had now become dank and chilled.

In the lane I enquired. 'But why the Dog and Cat? Why call it that?'

'It's suitably christened.' Kay shuddered. I felt her tremble as she made her observation. 'Most of the unwanted kittens, the unwanted puppies, and dogs and cats who have nearly got to their natural end, or who are too sick to get better, end up there. Vets are too expensive – a luxury beyond most pockets. Why, even the people in Padmore have to be nearly half-dead before they visit a doctor: funds do not run to preventative cures. Kindness to their pets is tempered by economic restraints. I am surprised by the generosity of spirit that abounds here considering the harsh existence most of the people live out. Of course, I cannot condone murder or senseless killing of anything that lives. I can't help thinking that environment has a lot to answer for. Daffodils or bluebells could not exist in a desert, but some cactus flowers are very beautiful when they eventually flower. What a struggle they must face to come into bloom.'

Janet Haycock loved these speeches, for that is what they were: Kay seemed to speak to the hedgerows and not to us directly. I noticed that Janet had lost the second button on her blouse and my curiosity was constantly drawn to a glimpse of part of her breast. I experienced a guilty pleasure from peeping at its curve and wondering what it would be like to cup the whole of it in my hand and place my open mouth about its nipple.

'It's been a delightful day, Mr Harper. I think we must part company here.' Kay spoke abruptly and I felt myself blushing with shame. Had she noticed my preoccupation with Janet's clothing? We had come to an intersection in the high street.

'I am walking back to Janet's house to have a chat with her parents about her future. Just a chat, mind you – I do not believe in plotting a destiny.'

'Perhaps I will see you later?' I almost pleaded.

'Without a doubt, Mr Harper. Only a blind or severely incapacitated person could avoid seeing their next-door neighbour.'

'I meant today. This evening, in fact.'

She shook her head. 'I'm afraid not. I've arranged to go to the pictures with my father – it's a Charles Laughton film. Such a fine actor, don't you think? With a single expression he manages to be both comic and tragic. I have an intuition that his personal life away from the screen holds some secret life, some secret sadness.'

'I think we all have secret sadnesses.' I managed to look into her eyes for a fraction of a second. 'We can't all be actors, Miss Roper.'

She returned my glance and said, 'Performance and reality lie close, Mr Harper.' As if to prove her point she took Janet's arm as though the girl were related to her in some way and marched purposefully away from me.

I can't remember how I made my way home that night. I do know it felt as though my whole frame were in some kind of turmoil. On one level I felt a degree of rejection, but in another way I felt excited and elated, it was as if I were enjoying the effects of some titillating transgression or drug.

It was in this heightened state that I found myself knocking on the door of Aileen Pugh, who occupied the other house in our turning. I had seen her on few occasions – she was an unremarkable, solidly built woman of around forty. It was said that she originated from Cardiff – her lilting South Wales accent and low voice were probably her most appealing feature. The tightly rolled curls about her head and the lipstick-blurred mouth did not seem to be part of her. She was recorded as a corsetry agent, but my mother had other ideas about her station in life.

'Don't speak to that woman, Patrick. She's scarlet. She's rubbish. Do be warned.'

'What's wrong with her? She's doing us no harm. You wear a corset yourself.'

'Not one of hers, I don't. How many women have you seen going there to be fitted up?'

'A few – maybe one or two.'

'Ah, one or two. That's not enough for a livelihood. Now, answer me this. Since when have soldiers and airmen needed to wear a corset whilst they are on leave? Tell me when? Well, there's four or five called there this week.'

'She might be related to them,' I suggested.

'She's old enough to be their mother or their auntie, I'll grant you that, but if all those young men are relatives then her mother must have been employed in a sausage factory. The quicker she goes back to Wales the better.'

Aileen Pugh opened the door and spoke. She said something about fittings and I explained that I had come on my own behalf and that my call had nothing to do with my mother.

'Strained your back, have you, lad?' she enquired sympathetically. 'Heavy lifting takes its toll even on the youngest. Growing men can have back trouble, I hope you're not going to get any taller, you'll end up like a poplar tree. Always bend your knees a little when you are lifting something heavy – it takes the strain off your spine. A corset can help for a . . .'

'My back is fine.' I spoke urgently and she understood my plea.

For further evidence she looked down towards my fly buttons and observed the aching bulge in my trousers which I could do little about.

'Oh dear, oh dear, you are in a bit of a state, aren't you? Cold showers are a cruel compensation and the effect is not lasting. You had better come in off the doorstep. If your mother sees you there she'll try to get me shot – or stoned to death.'

I followed her into the small sitting room that led off the kitchen. With one hand she indicated that I should place my fishing tackle near one of the two rexine chairs. There was a single bed in the corner of the room and close beside it stood a chest of drawers. On top of the chest of drawers were a jug and wash-basin, a bar of soap, and two or three neatly folded bath-towels. The curtains were drawn and a poster stuck on one wall said, 'Careless talk costs lives.'

She hardly spoke at all: the whole procedure was not too dissimilar from a medical examination. She took one bath-towel and laid it lengthways on the bed. From one of the drawers she took out a piece of rubber tubing – one end of it was attached to a spout and the other was fixed to an oval-shaped rubber receptacle. She placed this in methodical fashion alongside the towel on the chest of drawers. Then she gave me instructions as though I were attending a clinic for some ordinary kind of treatment – I could have been consulting a chiropodist about painful bunions or corns.

'Wash your hands, would you, love? There's water in the jug. Use the green towel – I've set it aside for you. Don't rush at it like a mad bull. I'll tell you when I'm ready.'

I watched her set free her stockings from her suspender belt and unpeel them from her dimpled thighs.

'Take your shoes and trousers off, dear. The buttons can hurt like hell if they are grinding next to your skin and shoes mark the bed covers.'

There was no brassiere under the pale angora wool jumper. She cupped a large breast in either hand and pushed them upwards as she looked down at them in self-admiration. 'Nice, aren't they?' She spoke as if she were referring to some choice fruit.

She looked towards me. 'You can keep your shirt and socks on – oh dear God, you're well blessed. It's a pity your dick can't fire bullets. I reckon you could shoot down a Stuker dive-bomber with that cannon.'

She picked a record out from a pile of three or four. It sounded badly scratched, but the turntable didn't reject it. 'I like a bit of music – do you, Patrick? I'll call when I'm ready.'

Aileen lay on the bed, lifted her skirt so that the bottom of it covered the dark red disks surrounding her nipples, then she raised her knees and parted her legs.

'Come on then, lad. Come on – let that lovely cock nestle into this warm nest. It's been out in the cold too long.'

I moved towards her, closed my eyes and let myself be guided. 'Gently does it. Gently . . . gently . . . oh I can feel it. Gently . . . That's it. That's nice now, isn't it?'

I couldn't utter any endearments – my relief was so great, speech had gone from me. Gracie Fields sang 'Wish me luck as you wave me goodbye' as I thrust to and fro. 'Cheerio – on my way – here we go,' she sang. At the point where Gracie began to yodel or make a noise that sounded something like yodelling, I came. It flooded from me in protracted spurts. By the time the song was finished, Aileen was properly dressed again and I was putting my shoes on.

'You'd better not call again, Patrick. Nothing personal, mind. And it's not that you weren't good – you were no trouble at all, took to it like a duck to water. With some clients it's all talk and no do, I can tell you. It's no easy job getting a marshmallow into a money box – but that is how it is with some customers, poor things. Think of me, Patrick – don't call here again. Your mother would cause trouble for me and I don't want to piddle on my own doorstep. You do understand?'

'Yes, Aileen.' I managed to find my voice. I felt relaxed and experienced no sense of shame or guilt. Nor did I feel cheated when she asked me for seven and sixpence.

'I hope to satisfy my customers but there are some who Delilah couldn't please. If you get into a state again, there's no harm in putting a hand to yourself for a bit of relief. If anyone tells you it affects your brain, they are talking rubbish. Even priests. And you're not a priest by any chalk mark – but I must say you are well blessed. I can vouch for that. What's wrong?'

She must have detected the look of dismay on my face as I began to forage through both my trouser pockets. At this time, Bevin Boys were paid three pounds per week and nothing more, and that was presented to you as if it were a privilege. 'The Government has decided that the essential manpower require-ments of the coal-mining industry should be met by making underground coal-mining employment an alternative to service in the Armed Forces and by directing to such employment a number of men who would otherwise be available for call-up service in the Armed Forces.' I counted out five shillings and threepence and thrust a hand back into my pocket knowing it to be empty. 'The method of selecting men for direction to this employment has been made public. It is by ballot and is strictly impartial. Your name is amongst those selected.' We looked at one another, both regretting the frugal resources of the times.

112

'I'm sorry . . . er . . . I'm afraid I'm short on cash, Aileen. Er . . . I can make the difference up to you next week.' I was honestly apologetic.

'No need,' Aileen responded matter of factly. 'You might get yourself all gingered up again by next week and a young man with your zest could be in a mountain of debt by the end of the month.' She accepted the five and threepence and dropped the coins into a jar that was placed behind the 'shy girl' statuette. 'That goes towards my wool shop. I'll open it when this rotten war is over.'

'Your wool shop?'

My enquiry seemed to surprise her. 'Why not a wool shop? I shall go back to Wales and I'll buy a shop in Neath. That's where most of my family are. I'll sell wool, woollens and baby clothes. When men get back from a war they need lots of love-making and everybody ends up with bigger families. The messages will change again. It will be "A woman's place is with her children" – they'll tell women their place is on their backs with their legs up at night-time and attached to the kitchen sink during the day. Their service in the factories will no longer be considered honourable. There's less justice for women, you know.'

'You sound like Kay Roper,' I said.

'Ah, Kay. You've set your cap for her, haven't you? No need to look down at my rug. There's more than one man in this village who would like to have Kay rooted in his back bedroom. I know that for a fact. She's spoken for.'

'Who? Who is it? Is he local or does he live in the town?'

Now it was Aileen's turn to stare at the rug. She made no reply to my questioning.

As she stared her expression changed from one of resignation to dawning horror. Suddenly, she screamed and leapt up on to one of the rexine chairs.

'A rat! A rat! Your bag! It's moving.' She pointed to my fishing satchel. 'Oh Christ in Heaven.'

The satchel behaved as though it were poltergeist-ridden. It moved and bobbed and bounced about the floor near to her feet. Aileen whimpered with fright as I took the bag up in both hands.

'Please, please don't,' she whined as I opened it – then she covered her eyes with both hands.

'There's nothing to worry about, Aileen.' I spoke soothingly. 'It's not a rat. Look, look it won't upset you.'

She studied the pike from between her fingers. 'A fish – what a whopper,' she said, and dropped her hands to her sides and began to laugh. 'Is it still alive?'

'No, I don't think so. Large fish like this one often convulse and twitch after they are dead.'

'How terrible to have a fit after you are dead. Though I suppose it's better than having one while you are alive. I'm partial to fish.' She heaved herself on to the rug and knelt before me and looked hard at the fish which I displayed before me. 'I suppose you cook this as you would cook cod, do you?'

'Yes,' I lied, as I could not prepare a boiled egg let alone a pike. 'Would you like it?'

'Oh no, I couldn't.' Aileen's response was unconvincing.

'It will wipe out what I owe you. Fair is fair, Aileen.'

'If you insist, Patrick – if you insist. Let yourself out quietly, would you, dear? It's dark now so nobody is likely to see you leaving. Mind the front doorstep – some of my guests fall arse over tit on that step. They will rush so when they have had their way.'

'Is he in this village? The man who Kay is keen on?' I whispered from the hallway.

'He's in her head. Off you go now, that's all you need to know.'

If there was a man in her life, I never saw him materialize. She had no male company about her apart from me and her father. She seemed happier and content in the company of women. I think her women would have died for her if necessary. Ivy Chaplin, Janet Haycock, my wife – they all adored Kay. Now she's dead, there's no getting around that fact – but I still feel the presence of her, she haunts me. She's in my head and I can't think she will ever go away. There's nothing miraculous about resurrection from the dead. It happens all the time.

6

'We would like your signature on the petition, Mrs Chaplin. I see that you haven't signed it yet. I think your name would carry some weight.'

'Why should my name carry any weight? The only Chaplin that I know who has any claim to fame was a comedian.'

'No, dear, I mean your background. If you signed and then put in brackets after your name, "retired headmistress".'

'I've known some head-teachers that would have been better employed as comedians.'

'Will you sign it? Then I can take it downstairs with me when I leave.'

'Place it over there, on the dressing table near the window. I'll look at it later. Right now I feel the need of a little nap. I think I have eaten too much Christmas pudding. I shouldn't have had any at all really, I've never liked it. Not even as a child, I never liked it, it was force-fed to me by my parents. That's it, dear, put the paper or the petition – whatever it is – near the table lamp. No, I won't look at it now. Later, later. There's no post today so nobody is being kept waiting.'

The worst kind of bullying is often gentle in its delivery. I was bullied into eating that pudding and I'm damned if anyone is going to make me do anything more today than I want to do. Bullying the old and the young seems to come naturally to some people. Ha, I shouldn't be hypocritical, I've bullied children. Made them eat when they didn't want to eat. Kay opposed me, but it was very much a case of 'waste not want not' in those days.

Oh, just think, I made those poor girls eat that dreadful bitter cabbage. I've probably put most of them off eating greens for life.

Kay's class all ate it without a quibble. She always ate her meal with her girls and their daily menu was her daily menu. She never joined the rest of us in the staffroom at lunch-times. I can see her dinner plate now – piled high with watery cabbage. I can hear her too.

'I have never had a pimple or a pustule or a facial blemish in all my life, girls, and it's cabbage like this that I have to thank for it. It keeps one's blood wholly clear from impurities.'

Her girls dutifully chomped their way through it like starved caterpillars. I felt that her example couldn't stand up to careful analysis as Kay always looked as though she had put on her make-up with a trowel. Any kind of eruption on her skin would have been invisible to the naked eye.

Oh, that pudding feels like a ton of bricks deposited in my stomach. Pulling me down . . . pulling me down. I can't even keep my head raised. There's nobody in the street to look at, everybody has either eaten too much or drunk too much – or they are alone and too depressed to move. It's Christmas, all right.

If this is dying, if this is dying, then it's not too bad after all. It's not sleep I'm drifting into – but some kind of dark all-enveloping torpor. This knotted body of mine has lost its weight and pain and is falling and drifting in an ocean of warm currents and I feel gently buoyant. I am naked and all of me seems to have settled or dispersed itself on the sea-bed. I have nobody, I have merged into this marine world. I have not just come to rest here. I have become part of this mystery. Are those elegant swaying clumps of seaweed my arms? These two pulsating starfishes – are they my breasts? These multi-coloured reeds and grasses – are they my hair? The outline of my body is indistinct. Blurred. Yet its centre is marked by a sweet, pink, marine anemone. This lovely sea-fruit marks my sex. It opens and closes, revealing just enough of its secret beauties and pleasures.

A sea-horse of ever-changing colours hovers about me and rides through my hair, it rests in the pastures of my armpits. It entwines itself about my breasts. Slowly, it approaches my sex. I open and reveal more. I unfold, I blossom. The sea-horse explores the recesses of my flowering with its tongue, it searches every part of me. We drift together. There is no fear ... I am glad to be abandoned ... I am pleased to move on.

God help me, if that's what an excess of Christmas pudding does for you I'll have some every day. I wish the dream, if that is what it was, could have gone on longer. What's this they want me to sign? I'm to sign a petition of complaint about a television programme that I've never seen. 'This programme has eroded the stability of our culture in its presentation of intimate sexual details that must have caused grave concern to thousands of decent-minded people who ... a man's faith.'

How the hell can it have given offence here when everything is edited by Mrs Organization who runs this place? I'm not signing it and that doesn't make me indecent. No fear.

'No fear,' that's what Kay said to me, those were her very words. I had gone over to her classroom hoping she would still be there after school. She was sitting at her desk making a rug. Kay could make anything she put her mind to with those long, dextrous fingers. She looked up from her task and welcomed me but continued pulling the coloured cloth through the holes in the sacking.

'You are still here, Kay. I'm glad, I was hoping you would be.'

'Not much point in going home on Wednesday afternoon. My women's interest group begins at half-past five and I like to be here when my mothers arrive.'

'Ah yes, I'd forgotton your group. Very remiss of me.'

In those times such a group would normally be concerned with sewing, cooking hints, flower arrangements and all the attributes that a nice woman of tidy background ought to have at her fingertips. Kay's groups consisted of working women from the village who had little time for such luxurious gentility.

I never attended, yet I had heard that Kay often 'led' discussions, and that extremely personal marital details and problems were aired and shared, and it was once reported to me that raucous songs were occasionally sung. I never took any action over this as there was never any kind of formal complaint. Illegitimacy was low in our village compared to some others and I'll swear this was due largely to Kay's 'personal health care' sessions with her group. If she did approach what were then taboo subjects, no one knew, as her female adult group never wavered in its loyalty to her.

'It is mothers only, isn't it, Kay?' I asked.

'Yes, it is something special for them. Older girls might benefit, but I think mothers are in need of some time to themselves. Away from the rigours of work or the stress of home.'

'I wasn't thinking of older girls, I was thinking of myself. You see I . . .' I began to cry but checked myself. 'You see, my husband is coming home next week. I haven't seen him in nearly a year. It's silly of me to be upset like this.'

'I wouldn't ever describe any kind of distress as "silly", and I don't think I could imagine any circumstance where the adjective could be applied to you. I know that you are deeply fond of Ralph, you mention him often – and always it is with the utmost tenderness and affection.'

'Tenderness and affection aren't enough, are they?'

I'm not sure whether I asked this question of Kay or for myself. She answered. 'In marriage, I imagine there has to be more. I can only imagine such things as I have chosen the single state.'

It was much easier to talk about my dilemma than I had thought it would be. I suppose after two years of marriage, I had reached a point of desperation. A desperation – I foolishly thought was peculiar to me. I felt a great sense of shame and inadequacy that I could not enter my duties as a wife in a fuller sense. I came from a family where the sexual act was never mentioned – I went to the altar not only a physical virgin, but an emotional one as well. My mother's words: 'I'm sure Ralph will be reasonable with you. I'm afraid you'll have to let him have his way with you from time to time. Something comes over men and they become animals. It's horrible while it lasts, but it's something that married women have to bear.'

118

For his part, Ralph was virginal too. There was nothing romantic about our honeymoon once we had stopped holding one another. I cried out in pain and he apologized for being so clumsy. I wonder now if he wept in private as I did in those first few months. Our situation was probably made more tragic in that we loved one another – yes, we wanted one another. I remember the unpleasant guilt I felt when the war took him away from our home and me. You see, my loss of his presence was also tinged with relief in that he was no longer in my bed.

I explained my situation to Kay, who did not interrupt me save for a nod of the head. She sat there like some great swan, her head bobbing a response from its long and slender neck.

'I am longing to see him, I miss his presence so much – but at the same time I am filled with dread. Dread of the evening – dread of that time before sleeping.'

'You do love him?' Kay made a very level enquiry.

'Yes, I do, I do. It may not sound as if I do.'

'You want him, do you?'

'Want him? Want him, Kay? I am married to him.'

'Sexual intercourse is not a technical exercise, Ivy. It is a physical and emotional pleasure. A great deal of its attraction is in the anticipation of it. Perhaps you have not anticipated it in a proper and full way.'

'I try not to think about it at all. When it happens, I am not part of it. I am a receptacle. Nothing more.'

'Oh, I don't think that sponge-like role suits you – I think you would be happier being more than that. Why not prepare yourself for Ralph's home-coming? Why not enjoy your own body?'

'Enjoy my own body? What do I do, eat myself for Sunday breakfast? I've no idea what you are talking about, Kay.'

'If you have never taken delight and satisfaction from your own body how can you expect to enjoy anyone else delighting in it? You should begin to touch yourself for pleasure.'

'Touch myself?' I whispered – knowing full well that Kay was referring to something quite unmentionable. All those years ago, it was considered unhealthy and even perverted for a woman to contemplate such a thing, let alone talk about it.

Kay took no heed of my scandalized tone. She bodged holes in the sacking with a sharpened wooden peg and added more pieces to her rug at a furious pace. As if hypnotized, I watched the pattern slowly emerge and listened to what she said.

'After you have bathed and showered yourself in perfume and talcum powder (I recommend Soir de Paris), lie down on your bed. Lie there naked. If there is some light music on the radio, turn it low and listen to it, feel comfortable within yourself. Feel glad to be alive. Offer gratitude that you are whole and not malformed, look at your hands. Raise your legs slowly – first one, and then the other. Admire them. Be grateful. Love yourself. Let the fingers of your left hand stroke and gently knead your left breast, caress its beauty and feel its response as the rosy nipple becomes proud and taut.'

I think that I must have sneezed at this point or coughed nervously. This did not deter Kay from eulogizing over a woman's body. In this case, my body, and it felt as though she were occupying territory which had formerly been my private domain. I had never explored it.

'With your right hand stroke the inside of your thighs and let your fingers finally rest on your pubic region. Circular movements with your fingertips give great stimulus and you will find that your clitoris will swell with pleasure at this attention. Slowly attend to the lips of your vagina, the labia minora and the labia majora will dampen to your touch and when they are wet and dewy with titillation, move your finger inside. Then enter your own rhythm – think of Ralph, share this dance of life with him.'

Once more, I cleared my throat. I wanted to say something, to express some kind of indignation, but only managed to say that I had a touch of laryngitis – a teacher's illness if ever there was one.

'It's a pathetic fact that the only pictorial sort of references women have with regard to men's bodies are largely in the depiction of saints.'

'That is a ridiculous observation, Kay. We see pictures of men all the time – in the newspapers, in books, and at your beloved picture-houses.'

'I never saw one that was naked – not anywhere. Front or back view. I've only seen pictures of naked men in religious settings. Otherwise, one would never know what they looked like underneath their clothes. The ancient Greeks thought there was nothing shameful about a penis.'

At this point, I was hoping I could faint. Certainly, the blood had surged to my head and I knew that I had blushed. Kay remained studiously unaware of my embarrassment; she took her powder-compact out, snapped it open and studied her features in the mirror. She dabbed at her nose and forehead and chatted on.

'You know, there is an island . . . I'm trying to recall its name, . . . Delos. Yes, Delos – that is its name – well, this place is full of priceless antiquities and buried statuary which reflect an enlightened civilization that existed centuries ago. At the entrance of the harbour visitors have to pass between two enormous penises which tower over either side of the sea-channel. Travellers could hardly have turned their faces away from pricks that size.'

'Kay! Please! Kay, your language. I must ask you to lower your voice and at the same time raise the tone of your descriptive powers.' I didn't look at Kay as I spoke: I didn't want to reveal the full extent of my shock and indignation.

'I'm sorry if I have upset you, Ivy. Our private parts ought not to be private when we are sharing them with someone else. Penis, testicles, vagina, clitoris, labia – these words are not the words of love-making but the vocabulary of a doctor's seminar. I have to confess to complete bafflement in terms of conversational correctness. A flaccid penis is acceptable – a soft cock is not. An erect penis is permissible, but a stiff dick is not allowed. If all this hurts your sensibilities, I'll say no more. Switch me off as though you had tuned into Lord Haw-Haw or Tokyo Rose.'

'I wouldn't dream of switching you off, Kay . . . you are not making a broadcast, are you? From what you have said, I gather it doesn't necessarily have to hurt one?'

'Oh, no, Ivy, ecstasy can be painful but it never hurts – with some degree of insight and relaxation you can be sensual and comfortable.'

Kay had somehow managed to transform a future dread into an adventure. It was as if she had invited me to explore some

121

exotic island which was outside my culture and experience. A place where luscious fruits and spectacular vistas abounded. I was prevented from asking how I could emigrate to these wilder shores of love by the noisy entrance of four or five women. They were the first arrivals of Kay's 'women's interest group.'

I observed that they nudged each other to note my presence and that their carefree manner was cast off as they nodded towards me muttering their 'good evenings'. I didn't know, or at least I couldn't put a name to, any of these women, yet their daughters all attended my school. At that time, it wasn't considered prudent to get to know the parents in an area like Padmore. It was tantamount to fraternizing with the enemy. Indeed, there was a sign placed just inside the corridor to the main entrance of the school which read, 'No parents beyond this point without appointment.'

It was meant to be forbidding. Making an appointment required a letter, a handwritten missive. There were few parents who took this up. As for telephone calls, there were only four people in the village who possessed the apparatus – the post office, the pub, the police station and Kay. (How strange that Kay should have one then – I've never thought of it until now.)

All the women wore identical blue overalls; these had become the uniform of female factory workers. Fortunately their head-wear allowed for some individuality as each turban was of a different colour or design. Any hair that peeped over their brows or to the side of their faces was encased in Dinkie curling clips or clamped into tortuous-looking wave-setters. If that group of women had chanced to walk under a giant magnet they would have been hauled off their feet.

The women seated themselves in a corner of the room and muttered amongst themselves. They did not seek to claim Kay's attention immediately and treated me with a sort of grudging respect. I was content with this state of affairs. I was a middle-class woman and these people were not of my grouping. The divides of 'class' in this village at that time were as defined as the Hindu caste system. For Kay, there were no untouchables, no unknowable group. I understand this now, but at that time it bewildered me.

'I think I had better be going.' I spoke regretfully.

'Thank you for your support by visiting us today. It is a timely visit, Mrs Chaplin. I had heard there were some unpleasant voices in the village and the town who had cast unfair comments and inane reservations about the validity of our group. It will be let known loud and clear that you have attended our meeting and that our activities meet with your approval.'

As I left, I couldn't help but admire Kay's social manoeuvrings, yet I felt a little disconcerted that someone who was younger than me could have such a detailed knowledge about an area of life which could only be respectfully confined to marriage. Had that side of life been respected in my own marriage? For me, the sexual side of marriage constituted some kind of mutual degradation which I was obliged by law to partake in. Yes, our marriage was consummated but the consummation was not appetizing or fulfilling for either Ralph or me.

I pondered over Kay's words and a great part of me questioned the accuracy of their message. How could a single woman, a spinster, know of such things? Presumably, her personal life – which seemed to evolve greatly around her father's comings and goings – was fairly sheltered. Had she learned these things by mixing with women who were not of her grouping? And what of those women? Was it any better for them than it was for me? Did they feel differently? They certainly looked different. Kay said that on Saturday nights when they attended the working men's club with their husbands they looked breathtakingly beautiful. 'They use quite a lot of lipstick, they wear their best dress, they remove the armoury from their hair, their eyes sparkle after a port and lemon or a milk stout and they become vibrant. It is as if they leave pupation and metamorphose into these entrancing forms just once a week. Perhaps it is the only time their environment allows them the luxury of such fragility.'

I got home intent on forgetting all that Kay had said. I thought if I made myself busy with domestic chores the ensuing exhaustion would bring me some peace of mind. I polished cupboards, chairs, sideboards, linoleum, banisters and tables until my arm felt like lead and my head felt muzzy with the smell of wax.

I needed to bathe but only ran a few inches of water as energy had to be conserved. Still, I was glad of this tiny puddle of comfort and afterwards I changed into my night-clothes. It was after I switched off the light when Kay's words came flooding back into my head. I had no need of a radio, I convinced myself I was dreaming – that what I was doing to myself was not really happening. Afterwards, I experienced no ill effects and slept more soundly than I had for months.

My husband returned home on a Friday afternoon. What a weekend that was . . . with its innocence and exchange of sweet and previously undeclared sensual confidences. I remember one of our neighbours banging on our front door – it was just a few minutes before noon.

'Ivy, I hadn't seen you or Ralph in the garden. I wondered if something had happened to either of you?' Her voice seemed to trail off as her eyes absorbed my attire. I was still in my night-gown. 'Are you well, Ivy dear?' she asked.

'I can't remember feeling better,' I replied.

'Oh dear, I seem to have called at an unfortunate time.' She stared past me to glimpse my husband who was crossing from the breakfast room into the lounge. Not an unusual occurrence except that he was naked save for his underpants . . . 'I'm sorry I called at such a . . . a . . . moment . . . but . . . but it's midday . . . and it is Sunday.'

'A day of rest,' I replied, 'and that is what Ralph and I are doing. Now if you will excuse us both, we'll take a little exercise.'

I think I must have enjoyed responding to her in this brazen fashion, and, in a way, I even relished her disapproval.

Just fancy, I had been married all that time and I had never seen my husband naked. Formerly, I had closed my eyes when he had lifted my night-dress up to my chin and then stabbed into my body with a hard part of him which stuck out from somewhere between his thighs. And in those early years of marriage, I could never have believed that sex could be enjoyed by women – nor would I have believed that a woman could even be a protagonist

124

in its varied themes and nuances. My ignorance was so great, I had not realized that orgasm could be shared and that women could savour it more times than men. I was supposed to be an educator, but knew nothing of these matters.

Oh, I learned quickly – this was a four-day embarkation leave for Ralph and every moment became precious. I taught him innate skills of love-making which had lain dormant in my being for so long. 'Slowly, Ralph . . . slowly . . . pause . . . oh, . . . oh, yes . . . yes.' There could not have been a more willing pupil anywhere in the whole world. How fortunate for me that my husband became my lover – that the two roles were as one at that time.

I remember him crying bitterly as I said goodbye to him on the railway station platform. It was a troop train and I was not the only wife there – there was no so-called British restraint in our parting. He clutched me to him, held me tightly in his arms until I could scarcely breathe, he spoke through his sobs. 'I can't bear the thought of being away from you – not even for a minute, let alone months . . . or years. I never knew. I never knew how much . . . how good it could be . . . Oh, Ivy.'

His letters from the front had always been of a chatty nature, full of the kind of details you think a pen-friend might be interested in. From this time on, they changed. I received the most passionate love-letters from him, so graphic that the censor occasionally blacked out some of the words. Mean bugger. It wasn't only a stiff upper lip my husband presented in his correspondence. I kept those letters, long after Ralph's death – they were private, thrilling and particular to me.

When I agreed to move in here, I asked after them. I shall never forget that sorrowing look I received from my God-loving, tambourine-shaking son-in-law. And I shall never forget his words.

'Sometimes, Mother, doing the right thing is very painful. I felt I had to do the right thing even though you might be hurt a little. I know you will thank me for my actions later. Yes – in your heart you will thank me through Jesus.'

'I never needed a messenger to convey my thanks. I'll do it now. What have you done? What do I have to thank you for?'

'I've burnt them. I've destroyed those disgusting letters. No one will ever know of their existence. Time can heal a disgrace.'

He looked into my eyes with that beatific expression, that look of patronage which I had come to detest. I gathered as much spittle as I could muster within my mouth and then let him have the lot. Right between the eyes. I was glad to see my contemptuous ammunition trickle down his face. If I was to be cast as a wicked woman then I might as well play the part with conviction.

I can hear him explaining my action away. 'Mother is not as she was. It's her age, you know, it is kinder to some than to others.'

I am not his mother – what's more, I am exactly as I was. My body has taken on the appearance of one of those old women in a Grimm's fairy-tale. Why are age and infirmity usually correlated with wickedness in those stories? They all think I'm perverse in this place. I'm made to feel like a cabbage amidst the orchids. This rarefied atmosphere is stifling the life out of me. Ah, there's Janet Haycock . . . I suppose they'll keep her waiting downstairs a good half-hour before they let her come up and see me.

I would recognize that girl's walk anywhere, she's like a moving lighthouse – her head is going in all directions. Has she ever missed anything? It's a wonder she doesn't have to wear glasses. I reckon she could scan those library shelves in twenty minutes and tell you which books were there and what colour the cover spines were. She's head librarian now – when she first worked there the place was not much more than an outsized wooden pigeon pen. It was well attended, though – and it had more books. The place is half full of videos now. Yes, women began to read more. Kay said that they would and she said that they would write more: 'If men don't write about women fairly and knowingly, then eventually women must write about themselves.'

It looks as though Janet has dyed her hair. I can't remember it being such a rich, chestnut brown colour the last time I saw her.

My daughter doesn't like Janet visiting me. She regards divorcees as semi-failures or something less than decent. Janet was the first woman in Padmore to be divorced. It was granted in her husband's absence. I always wondered if he had deserted her for another woman, but Kay seemed to think it was more likely to be another man. Janet still wears her hair as if she were Ava Gardner or Veronica Lake – it's falling half-way over her face. If she let it fall over the other side of her brow she could hide the birth-mark. I'd never mention it to her as she can be very contrary at times – but I do like her.

There, I'll just spill a little water over this petition. That's it, just a dribble here and a spot or two there. Mmm . . . very hard now to make out any of the signatures. It's no loss as most of the people didn't know what they were signing anyway. Kay didn't let her hair down too often. I expect Janet has contacted Patrick Harper about Kay. He was as much a part of Kay's fan-club as she was and I think he may have been a little jealous of her. Ah, he was – just as I was. We all wanted to be first in Kay's affections. From Kay's point of view I suspect we were all equal – except for Daddy . . . he always came first . . . that's where her heart belonged.

7

'I'd better be leaving, Mr Harper, I've kept you long enough. I thought I'd just have a few minutes with you after seeing Mrs Chaplin. Good Lord, my watch says half-past eight. Can it be that late? Have I been here that long?'

'Yes, that's the right time. I wouldn't say it was late, though. Time goes quickly in good company, Mrs Read.'

'Oh, do call me Janet. I still am Janet Haycock. I hated changing my surname when I got married. I think it's quite wrong for a woman to have to give up the name she was born with.'

'You sound like Kay.'

'I suppose all of us who knew her, echo her sometimes.'

'Not a bad thing, Janet. I'll come to the door with you.'

'I'll call again close to the New Year when more is settled. There will be an inquest, of course. We will all keep in touch. Goodnight, Mr Harper.'

'Patrick. Call me Patrick and call before New Year. I'd like that. I really would.'

'Goodnight, Patrick. I'll call before then – but I'll telephone first.'

'No need. You are welcome at any time. Any time at all. Goodnight.'

Well, what about that! I kissed her on the cheek as if I had known her for years. How stupid! I have known her for years. I like a woman to wear scent – Janet smelt of it ... of ... something floral. God knows in my business I ought to recognize it. I can still smell it here in the hallway. It's lily of the valley, such a secretive little flower, but bold in perfume.

I wish I could be more adept with women. I mean socially adept. If I like a woman, I can't help taking in her every feature, and I had lapsed into this habit with Janet just now. She caught me at it and challenged me.

'The mark on my forehead seems to be fascinating you, Mr Harper. I had mine before Mr Gorbachev had his. Do you stare at his drop of port wine when you see him on television?'

'I don't look at Mr Gorbachev in the same way as I look at you. I'm sorry if I've upset you in any way, I was not looking at you critically. Quite the reverse – I think that it suits you. Do believe me.'

'I do, I do.' She clapped her hands with pleasure. 'I view it in the same way myself. For years I hated that mark, but now I want to show it off as though it were some type of adornment. Does that sound silly or far-fetched?'

'No, not really. I feel much the same about this.' I rolled my shirt-sleeve as far up my arm as it would go and revealed the long serpent-shaped scar that ran like a railway track from my wrist to the top of my shoulder. 'We all have our marks.'

'I was born with mine. It has been with me always,' she said.

'I earned mine and I've got it forever,' was my response.

She knelt beside my chair and commented that my mark was red, blue and purple in colour. She ran her finger over part of it to feel the difference of texture in skin tissue. That's when I caught the first whiff of her scent and it occurred to me that a woman who was – well, to put it squarely, ample, over fifty – was still . . . not 'still', no 'still' about it, she was attractive.

I ought to be past such pleasant meanderings – I felt I was until today. And today, I'm bloody glad of this great scar. It's brought me more attention than a medal might have done – who would have thought the pain and horror of its origin would actually bring such an exquisite reward?

22 February 1944: 'Ministry of Labour and National Service – Allocation: Men are mainly required for coal-mining in Durham,

129

Lancashire, Midlands, Northumberland, Notts and Derby, York-
shire, Scotland and Wales. On completion of training at the
Training Centre you will be directed to a working colliery. Any
preference for employment in a particular area which you may
have expressed in reply to this notification will then be taken into
account as far as possible, even if you have been required to
undertake your training in another area.'

My mother had never travelled further north than St Albans
and felt that the Midlands was the only choice of area she could
cope with. 'I'm sure I couldn't understand what people were
saying in those other places. It's bad enough here, the accents
make English sound like a foreign language. Thank goodness
none of them are allowed to speak on the wireless.' After my
training was completed, I was put to work as a trammer. It was a
set wage we received: sixty shillings a week. Bevin Boys were not
allowed to earn more.

Most of the day I stood alongside two long metal-coiled ropes.
The one was approximately chest-high and the other close to
floor-level. As the heavy steel tubs clattered in, I would uncouple
the full ones and clamp the empty ones ready for winching to the
coal-face. It was back-breaking, tedious work which required neat
footwork as the tubs came hurtling in at a tremendous rate. There
was little or no time for pause and any conversation with my
workmate was conducted in a series of shouts and loud
observations.

'Move! Move – fucking move. Move, Patrick. Move!' I heard
this shout, I grasped its urgency as it verged on a scream. A male
scream was a rare thing to be heard in a colliery. I did move – but
not quite quickly enough.

The pain seemed to invade my whole body. I could not call out,
the agony was so great it left me speechless and without breath. I
had heard the great clanking noise as the full tub had cast off its
moorings and hurtled back against the empty one. The two tubs
now lay close to one another. Only my left arm kept them apart.
I watched as the blood – my blood – bubbled down the steel sides
and dripped on to the rails.

Jack Edwards bawled and shouted for assistance as he heaved

lumps of coal from the tub. He went about his task with a demonic fury – he seemed possessed by an outer strength. Never have I seen anyone work at such a frantic pace.

'Hold on, Patrick, I'll get this unloaded. Take the pressure off you . . . Where are the other fuckers in this shit-hole? Help! Help, for Christ's sake, help! Come fucking quick. Get your arses here – move, move yourselves.' He shouted as he worked.

I glimpsed three other miners running towards us. I saw anguish and concern on faces that were usually without expression. My arm felt numb but my ankle had begun to throb with pain – my trousers were wet and stained a dark crimson. I smelt the blood. It was then, it was at that moment, the moment I smelt my own blood, that I fainted.

'They have managed to save your arm. It won't be cut off. The sister told me amputation was not a consideration in your case. If you had lost an arm, at least it would have been your left one, not your right one. You would still have been able to work, there are quite a number of one-armed postmen nowadays. It's a safe and secure enough job.'

These were my mother's first words of comfort on her first visit to the hospital. I had been in the place for five days before she called and her presence hardly did much to lift my spirits. I had no intention of becoming a one-armed postman but was in no fit state to think of work of any kind. It seems harsh to ponder on it, but I'm sure on the few occasions when my mother looked into my eyes she saw pound signs where my pupils should have been.

'I'm surprised they have put you in this bed.'

'What's different about it?' I glanced about the long ward. 'All the beds look the same to me. They are standard hospital beds. This one is comfortable enough.'

'No, I mean in this position. At the bottom end of the ward. At the lift exit. I do hope this accident hasn't affected your brain as well as your arm and ankle, Patrick. You know which patients are placed here, don't you? You know who this position is usually reserved for?'

131

'No, I don't know,' I muttered through clenched teeth. I wanted to shout at her in rage.

'Serious cases – only the most serious cases. The bed in this position is usually for fatalities. Deaths. It's more practical to have them here.'

'Practical?' I groaned.

'You've no thought for other people, Patrick. It wouldn't do to trundle a dead body down the whole length of this ward, would it? Apart from upsetting people, it wouldn't look right. Appearances count for something. I've always tried to instil that into you. If someone passes over to the other side where you are lying, they can be slipped out quietly through the swing-doors and into the lift and taken down to the basements. I suppose it must have been touch and go with you for a time. You are a lucky man.'

'I don't feel lucky.' I looked at my arm suspended on splints and wires, fixed above my head in a position of permanent salute. I glanced down at my leg encased in white plaster of Paris. 'If I'm lucky, I bloody well shudder to think what it's like to be unlucky.'

'Now, Patrick, there's no need for that kind of language. You know it affects me badly, I'm not accustomed to it. No need for swearing. Count your blessings. The sister says they have given you Mr Fleming's wonder drug. She said gangrene would have set in if you had met with this accident five years ago. She had the audacity to tell me the drug was taken from things that had gone mouldy – or from mould. What rubbish. Some of these young things today think they know everything. Penicillin, that's what the drug is called. Taken from mould indeed. She's Irish – the Irish will believe anything.'

I remember groaning with exasperation. Fortunately she mistook the cause and interpreted it as physical pain. She chanted my injuries as though they were a shopping list, or some kind of domestic litany she had to lodge in her mind. She never asked how I was, or how I felt.

'You've a compound fracture of the left ankle and a hair-line fracture to the shin. Your left arm is broken in three places below the shoulder and in two places between the elbow and the wrist. There are multiple lacerations but no main arteries have been severed. You have forty-seven stitches in your arm – but there's no doubt that you will mend again. You'll be able to go back to work – they say in about two or three months' time.'

'Not as a one-armed postman then?' I couldn't keep the acidity from my tone.

'No need to be sarcastic with me, Patrick. Not after I have travelled all this way to see you – and you know how buses always make me feel nauseous. Oh, I forgot. Don't worry about money. A man has called round from the colliery with something called your "compo" or "box" money. I get it each week. Really, it wouldn't be enough to manage on but it was supplemented with a gift.'

'A gift?' I asked.

'A sum of money – from the colliery owners, I suppose. It will be enough to tide us over until you are working again. It's very considerate of them, don't you think?'

It was impossible to conceal my anger any longer. 'You know full well where that money came from. It did not come from the colliery owners. The owners of the colliery live in an estate in the heart of Dorset; they are not even aware of my existence let alone my accident. It was the men from the village, my fellow miners, who gave you that money. They always have a collection in such circumstances, they always give to their own. The people you despise gave you that money – and you know it.'

I watched her straighten her clothes, or at least go through some motions of adjusting her dress. I expected a cool, cold barb from her. And that is exactly what I got.

'I had better be leaving now. I can see that you are not quite yourself. The smell of hospitals always gives me migraine so I won't call again unless I'm sent for. It wouldn't do for both of us to be laid low, would it? Don't worry yourself about the home – our home. When you get back it will be just the same as it was when you left it. Clean and paid for.'

She patted the side of the bed as she stood up and somehow managed to break into a brave martyr-like smile. 'Don't let this business cheapen you, Patrick. Remember what sort of people we are.'

133

I listened to her heels as they clicked themselves down the length of the ward and felt the utmost relief when the sound gradually faded away. I suppose I should have felt guilty for not feeling much affection for my only blood relative. I thought of her final words – 'Remember what sort of people we are' – and, strangely, they lightened my mood for they made me think of Kay. Two days before my accident I was answering her queries regarding onion sets – we moved on to other horticultural issues like gooseberry and redcurrant shrubbery. Then I began to complain in general terms about the village itself. I still felt as though I was an interloper, a tolerated guest – even an outsider at times.

'I think you ask far too much, Mr Harper. If you entered all the social mores of this village and its surroundings I believe you might suffer more than you do now. I don't think it's altogether a bad thing to be a little estranged. Each and every place has its own brand of parochialism. It would strangle me to be at the hub of such density of collective leisure and work. No – I think, like me, you will always be a little apart, wherever you are.'

'Apart? Apart from what?' I asked, wishing I was on a desert island with this exotic woman rather than talking to her in my back garden.

Her father shouted for her from an upstairs bedroom window. He sounded as if he were in the middle of some emergency or as if Kay were about to be cut off by some incoming tide.

'Forgive me, I must dash. My father . . . you heard him? He is the centre of my universe. I would not be the person I am without him – I doubt if I would be a person at all . . . I must dash.'

It must have been two or three days after my mother's visit. I felt drained and exhausted – I guess more from lack of sleep than discomfort from my injuries and wounds. The ward was stifling hot, I seemed to have gone through a series of cat-naps which were closer to hallucination than to sleep, and I was in a state where dreams and realities were without barriers.

'How wonderful to see you again, Mr Harper. I hope you don't mind – or consider it in any way presumptuous for me to call and see you. If it is too painful or bothersome for you to see anyone at present, I will quite understand – just give me a signal and I will quietly drift away . . .' The voice seemed to speak to someone else. 'Poor dear man, he's so hurt . . . Oh it's so unfair.' I didn't open my eyes because I wanted this particular dream to last. Then I got a whiff of her scent. I spoke out. 'Don't go, Kay. Please don't go. Stay here by my side. Please stay.' 'Of course we will stay. We intend to be here right up until the end of the visiting period. The half-hour will be as precious to us as it is to you.' I opened my eyes – and there she was. Even the sight of Janet Haycock sitting at her side could not diminish my gratitude. I can't remember what we talked about. I must have spent most of the time listening as I had my mouth full. Janet Haycock had donated her week's sweet ration to me – she unwrapped each chocolate with excessive care.

'Open, open wide,' she would say – and then pop one into my mouth. Helplessness at the hands of a generous girl gave me unsuspected pleasure. I think she enjoyed the commandment. I know I enjoyed the consequence.

There was no promise forthcoming that Kay would call again. I must have willed her back into that bloody hospital. Good timing never seems to be on the side of unrequited lovers and I was no exception.

The far doors of the ward had been flung open and a mass of visitors pounded their way down the linoleum as though they were rushing to get to the best seats in a threepenny matinée show. I could hear their hushed chatter and the clattering of chairs as they took their seats at the various bedsides. A screen still shielded me from their sight but they brought non-institutional noises in with them. I hoped that their babble had drowned the sound of my last successful fart and heralded the delivery of my final turd into the bedpan which lay beneath my buttocks.

A fretful staff nurse removed my bowel entry from its mooring just as Kay arrived. The stench of me was all about us. The staff

135

nurse spoke to Kay almost as if I wasn't there, as if it were her humiliation and not mine.

'Sorry about this, we've been rushed off our feet today. It's been one emergency after another. The sister ought not to have let you all in – not just now, anyway.'

Kay smiled and nodded sympathetically as the nurse cast a towel over my steaming excrement and bustled herself and my shit out of the way.

I can't explain this – not even to myself – but I began to cry. Not in a loud demonstrative way, there was no noise – but I could feel the tears wet upon my cheeks.

'Oh please, please, Mr Harper. Please. Don't cry. Don't upset yourself. Please.'

'I'm so ashamed.'

'You have no cause for shame.' She knelt by my side and took a small phial of perfume from her handbag. She dabbed some on each of her wrists and then sprinkled it liberally on my brow and the hairs sprouting near the hollow of my neck.

'I don't think men are supposed to wear perfume, Kay.'

'They have in the past, Mr Harper, and I'm sure they will take up the habit again in the future. You are setting the pattern – we ought to record the time and date. All adornments and perfumes were made for both sexes – the Puritans have a lot to answer for.'

Her scent was all about me: she had even dropped a little on the single cotton sheet that covered me. In less than a few seconds I was assaulted with a different kind of embarrassment which in a different way left me as socially maimed as I had felt before.

My prick had thrust itself through my pyjama aperture and had struck out to achieve a swift, bold ascent. I lay there with my arm still in scaffolding while my prick resembled a tent-pole beneath the sheet.

'Oh dear,' Kay muttered breathlessly through her vivid lipstick.

'I'm sorry.' I murmured. 'Take no notice and it will subside – oh . . . oh . . .'

'Are you in pain, Mr Harper?'

'No . . . no it's just this,' I referred bashfully to my erection, 'it aches. I'm sorry.'

I said no more. I watched her as she slowly lifted the sheet from my body. She remained kneeling as though in prayer and regarded my dick with reverence rather than shock. She touched it lightly before taking it gently in her hand (how is it possible for a woman to masturbate a man with more sensitivity than he himself?).

'It is beautiful, Mr Harper, it's aching with impatience . . . what a passion . . . what a flowering . . . what a magnificent head . . . a king of pricks – I'll accept his nectar.'

I watched her lower her head, I saw her lips part and then almost fainted with pleasure as she took my cock into her mouth. It seemed to traverse all the way down her long neck as her head bobbed back and forth. My climax flooded from me and the process shook my whole frame with the intensity of pleasure and the relief I experienced. I called out in a long, harsh wail: that strange male sexual sound which is half ecstasy and half pain.

Kay assured the worried-looking staff nurse that nothing was amiss. She lied with all the assurance and authority of one of our present-day politicians.

'I'm afraid I let my handbag slip from my grasp as I searched for my powder-compact – everything always seems to make its way to the bottom of a handbag, doesn't it? Mr Harper is very cross with me for being so careless,' she made a tut-tutting sound, 'and just look there, I've even got my lipstick smeared over the sheet.'

'I think I'd better remove this screen. It shouldn't have been left here,' the staff nurse responded in an offhand, almost insolent manner.

'Do do that, my dear, I wouldn't want anyone to think that I was responsible for its presence.' Kay met discourtesy with more discourtesy and the nurse left us alone – but now exposed to the rest of the world.

'That was wonderful, Kay.'

'I have another treat in store, Mr Harper.'

Kay bent down and reached for a brown paper carrier-bag which she had placed underneath the bed shortly after her arrival. I couldn't imagine a treat more delectable and tantalizing than the one I had already received. I wondered if she were going to do something even more daring and shocking – here in the open ward, in front of everyone. There was no doubting her ingenuity – she had more tricks up her sleeve than a conjuror, she was so clever with her hands. I felt my cock twitch and swell into semi-arousal in anticipation.

'There, what about that?' She removed the cloth from the top of a white pudding basin. 'It still has the skin on it. I think it's a minor miracle it has remained intact throughout the journey.'

'I suppose it is. Yes, it is.' I didn't want to sound ungrateful but the rice pudding seemed to inhibit my appetite rather than quicken it. There are times when food of any kind seems entirely inappropriate. The pudding acted like some type of buffer to the proximity and intimacy I was hoping to achieve with Kay. I felt – rightly or wrongly – that she was acting rather callously with regard to what had gone on before. I wanted to mutter sweet words to her, whisper private endearments, and personal longings – and all she could do was produce a rice pudding. One minute I was treated like a man, and in a moment I was being regarded like a child. 'I can't eat it.'

'Can't eat it? Don't you like rice pudding? This one has a clove or two in it. I thought it would appeal to you, Mr Harper.'

'Please stop calling me Mr Harper. It's as though I am an ageing, corner-shop newsagent rather than a man who has just made love to you. You are being ridiculous.'

'I am sorry if you are upset. However, it does have to remain that way – I mean, you must still be Mr Harper. I'd better go.'

'Please don't, there are still fifteen minutes left. I'd like the pudding but you'll have to feed me. I can't negotiate it very well with one hand.'

'How silly of me not to realize. There's a spoon here on your locker.' Kay tucked a handkerchief in baby-bib-fashion over my pyjama front. As she leaned forward she whispered into my ear, '*You* did not make love to *me*, Mr Harper.'

'What?' Once more, I was beginning to feel a sense of outrage. Kay dug the spoon into the pudding. 'You like the skin? So do I. No, *you* did not make love to *me*, Mr Harper. I made love to you. Now, open your mouth. There, that tastes good, doesn't it?'

As she spooned the sweet sticky rice between my open lips and on to my waiting tongue she banished all indignation and anger from me. I was as much charmed by her absurdity as I was by her mysterious composure. After she had left, I concluded that Kay had done what she had done out of compassion more than anything else. There and then, I decided to make myself pitiable to her when I eventually got home again.

I ought to feel drained and exhausted and sad and miserable at the end of such a day. I do feel sad. Sadness is all about me now I'm home again, now that I am alone. Yet, however sad I may feel, I sense there is a kind of exhilaration to all of this. It's Kay who has created it. Even her death has excited us almost in the same way as those first heady, giddy years – those war years which heralded her arrival.

By her death, Kay has once more brought all three of us on to the dance floor. Right now, right this second, I'd like to ask Patrick Harper to dance – his awkwardness was always so appealing. He is a man who is entirely without artifice and he has never been able to hide his feelings.

Oh, I have to laugh at the thought of his expression – his abject disappointment – when Kay used me as a chaperone. I'm sure I could have extracted bribes from him to make myself scarce. His eyes would light up when he saw Kay, but when my presence was noted he could not hide his frowns or signs of dismay. 'Oh, it's you, Janet.' This was the nearest I ever got to receiving a greeting from him. I can hear the empty inflection in his voice. And now we are all on the dance floor again and the band has yet to play our tune.

8

'Oh, it's you, Janet.' As he spoke, I wasn't sure whether his pained expression was due to the aftermath of his accident or to my presence.

'It's Empire Day, we have a day off school.'

'One day off and you choose to spend it with your teacher? I never spent any of my holidays in the company of any of my teachers.'

He looked at Miss Roper as he said this. She sat perched bolt upright on her chair, which was drawn close to his bed.

What an ungrateful pig, I thought. After all the sweets I'd collected for him – toffees, chocolates, liquorice allsorts. Precious goods. I no longer felt obliged to feel sorry for him. Pit accidents were common. Why, there was hardly a miner in the village who hadn't been injured one way or another at some time. Blue scars were part of the job.

'You never had a teacher like Miss Roper, did you?' I retorted sharply.

'I wish I had,' he said. 'I would never have gone past the school gates.'

I felt the blood rush to my neck and face – not from embarrassment, but from fury. How dare he think about Miss Roper in *that* way! He was no better than some of the boys in the village who stared at your blouse as if you weren't wearing one. I glared at him. I knew that I was in some way jealous of him. Was it that he could declare an interest and I had to keep silent? Was my love for her any more pure than his?

In my most private, passionate, adolescent dreams and thoughts I never imagined myself in the arms of a man – if I ever touched my own breasts or stroked my own nipples, it was Miss Roper I thought of. It was the crook of her arm my head rested in, it was her deep dark blue eyes that looked into mine – and it was her lips which kissed me.

My mother had given me a little, battered book called *The Facts of Life* which somehow made romance and marriage look like the rudiments of carpentry or house maintenance. It all looked like a series of technical exercises which culminated in something called 'penetration'. I didn't savour the idea of being stabbed between the legs by something which looked like a spear-head which stuck out from men in a funny way.

At this time, I vowed never to marry anyone unless it was Miss Roper – and I'd never heard of a woman marrying a woman. It was horrible to think that Mr Harper wanted to stab Miss Roper with his spear-head and I felt pleased that he was temporarily incapacitated.

'Boys aren't allowed near the school gates.'

'Pardon me?' he enquired.

'You couldn't hang around near the gates for Miss Roper. Boys aren't allowed there,' I said.

'I'm a man.'

'Oh really?'

Miss Roper coughed. 'Ahem, ahem, Janet, I'm surprised. There is no need for that kind of familiar talk or rudeness. Mr Harper is neither a boy nor a man – he is a gentleman. Please remember that.'

Duly silenced, I sat there feeling morose and cheated. I eventually intervened in the conversation by whispering a request into Miss Roper's ear.

'It's at the end of the ward, dear. Turn left and it's the second door down on your right. It is marked on the door, "Ladies". We have another twenty minutes here so you had better go now – you don't want to go on sitting here feeling uncomfortable.'

When I got to the lavatory, I hitched up my frock, lowered my knickers and wept. If I was red-eyed on my return neither Miss

Roper nor Mr Harper sought to mention it. I wondered if either of them would refer to my hair. I had clipped it back away from my brow whilst I was in the toilet: I thought my birth-mark – glowing like red embers – might cause them to feel sorry for me, or at least force Miss Roper to give me her undivided attention. She hardly paused in her conversation.

'Ah, you're back with us, Janet dear.' She turned to him. 'My father always insists on sitting in the balcony. There's not a great deal of leg-room in the Tivoli, is there? It was a musical – but you know, I sat throughout it as though I were in a hypnotic trance. Boredom can do that to one. I would have thought a tuneless, plotless musical would hold little interest for anyone, yet my father adored it. He is very fond of Carmen Miranda – have you seen her? She is referred to as the Brazilian Bombshell. I must say that she overcomes her handicap very successfully.'

'What's wrong with her, Miss Roper?' I forgot my resentment – was Carmen Miranda deaf? Or did she have a glass eye or something like that?

'I noticed her shoes – the skyscrapers of footwear. I paid attention to her elaborate head-dresses of fruit and flowers that towered high above her head . . . and as she twitched and jigged and grimaced and rasped out monotonous music from her huge mouth, I mentally removed her shoes and took away her head-dress. And what did I see?'

'What, Miss Roper?'

'What did you see?' Mr Harper wanted to know too.

'I saw a dwarf. I saw a vivacious midget. It caused me to reassess her performance – the woman has courage if nothing else. I said as much to my father but he did not seem to appreciate my observations.'

I sympathized with Miss Roper. I knew how she felt about Carmen. I was relieved to know that she was capable of petty jealousy too, and I felt consoled by her discomfort.

'Your hair looks better that way, Janet.' Mr Harper said this as a statement of fact rather than as a compliment.

'Yes, it does look interesting, Janet. Clearly, courage is not limited to Hollywood glamour queens.'

Miss Roper rummaged through her bag and drew out her powder-compact. People had begun to leave. She gave a little flutter of the hand to Mr Harper and I nodded grudgingly. She said that the village wasn't the same without him and made me concur on this point when I hadn't missed seeing him at all. In four days he would be home again, and I wondered if I could bear the thought of him living so close to my beloved and looking at her in that soppy way. I was tempted to fall on his arm and cause a temporary set-back in his condition which would detain him a little longer in the hospital, but decided against it. I seemed to have had enough punishment for one day. Disapproval from Miss Roper was as bad as receiving twenty lashes of the cat o'nine tails.

A heavy shower beat down on the pavement outside the hospital. It benefited me as Miss Roper took my arm and urged me to run quickly over the hundred yards or so to the bus stop. What a pleasure to be running wild and free, arm in arm with Miss Roper, when poor Mr Harper couldn't even walk. 'Oh, Janet . . . oh . . . I'm out . . . of breath . . . Oh, Janet . . . what fun . . . how invigorating . . .' I can still hear the clicking of those high heels.

'Perfect timing, there's a bus due in four or five minutes.' Miss Roper glanced at her wrist-watch. 'I want to be back home before my father arrives.'

A group of middle-aged workmen had paused from extracting some iron railings that enclosed the office buildings which stood opposite. Their gaze was direct and wholly undiluted: they stared at Miss Roper's legs as though they were evaluating some piece of property that could be bought or leased. Miss Roper was aware of this interest and almost seemed to encourage it. She called out to them in her friendly, fluting tones.

'Terrible weather, isn't it? Not to worry – it won't last long, just a heavy cloudburst.'

'It's ruined your stockings, missus,' one of them called out. The others laughed.

I studied Miss Roper's legs for signs of a ladder or holes. There were none, but those long 'Tiller Girl' appendages now looked totally unprepared for any high-kicks. The rain had caused the sand stains to erode so that her legs were now a strange shade of orange and her knees, shins and calves were criss-crossed with white estuaries.

'Oh, Miss Roper . . .' I exclaimed sorrowfully.

She merely threw back her head and joined in the men's laughter.

'Next time, I'll try gravy browning.' She half turned and displayed one of her legs more fully to the workmen. 'If it rains they'll be good enough to eat. You must admit – the shape is good.'

The men shouted agreement and cheerfully resumed working. I felt furious with Miss Roper for cheapening herself in such a way. It wasn't the first time that she had displayed this common side of her nature. That day I felt less accepting of it. The bus arrived and she climbed upstairs; I was sure she did this so that all and sundry could stare at her bespattered legs.

As the bus pulled away I said, 'I don't like boys.' I'm sure Kay realized this was a judgement on all males, whatever their age.

'Don't you, dear? I wonder why?'

'They are cruel, Miss Roper, you don't know how cruel they can be. There is a gang of them in the village who do terrible things – things so horrible I can barely tell you of them.'

'What sort of things?' Miss Roper's question now lacked any patronage and carried with it a trace of concern.

I couldn't let this opportunity for exposing male wickedness pass.

'They put Mrs Armitage's two kittens in the water barrel outside her drain-pipe. One was black and white and the other was ginger. They let them struggle and paddle about on top of the water and pointed and jeered at their little pink tongues calling for help as their throats filled with water. They counted how many bubbles each kitten produced before they were finally drowned and they left them in the barrel until they were dead.'

'How sad . . . how very sad. Did Mrs Armitage want any more cats?'

144

I didn't answer Kay's question, but increased my narrative tempo in terms of male sadism and cruelty.

'They took a fledgling hedge-sparrow from its nest and placed it in a matchbox. They drew a picture on the matchbox cover and coloured it with wax crayon, then they attached an elastic band to one end of the matchbox and looped the other end over the bird's head. They closed the box and gave it to that silly Valerie Harvey – she's boy-mad, she'll do anything they ask her to do. They told her it was a present, they told her to push the matchbox open. And she did. When the drawer opened it pulled the little bird's head off. She beheaded it.'

'Unwittingly, Janet – it was not Valerie's fault. Don't make her lack of insight sound like criminality.'

'She shouldn't have trusted them. She knew what they were like. She was there when they caught the large green frog with the yellow eyes near the edge of the Horn's pool. They trapped this frog and one of them held it whilst the other one – the other one . . . the other one poked a straw up its bottom and then put his mouth to the other end of the straw. Oh, it's horrible, horrible. Then he blew and blew and blew until the poor frog was inflated just as if it were a balloon. It was three or four times its proper size. They placed it back in the pool and watched it float and spin – this way and that, it could no longer govern its own direction. All the boys had catapults and they took pot-shots at the frog until one of them scored a direct hit. It exploded in front of our very eyes and bits of skin and giblets were dispersed all over the pond. And you know what those boys did then, Miss Roper?'

'What did they do, Janet?'

'They cheered. They congratulated one another and cheered.'

'I've never joined a group or a gang. War forces us to make harsh collective decisions. There are girls who are just as cruel as boys, Janet. Not all boys wish to play Follow-my-leader. An evil leader spawns a multitude of crimes.' She sighed and sought to change the subject by pointing to the fir trees on the skyline.

'They look so graceful, so perfect in their symmetry set against the light grey of the sky. Almost Gothic . . . or phallic.'

'What is Gothic and phallic?'

'Oh dear me. I forgot myself. Architecture. They are both forms of architecture. One is older than the other. Now, tell me about your preparations for your new school, Janet. The class will miss you.'

This tepid reference to my future leave-taking seemed sadly lacking in emotional resonance. I felt as though my affections were being placed on ice. I drew in my breath, paused – and then spoke in a rush of words.

'The class won't miss me. I don't care whether they miss me or not. But will you miss me, Miss Roper? Will you really miss me?'

'Janet, you are not going away. A Poor Girl Trust scholarship only takes you to a different school. You will be returning home each night, you will still be living in the village.' She turned her face away from the passing landscape and looked down into my eyes. 'Nor will it take you away from me. You will always be close to my heart wherever you are. Now, do let's stop plotting your destiny. It is only your concern – only you are responsible for its future shape and mould.'

For the rest of the journey I listened to my heroine's quiet raptures on the scenery we passed through. The gorse, the firs, the heather, the high pit-stacks, the silver birch trees – all were pointed out. She apologized for an inadvertent loud burp and I remember feeling relieved at receiving this token of proof that my loved one was human. Nevertheless, the bus ride was the highest point of my worship for my goddess. She could have asked anything of me: as it was, she asked or demanded nothing.

Her father met us off the bus and threw both his arms about her in a demonstration of paternal affection. You would have thought she was returning from a world tour rather than a five-mile bus ride. As we walked through the village, he let his hand rest lightly upon her shoulder and she chatted on to him in the same girlish manner that I had chatted to her.

They said goodbye to me on the corner of the street and, as I watched them stroll away together, I knew that Kay's thoughts no longer dwelt with me.

My mother was getting ready for her evening's work when I

got home, and was in the process of packaging her jam sandwiches.

She nodded her usual, silent greeting, but was greatly taken aback when I put my arms about her and kissed her on the cheek and brow. 'I love you, Mam,' I said.

She gently levered me away from her and completed her job of wrapping the grease-proof paper about her food. She smiled in her own sad kind of way before she spoke.

'And what has got into you, young lady? Whatever has got into you?'

'Nothing,' I replied. 'Can't a daughter kiss her own mother?'

'Yes, she can – at a wedding or a funeral. Or maybe even at other times if she's gone funny in the head. Try those shoes on. I got them today from the club. I can take them back if they don't fit right. I want you well turned out on your first day in your new school, even if you have gone daft in the head.'

The shoes felt comfortable and, as I walked up and down the room which was our lounge, sitting room, and dining room, it dawned on me that I would still be at school when some of my village classmates were married. Spinsterhood held great appeal for me then. I would be like Miss Roper. I would have a room and a bed all to myself. And even if the Germans came and took over the village, I'd still look after myself and I'd always sleep alone.

9

'Mrs Chaplin? Yes – it's me, Miss Roper. I won't be able to get to school today.'

'What is it, Kay? Are you unwell? Did you contact a doctor?'

'Am I unwell? No, I don't think so. I don't think that I am ill.'

I felt deeply unnerved sitting behind that large barrier that is called a head-teacher's desk. I had never known Kay be late for school, let alone take a day off. Her voice sounded empty and void of its usual swooping cadences and animation. She talked as if she were recovering from chloroform or some kind of concussion received from a severe blow about the head.

She had seemed in good form the previous night. The two of us had gone to the cinema – an 'Old Mother Riley' film. I had found it inane but Kay had laughed and chuckled at the antics of the old woman who flapped her elbows about and shrieked like some prehistoric bird while her snobbish daughter muttered despairingly, 'Oh Mother, oh Mother.' Kay had relished it all and left the cinema in high spirits, seemingly invigorated by the nonsensical escapism of the celluloid farce we had sat through.

I waited for her to explain her absence but no further words were spoken. I could hear her breathing and I spoke into the mouthpiece very slowly. I must had sounded like Anne Driver doing her music and movement lessons over the radio for young children.

'Now, I know you are there, Kay. I can hear you and I am sure you can hear me. Please tell me what is wrong. Are you worried about something? You can tell me in confidence, I will respect it

. . . There's nothing you cannot tell me . . . I'm so worried about you and I . . .'

'He's dead.'

'What's that you are saying, Kay?' My first thoughts were for my own husband and I couldn't help the question rushing from my lips. So many wives lived in a permanent state of dread in those times.

'He's dead.'

'Who, Kay? Who is dead?'

'Peter. He is dead. An accident.'

'Who?'

'My father is dead. I am unable to attend school today.'

The clicking of the telephone being replaced and the smug purring sound coming from the earpiece prevented me from offering condolence or comfort. I was tempted to ring back in an effort to glean more information but on slight reflection decided against it. It would have meant me donning my head-teacher drapes: 'I'm so very sorry, so very sorry. Of course, you are allowed three days' absence on death of spouse and in the case of parents, one day for either a mother or a father.'

It was a relief not to have to churn out this 'officialese' – in my diary, I recorded Kay's absence as due to severe menstrual problems. Such illnesses were never questioned by our education officers and administrators – it was an all-male enclave. All of them regarded women's illnesses as if they were some kind of alien territory, even though all of them were married. I thought of Kay's distress and felt some injury and sense of loss for myself. It was a secret loss.

Peter Roper had often reared up at odd moments in my sexual fantasies and he had also played major roles in erotic dreams which sometimes occurred during my husband's absences abroad. Could I no longer expect my subconscious to reveal those red tufts of hair nestling in his armpits? His broad hands with the square-shaped fingertips delving urgently into my crotch until it was wet and openly inviting more of him to enter – were these dreams to be denied me with the advent of his death?

'Mrs Chaplin – Mrs Chaplin . . . is anything the matter?'

149

Although Mrs Pickett stood directly in front of my gaze I had not sighted her. The shock of Kay's fearful information and my preoccupation over the matter left me with my eyes wide open but unseeing. For once, I was glad of Mrs Pickett's presence. It brought me back to the re . . . ah, I was going to say the real world, but the world of a school is no more real than anywhere else. It did bring me back to my livelihood – which in those days was better than that of most people who lived around me.

'Sad news, Mrs Pickett, I'm afraid – very sad indeed.'

'Not your husband . . .?' The expectant half-gasp of horror and foreboding seemed to crackle all about Mrs Pickett's tight curls like electricity.

'No, no, nothing that close,' I lied.

'Oh, thank God. With things looking so much better now it would be dreadful news indeed. I think it's so much worse to hear of people being bereaved or having loved ones badly wounded at the end of a war rather than at the beginning, don't you?'

'Not really, no. Death is death and wounds are wounds. I'm afraid Miss Roper will not be in school today.'

'That is unusual. Her attendance is diligent normally – even vigilant at times.'

Mrs Pickett stood with her legs slightly apart clasping both hands towards her bosom as though she were encapsulating some beautiful butterfly in her grasp.

'Her father is dead. Of course, she is very upset and shocked. I shall take her class today – there is no need to make any timetable alteration.'

'Are you sure, Mrs Chaplin? There is no point in exhausting yourself if coverage can be arranged without it. We can't have the headmistress overtaxed, can we? What would we do without a captain for the ship?' This woman, who would be delirious with joy if I were swept overboard at any minute, smiled brightly. 'Just give the orders.'

'Instructions might be a better word, Mrs Pickett.'

'Same difference, I would say.'

'No, an instruction may be questioned. An order is to be obeyed.'

'For just a teeny moment you sounded ever so slightly like Miss Roper. I suppose it is inevitable for speech patterns to become contagious when one is working in close proximity with others. What happened to her father? It must have been sudden. Was it a heart attack?'

'Yes, it was sudden.' I avoided answering her other question by collecting some papers from my desk. She had no idea that I was as ignorant as she was concerning the details of Peter Roper's death. 'There's no need to make any timetable changes or alterations. I'll take Miss Roper's class. The running of the school is as usual – except that I am available only in case of emergency.'

'You are thinking of taking the class for the whole day?' She said this as if I had never undertaken such a task before, as if I were about to attempt something verging on the miraculous. She was a mistress of the gentle insult.

'Yes, the whole day,' I replied.

She called out to me as I placed my hand on the study doorknob.

'You'll want me to cancel assembly, of course?'

'No, don't bother.' I spoke with my back to her. 'I'll take Miss Roper's class in with me and send one of the girls round with a note when I am ready.'

I feel certain Mrs Pickett got some kind of weird satisfaction in school when one member of staff or another was absent. There were no such educational luxuries as supply teachers in those days and just one teacher away left a surplus of over forty girls scholastically marooned for the day. The teachers that were in school absorbed a strain which was – in most cases – beyond their capabilities. There were screams and shrieks for order before the afternoon was over and such days were fraught with tension.

The situation was worse during the winter months – and this particular January of 1945 seemed to have brought great waves of influenza and bronchitis along with its sleet and chill winds. The outlook in terms of the war was cheering and optimistic, but at home we still had inedible stuff made from powdered eggs on our toast and our social forecast matched the weather more than the political future outlook. I wonder if the perpetual jauntiness and general brave fronts that we all put on had begun to tire us. I should think most of us felt as if we were performing for ENSA much of the time. I must say the show went on . . . but the performances were beginning to creak.

Most of the girls in Kay's class were behind their desks by the time that I had crossed the playground and entered the classroom. Yet again, it was 'sunny-side up' time and I greeted the girls with a forced brightness and enthusiasm. There had to be no display of grief, no show of regret: any sniff of despondency would have been close to mortal sin. Be brisk. Be cheerful. Be busy.

'Good morning, girls.' My words received an echo that was polite but apathetic.

'Surely you can all do better than that? I'll try again. Good morning, girls.'

The second greeting was louder in volume but still remained lacking in enthusiasm. I decided to call the register before explaining the reason for my presence and Kay's absence. No girls were late-comers and there were two absences. One was due to diphtheria and the other girl's mother had been delivered of a child the previous day.

'Alice's mother has had a baby, miss. Alice has got to look after the house – her auntie left a note with my mother.'

A new arrival often meant that one of my adolescent girls took a week's maternity leave on behalf of her mother. Home skills were passed on as of necessity rather than taught in school.

'Now pay attention, girls. Look this way – I want your full attention.'

They watched me close the register, it was really quite unnecessary for me to ask this of them. They sensed a dawning drama: Kay was never away. I could feel the collective concern in that room. I fixed my eyes beyond the heads of the girls and spoke to a wall-chart which gave out clear information on our idiosyncratic coinage system.

'I'm afraid that Miss Roper will not be in school today.'

There were groans and sighs. I held up my hand as though I were taking some oath and achieved an instant silence. I continued, 'I shall take this class for today. There will be other demands on my time on occasion. I must ask for your help and co-operation as I may have to leave you on your own – and I have to feel that I can trust you all to behave well while I am out of the room.'

There was some sense of relief at my words: better to be with me than split into smaller groups and dispersed like poppy seeds throughout the building. Better to be with me than spend time chanting tables which they already knew with Mrs Pickett.

Now that the atmosphere had lost some of its tension, I looked directly at the girls and spoke quietly. 'I have sad news, girls. Very sad news. News I wish I did not have to relate to you. It concerns your teacher – Miss Roper.'

The girls sat quite still – there was no shuffling, no whispering. One girl who had opened her exercise book closed it; she brushed the hair away from her brow and looked at me with the thoughtfulness of a young woman not a child. I could no longer maintain my cheerful façade before these girls.

'Miss Roper will not be in school today. It is a very hard time for her – you see ... er ... her father met a sudden death yesterday. Her father is dead. I'm sorry to have to tell you this sad news, girls, but I feel you should know the ...'

'He is the most important person in her life, Mrs Chaplin. He wasn't just her father. He was the most important person in her life. She told us that – he was even more important to her than us, she said so.' It was unusual for a child to call out in class without permission to speak. I looked in the girl's direction but was incapable of mustering an admonition. She continued, 'She was devoted to him, miss, that's why she wasn't going to marry anyone, she told us, Mrs Chaplin – and my mum will be ever so ...'

There were noises from the other girls. 'Ssh ... ssh ... ssh ... Elsie ... shush, Elsie.'

It was at this point that all my decorum cracked. No, it didn't crack, it collapsed completely. I must have sat there in front of those girls and blubbered and sobbed for at least five minutes. Indeed, I was so overcome with grief – or was it anger? – that I forgot or became unaware of their presence. Like all rainfall, my tears began to subside. I felt a gentle tap on my shoulder and through my reddened eyes I perceived something which looked like a teapot. I blinked and swallowed and breathed in deeply. 'Shall I fill the ink-wells, Mrs Chaplin?'

A tall girl stood beside me. She had let one hand rest lightly on my shoulder and with the other she held the ink-well pourer. Somehow I managed to recover myself.

'Yes, do, dear. How thoughtful of you.' I turned to find another girl on the other side of me.

'The rabbits, Mrs Chaplin.'

'Rabbits?'

'Yes, Mrs Chaplin, it's my turn to feed them. It's usually done first thing. They always seem hungry.'

I smiled and nodded assent. Kay's rabbits were known throughout the village. In the years that she had been with me, there was probably not a single family that had not eaten one at one time or another.

I stood and ventured to allocate some morning tasks and duties but found that nearly all of the girls had begun to occupy themselves sensibly. After ten minutes or so, all of these girls, over forty of them, were dutifully employed in one kind of educational study or another. If ever Kay Roper needed a reference or a testimonial as a teacher, then surely this was it. Yet, somehow, I felt that this display of application and aptitude had more to do with love than with training.

This was a way of passing on respect and condolence to Kay, and probably for the first time I felt . . . I felt human in my place of work. Quite suddenly, I felt an overwhelming sense of gratitude towards these girls but could think of no suitable way to declare it.

I wandered between the rows of desks and murmured encouragement to girls who were involved in laborious dictionary searches or practising handwriting exercises. Some were setting shopping bills for one another – 'Four pounds of tomatoes at twopence a pound is a bargain by any standards, Rosie. No, don't change it, you will have a queue outside your shop before lunchtime.'

Mrs Pickett entered the room without knocking on the outside door and looked around as if she had just arrived from the Ministry of Defence.

'I'll let the rest of the staff know that assembly will be cancelled – we do not want to set a pattern, Mrs Chaplin. You are taking on too much. I'll step into the breach.'

'No need, Mrs Pickett. I am keeping to my original instructions. We are having morning assembly as usual and you have no need to step anywhere. Just attend to your own duties today. The vicar's wife has volunteered to answer the office telephone. I have every intention of taking assembly this morning. I will let you know if there are to be any changes later in the day, but I cannot see that there will be.' I dismissed her with a 'Thank you' that was as sweet as treacle.

Some fifteen minutes later I wrote out a note requesting teachers to bring their classes to the hall for assembly. I sought a messenger.

'Now, I wonder who Miss Roper would choose.'

I didn't expect an answer to my question. Normally, our village girls were modest in proffering an opinion on anything. To my surprise, at least five hands were raised, not to be volunteers but to answer my question. They all seemed quite certain who Miss Roper's choice would be. 'It would be Esther, Mrs Chaplin.' 'She'd choose Esther.' 'Esther.' 'Esther.'

I imagine the Brackenburys would now be viewed as a 'problem family' – there must have been at least fourteen children. Mrs Brackenbury seemed a good deal younger than her husband, although on the occasions that I had seen her she was always swollen with pregnancy. She came to school each time she received any kind of letter or form. It would seem that neither she nor her husband could read very well and what speech she uttered was usually monosyllabic in delivery. The children, like their parents, were irredeemably backward. Unfortunately, none of the brood were graced with good looks – they were wall-eyed, pale, often lousy, and had a characteristic odour. This sad physical and intellectual deprivation set them apart from the rest of the school. With their wretched clothing and their general inadequacy they became the butt of both children and teachers. I realize now what a terrible, painful place school must have been for them to be in.

I called Esther to my desk and, apart from a little fading impetigo close to her mouth, she looked unusually tidy for a Brackenbury girl. Nor did girls draw back from her in exaggerated recoil, there were no grimaces, no girls held their noses as they did in other classes, no shame was thrust in Esther's path.

'Well, Esther, so you are to be my monitor for today?' I knew I sounded coy and false but went on, 'Everybody says Miss Roper would have chosen you. I wonder why?'

The innocence and truth of Esther's answer lacerated my emotions and chastened my attitude; it was immediate and telling.

'She loves me, Mrs Chaplin. She tells me every day. My Mam says she would die for Miss Roper 'cos she's been good to us like nobody else has. She's the only one. That's what my Mam says.'

'Miss Roper has been good to me too, Esther. When we are settled in the hall I'll let you take the note round.'

It was a cold dry day full of harsh gusts of east wind. By the time the class had crossed the playground and were seated in the hall most of the girls were rubbing their goose-pimpled forearms and bare legs. It was a two hymns and an 'Our Father' assembly. After my exchange with Esther Brackenbury I felt incapable of delivering any kind of homily concerning behaviour or achievement. I did say something but I had not considered it before the moment of dismissal.

'As you are probably aware, girls, I am taking Miss Roper's class today and I must tell you all what delightful company I find myself in. It is not only a pleasure, but a privilege to be with them.'

I expected Mrs Pickett to faint as I had never spoken in such a way before. I noted that some of the girls had begun to smile as though some long-awaited victory was now in sight.

I continued. 'It is such a very cold day – so cold – that I have decided that any girl who wishes to stay inside the building at lunch-time may do so, as long as she occupies herself quietly. I shall stay in class as Miss Roper usually does when the weather is inclement. Any class-teacher willing to do likewise will earn my gratitude. If a class is to be left unsupervised, I will choose older girls to act as monitors.'

I dismissed the girls class by class and was surprised as other teachers came up to me before they left and quietly informed me that they would be in their classrooms during lunch-time. This meant that Mrs Pickett would have the staffroom all to herself. The thought of her sitting there alone gave me much quiet satisfaction.

Our morning break was referred to as 'milk time' and Kay's class were as well organized in this as they were in other matters. I'm sure Lord Woolton, who had conferred this free beverage for the nation's children, would have appreciated its value if he had been able to see those girls drain their drinks to the last drop. I was never much of an accountant but I can never believe it is to anyone's economic good to tip thousands of gallons of milk away as they do now: it is a market form of balancing books that seems more criminal than political to me. It would be sad if rickets came back – people forget their own history. I suppose it's a matter of progress going hand in hand with selfishness – no one wants to be reminded of ills and troubles if they belong to somebody else.

I couldn't for the life of me see why those cardboard milk-bottle tops with a perfect round hole in the middle should be so carefully prised from their moorings. They were given to Esther who washed all traces of milk away from them and left them positioned on the side of the sink to dry.

Surely this was taking hygiene too far? After all, most of these girls lived in homes without a bathroom – and at least half of them had to walk to the tops of their gardens to go to the lavatory. Was it wise of Kay to offer such a double standard? False or unreal expectations would often cause problems at home for our village girls.

Janet Haycock was a case in point. I don't think her mother ever forgave her for going to the grammar school. Janet did well, but at that time few seemed to want a change in the order of things. Kay was one of those few, although I don't think that I was: there were layers to our snobbery. Kay never seemed part of any stratum – if she had a group loyalty it was closest to the mothers of the village. I can hear her now.

'They are not valued. In films and on the wireless they are portrayed as dim-witted comediennes or harridans. At best they are granted a jaunty optimism of outlook. They rarely appear in books nor do their children. How many of our girls have gone to boarding schools? How many of our girls have sat astride a pony, let alone owned one? How many of our girls have overcome disappointments at ballet school?'

'You can't make a purse out of a sow's ear, Miss Roper.' Mrs Pickett had sounded so sure of this.

'You could make a hairbrush from it, Mrs Pickett. I believe the Chinese have been doing it for years.'

I suppose the closest I ever got to burglary, or imagining a burglar's satisfaction in his appalling pursuits, was by being in someone else's classroom. There was a great sense of order to Kay's classroom: the cupboards were beautifully organized, each shelf was labelled clearly and all stock carefully sorted out. A chart that was pinned on the inside of the cupboard doors puzzled me. There was nothing complex about it – just an up-to-date class list with a flower and a number next to each name. I had checked the DOBs in the class register and the numbers had nothing to do with birthdays. I sought enlightenment from the class.

'Tell me about this chart, girls. I cannot make head nor tail of it. It's not birthdays or holidays, and it has nothing to do with the weather.'

There seemed a great deal of reticence and lack of enthusiasm as to who would answer my question. They all knew the answer, I was sure of that. The girls glanced covertly about at one another, some of them lifted their desk lids as if by hiding behind them they could opt out of their presence in the room.

I spoke more firmly. 'Close your desk lids. Close them quickly. I shall require at least one hand raised in answer to my question. Thank you. Now, please explain the meaning of this chart. It does not look as if it needs much of an answer. Please do not make me feel as though I am interrogating a bunch of German spies.'

After some nodding and a whispered consensus as to who

should answer, three hands were slowly raised. I chose a girl whose eyes were guarded by thick-lensed spectacles.

'They are for when we have visitors, Mrs Chaplin.'

'Visitors? Visitors, I would know if there were any visitors coming to the school. Or at least I should know. Which visitors are you referring to – parents, friends? Who?'

'Not people, Mrs Chaplin. It's when we come on. Our monthly periods. Miss Roper calls it flowering time.'

I had wondered why we had experienced no schoolgirl pregnancies whilst Kay had been in charge of our older girls – and here was part of the answer. Oh yes, there is nothing promiscuously modern about schoolgirl mothers. Up until Kay's arrival there had always been at least one a year in my school.

'I don't know how they can ever know what to do – let alone get themselves into this state.' I had tut-tut-tutted in irritation when Kay brought before me a small, thin, pasty-faced child. This was in Kay's first term – not more than a month after her arrival.

Kay's mouth had twitched. 'The "state", as you put it, Mrs Chaplin, is not self-induced. Nor is it always a question of coercion, passion or technique. It can be arrived at by force.'

'You are not standing there and suggesting . . . surely?'

'I am suggesting nothing, Mrs Chaplin. I am saying that most of the village girls will have heard their parents . . . will have heard their parents making love . . . They will have heard the noise of sexual congress. They would not necessarily know how a baby was conceived. And I hazard a guess that they would not know that conception could be either thrillingly pleasurable or painfully horrific. I shall do my utmost to see that girls in my class do not conceive before they wish to.'

We actually used an expression at that time – such a child 'suffered early maternity' – and without a doubt it was a suffering. The babies were usually brought up by the grandmother and absorbed into a larger family network. Paternity was rarely declared – and when it was, payments were a pittance. As often as not, the phantom fathers – that is, fathers who were never named – could be found within the family. Like huge cobwebs, large families have always had their secret bleaker sides.

Lunch-time revealed the attraction of the milk-bottle tops. Kay was marvellously skilled with her hands – she could knit, crochet, rug-make, weave. She did these things as though she had been attuned to them all her life. She would have made an ideal companion on a desert island. She was the kind of encouraging, inventive teacher who could pass on practical skills to even the most clumsy children.

The girls sitting before me did not remain idle. They worked as they talked. Some knitted, some worked on rugs, and some twirled different coloured raffia about the bottle tops. There were at least three completed shopping-bags. I had caught sight of some of the women using them in the village and had put it down to some new vogue or odd bit of parochial fashion. Now I knew. Had Kay been the source of other village fads? The multi-coloured knitted toques that some women wore over their curlers on cold days, the patchwork headscarves, the embroidered aprons that had commenced their lives as potato sacks, and those lurid, brightly painted necklaces made from small fir cones – they had all emanated from this room. This room was their source.

'Who do you think invented weaving, Mrs Chaplin?'

I had paused to watch the girl who worked with such confidence on the crude loom assembled on top of her desk.

'I ought to know.' I was wishing I had never stopped to admire the skill. It was generally assumed a head-teacher knew everything and I wasn't too happy to see such inflated faith punctured so early in the day. 'The name has slipped my mind – it's just this moment gone from me. I'm sure I know, but I just can't think of it.'

'It wasn't a man, it was birds, Mrs Chaplin.' The girl responded politely but did I detect a note or trace of superiority in her voice?

'Birds, birds? What do you mean?'

'It's true, Mrs Chaplin. Miss Roper told us. Then she proved it to us. Look at the nest on the interest table. It's last year's. It belonged to a thrush, look how it is made. It's woven, Mrs Chaplin, the birds did it. We have a lot to learn from nature and Miss Roper says . . .'

I remember smiling to myself. Great changes were being mooted for education after the war was over – there were to be all sorts of opportunities for all sorts of children. The whole social fabric which then existed was to be blown away. I felt sceptical about this, as I did about other things. Even now, with all the changes, I feel that most children are only deeply affected by having the good fortune to be taught by a few committed and skilful teachers. They could abolish all schools for all I care; it's good teachers who count, and perhaps five or six years' good service is all one can expect of them before they are burnt out.

At the end of that day, I felt better and more satisfied than I had done in years. I was physically tired but to my surprise and astonishment I found that I had enjoyed the company of the girls. I dismissed them promptly at four o'clock and asked them to tidy their desks before they left and then leave in their own time.

I sat behind Kay's desk and browsed through an exercise book which she had converted to her personal school diary. Some entries amused me, whilst others could only mean anything to the author as their message or reminder went beyond the realms of obscurity to a stranger. For Tuesday night it read: 'Rosalind Russell film – Wednesday Greer Garson 5.15 performance. 11.15 Tagliatelle check out details.'

Before I could dwell any longer on these cryptic reminders, I became aware that the girls had formed themselves into a single file which stretched from the left-hand side of my desk and wound its way more than half-way around the classroom.

The first girl stood at my side and I was at something of a loss to know what to do. Most class-teachers have routines and rituals which apply only to them, not unlike the variabilities in the Church of England in some ways; a visiting teacher or a visiting vicar usually follows the patterns that have been set. I had been teaching long enough to know most of them – but this long line of girls at the very end of the day baffled me. I had already dismissed them and here they all were, their faces wreathed in smiles as though they expected a huge piece of cod or a couple of strawberry plaice from a well-supplied fishmonger.

I recall sniffing – it must have been the fish queue that brought it to mind. The girl nearest to me had been liberal with her

'Californian Poppy' and I imagine a few dabs had been passed on to some of her friends. Kay had settled this particular issue a few months back.

'I believe some of your girls are wearing cheap scent, Miss Roper. You may not have noticed it – there are a lot of heavy head colds travelling around.'

'I never suffer from colds, Mrs Pickett.'

'You are aware, then, that some of your girls are wearing cheap scent?'

'Expensive perfume would be beyond their means.'

'You approve of them wearing that stuff?' Mrs Pickett's questioning had begun to sound like a counsel for the prosecution in court.

'If they wish to wear scent, I have no objection.'

'Soap and water are all our girls need, Miss Roper. I may sound old-fashioned but I have experience of these things.'

'I don't think you do – I don't think that you do have any experience of what our girls' lives are like. If you did, you would not be recommending soap and water.'

'I beg your pardon, Miss Roper?'

'No need to beg, Mrs Pickett. I have some facts for you. There are forty-five girls in my class. Only three of those girls live in a house where there is a bathroom. The rest of those girls are lucky if they manage to bathe once a week. When they do bathe it's often necessary for them to share the bath water with two or three other persons in the same household. Tin baths are cumbersome things – perhaps you have never used one. Ten of my girls have to climb into the wash boiler – when they get the chance. We all have our natural odour, Mrs Pickett. Some of us like to enhance‾ it a little, even disguise it on some occasions.'

Kay took a dark blue bottle from her handbag and sprinkled scent on the inside of each wrist, 'There are no rules in this school as to how we should smell, are there, Mrs Chaplin?' I could only shake my head. 'I never thought there could be. It would be dreadful to have to mention or even hint that a colleague or fellow teacher was … was … er, malodorous. Not even such a possibility could arise in this school, of course.'

162

The girl's wrist was thrust somewhere between my chin and bosom. She must have watched Kay applying her 'Soir de Paris'. 'We shake hands now, Mrs Chaplin,' the girl whispered and I took her hand. And this was followed by other hands. 'Goodnight, Mrs Chaplin.' 'Goodnight, my dear.' 'Goodnight, Mrs Chaplin.' 'Goodnight . . .'

This simple yet effective way of rounding off the day seemed to epitomize the highly personal nature of Kay's approach to teaching – ah, I laugh, I hear her voice.

'No, Mrs Pickett . . . teaching is not just a matter of instruction. If I had wanted to be an instructor, I should have taken up the management of dogs.'

By the time that I had returned to my study, it was almost dark enough for me to need my torch in order to find my way across the playground. On nights such as this when black, low-lying clouds blotted out the moon and stars, venturing outside without some illumination was like entering the world of the blind. In a few minutes, it was possible to feel directionless and lost.

'Hello. Hello, Kay? It's me, Ivy. Look, I don't expect you in tomorrow as it's Friday. Just take the time away – I can sort things out with the office. This must have been a terrible shock for you – quite terrible. There's no need to talk about it now.'

'I have nothing to say. I have said it.'

Kay's voice sounded flat and empty of all feeling. I tried to imagine her on the other end of the telephone, but her voice gave away little of her feeling. It was not the voice of the woman that I knew. I tried to bring part of the being that I knew back to me by ploughing on with details of my day.

'Ah, your class were a delight, Kay. The girls were so biddable and charming. I mentioned what had happened. They are with you in spirit – for that matter, so am I . . . I could call round now . . . it might be better if you talked about it a little . . . a grief shared does sometimes help in these . . .'

'No. Please do not call. I am not available to callers.'

I felt the need to keep her with me, the need to communicate with her. However, the odds were against this. I asked where the accident had taken place, and she mumbled incoherent responses.

I heard 'railway lines' and 'ought to have seen the signals' – and did she mention Crewe, or Carlisle? I can't be sure. I sought to lighten the time by lapsing into anecdotes concerning school. It was not a world that Kay wanted to consider any longer – she cut in before I could complete a sentence.

'I am not returning.'

'No one would expect you to, Kay dear. I'm sure it's possible for you to obtain a doctor's certificate for a couple of weeks or so. I can tell that you are deeply grieved. Deeply shocked.'

'A doctor's certificate?'

'Yes, it's quite in order – something like "nervous debility" will cover your absence.'

I was disconcerted – no, more than that – shocked to hear Kay chuckling on the other end of the telephone.

'Is that what would be written on the medical certificate? Nervous debility?'

'Well, something like . . . They have phrases which all mean the same thing for these situations – it's purely for office purposes. Contractual reasons – don't you see?'

'No, I don't see. If I did send in a medical certificate I would never allow any doctor to make such a diagnosis about my present state. I am not nervous. I am not debilitated. I am fucking broken-hearted and I am never, never going to teach again. This woman who you are talking to cannot . . . is not . . . is not fit to teach because of a broken heart. It is an injury that is slow in mending. I have written to you, Ivy, I have written to your precious education authority. My messages are simple and clear. I have resigned from my life as a teacher. I must go now. I beg of you to leave me to myself. If you have any affection for me, you will respect my wishes.'

Is it possible to accept the wishes of someone you think is temporarily deranged? I asked myself this question over and over again. Surely Kay must be more than merely grief-stricken? She could never have used such foul language if she had been right in her mind.

Her letters of resignation duly arrived. They were well con-structed and harshly to the point. This is more than I can say of the official letters which were sent to her. 'You have reneged on your course of duty in such a way that is shameful to your profession. We do understand that you have genuine cause for some distress, but to leave your position in this manner and at such a time, with little thought for your fellow teachers and even less thought for the welfare of your pupils, leaves us no alternative but to recommend to the Ministry that . . .'

Kay never taught again and never crossed the threshold of a school playground. I often wondered if I should have attempted to persuade her to see a doctor; if I had, I doubt if I'd have been successful. For days, weeks, months, she refused to see anyone. She withdrew from us all and nursed her own grief, looked after her own war wounds, and we were never to see her again.

We eventually saw a woman who carried her name, who spoke as she did, whose eyes were the same colour, who lived in the same house. But was it . . . was this person Kay Roper? Kay Roper who had captivated? Kay Roper the enchantress who . . .?

I would have laid any odds against her staying in the village . . . but she did stay. Oh, the language of my environment is computing itself into my brain.

I'm in one of my very favourite places. Janet Haycock brings me here once a week – sometimes twice if I'm lucky. Everyone at the home for biblical simpletons where I sleep thinks she has taken me for a drive. An outing. They imagine I'm sitting in her car sipping tea from a flask and eating digestive biscuits. It would bring them all to their knees if they knew I was here in a betting shop.

Boxing Day (I wonder why it's called that?) is wonderfully busy. Everyone is so relieved that Christmas Day is over – people without immediate family about them are supposed to die on Christmas Day. If not, then hibernation is their only choice. My God, they've all come out of the woodwork for today's racing.

I enjoy the duplicity of being here almost as much as I do the racing. It's much warmer than that home and I've made a few friends. There are more people of my age or thereabouts here in the winter-time. It saves a few pounds on their heating bills.

A young Irish man has just laid an each-way bet for me and has returned with my slip, my change and also the gift of a cup of coffee. There are a group of these men – so rough in appearance and ruddy of complexion. Most of them seem to have huge great hands – but beneath this heavy, lumpen exterior I have detected a gentleness and raw form of courtesy. I feel more secure with this collection of itinerant Irish road-workers than I do with most of the people in that home. I love to hear them curse if they lose and blaspheme from joy if they win. I like this declaration of feeling.

I do wish I had got to know those working parents better all those years ago: I missed out on a lot. Kay knew them. I wonder? I wonder? Did they know her any better than I did?

Here's Janet come to collect me, nodding to everyone as if she were Lady Jane Grey. She always was a bit forward, even as a girl. She looks a little flushed, not unpleasantly so, it is not a harassed look – more of a glow. If I didn't know her age and circumstance, I'd swear she had been with a man. If not wholly, then a damn sight near it.

'Any winners, Mrs Chaplin?'

'No, but enough horses in the frame for me to be in pocket.'

'I've just been over to see Mr Harper. There's a meeting arranged over at his place for the day after New Year.'

'You shouldn't have rushed over to get here, this shop is open until six tonight.'

'I didn't rush.'

'Oh, didn't you, dear? I thought you looked flushed. Your eyes are bright too. Hope you are not coming in for some flu or blood pressure. I wonder how you could have come by such a high colour. It's not as though . . .'

166

10

Janet Haycock called round, she's not been gone more than twenty minutes. She said that she'd just called on spec, I don't believe it though – it wasn't just a fleeting whim which caused her to call. She wore a nice pink jumper, fresh lipstick, and a bit of dark blue eye-shadow. And that was only part of it – she gave me half a dozen mince pies all nicely arranged in curly paper cups. It's not possible to dress up and pack away mince pies all on a whim. No, it's not, she's been thinking on me, and I'm glad because a lot of my mind has been occupied with her. So much so, that I dreamed about her last night.

It's funny how dreams are often sexual but they never seem to be pornographic. Mine don't anyhow. I'd love to be able to recall all the crazy details of that dream. I know, at one point, the two of us were on a raft and it wasn't clear whether we were drifting on land or sea. For comfort's sake we were stretched out end to end and somehow my prick was lodged between her breasts.

I could feel their softness pressing on me – and what's more, Janet was using my prick as though it were a microphone. She spoke to its helmet and described what she could see . . . and her words were transmitted to my brain through my prick. The more luxuriant and lush the landscape became the closer she got to my prick – eventually she was barely whispering and as her lips moved they touched my flesh. I woke up this morning with an erection and I left it there as it made me feel doubly alive.

When Janet left me today she offered her cheek for me to peck before I opened the door for her. I ignored the bit of rouge on her

167

cheek and kissed her full on the lips. Not long. Not lingering. But long enough to let her know that I had some feeling for her. Of course, for a lot of the time we had talked of Kay. I suppose in talking of her we talked about ourselves too. When you begin to get fond of people, it's a funny thing . . . you want them to share your past . . . or some of it . . . enter it . . . be part of your life that has gone . . . to enter your memory and play a role and . . .

After three weeks or more, when I'd seen no sight nor sound of Kay, I saw this woman standing close to the forsythia near the bottom of the garden. The early dazzlingly yellow blossoming of that shrub has always astounded and baffled me. At a first glance I thought my eyes were deceiving me. It was just one of nature's mirages. I looked again from my position behind the curtains in the back bedroom window.

There was a woman standing there. It was a cold day but she remained inactive and still. I asked myself if it could be a relative of Kay's, although she'd never mentioned relatives to me. Perhaps it might be a maiden aunt come to look after her. I hoped that this would be the case as we were all worried for Kay's welfare.

She'd never left the house for well over two months since her father's death. She'd stopped working and withdrawn into herself completely. Aileen Pugh did her shopping for her and I could get little or no sense from her – 'She's grieving, Kay's grieving, she's not the woman she was, she's stricken to the core with grief.' This was all Aileen offered in any explanation or answer to my questioning.

I'd knocked on Kay's door on several occasions. It was always the same empty answer spoken in the same expressionless voice: 'I'm not available for callers, Mr Harper, but thank you for your concern. I'm not available to anyone.' I'd stand there on the front doorstep and hear her footsteps patter away, away from me down the hallway on the other side.

The woman caught me looking at her from my position close to the bedroom curtain, and I waved in a friendly manner but she immediately turned away from my attention so that her back was to me. For good measure, she pulled up the lapels of her jacket and all I could see of her was the back of a dark brown coat topped by a crocheted beret. Whoever she was, I now felt some relief in the knowledge that Kay was no longer alone. My feelings for her were still strong – I still wanted her and I dreamed of being able to place my arms about her and comfort her. The dreaming went further than comfort – it was more ambitious than that . . . I hoped that in her despair and sorrow she might turn to me for love. Physical love. Kissing away someone's tears is often an excuse or a beginning of something more. Pity is often used as a stepping stone for passion – I don't suppose we can help our natures.

It was that very day, not more than an hour or so later, that I caught my mother out in one of her little deceptions. She was in the lounge and had the wireless tuned into Tommy Handley – not that he ever raised a smile from her. Laughter would surely have cracked her face.

'There's a woman staying with Kay. I've seen her in the garden. I saw her from the back bedroom window.'

Now this was the kind of news my mother would normally have delighted in – the greater the leeway for grisly conjecture the better she liked it. Yet there was no response. Even her expression gave away nothing, her face seemed to be set. At first, I wondered if she might be having a mild stroke and I shouted at her, half panic-stricken.

'Can you hear me, Mother? You're making me sound like Sandy Powell.'

She glared at me, eyes bulging, lips compressed tightly together. She looked distraught and angry as she clapped the palm of her hand over the bottom of her face and chin and then rushed from the room. I saw that she had brushed her magazine on to the carpet and, on picking it up, I watched four or five toffee papers flutter from inside its pages. I placed them back inside the magazine and saw that she had a half-pound bag of toffees secreted down the side of her chair cushion.

At the time, this family delinquency wounded me quite deeply. Throughout the rationing period she always maintained that she had sold our sweet coupons in order to make ends meet. Now these 'ends' had jammed her false teeth together, she was locked in a trap entirely of her own making. I felt little pity for her. What was most sad – very sad – was that I had lost any respect for her. I neither honoured my mother nor feared her any more.

I called out from the hallway to say that I was going to see Aileen Pugh for an hour or so. She never answered but I did hear her splutter before I closed the door.

'Can I come in?'

'I'm not working – and if I was – I've told you I can't take on any more customers. Oh God, that wind's cold enough to stiffen a parson's nose.'

As Aileen began to close the door I pleaded, 'Just for a few minutes – a neighbourly chat is all I want. Just someone to talk with. I mean, only company – nothing else. I promise.'

'Promises from men are made in heaven, they're not kept on earth.'

She stood there and looked at me as though she were exercising some pleasant forbearance for a favourite child. Her hair glittered from an excess of curling pins and an unequal amount of heavy rouge on either cheek gave her a lop-sided look. The lipstick on her mouth was badly applied or had been smudged so that there was no shape to her lips. I wondered if she already had someone in there with her.

'I'm sorry if I've come at an awkward time. I'll call later if . . .'

'There's no one here. I'm on my own.' She had read my thoughts and I felt ashamed of my crudity. 'I can't leave you standing there.' She made a grunting noise that resembled the sigh of a disturbed animal. 'I'll make us some tea. Well, you can have tea, I'll have a port and lemon. Give myself a treat. If I don't treat myself, no other bugger is going to . . . not tonight . . . or other nights. Close the door behind you.'

She surprised me by giving me a couple of home-baked rock cakes with my tea and telling me to draw my chair closer to the fire.

'What are you thinking of, lad? You have a funny look.'

'I was thinking that I would have liked you for a mother.'

170

'Well, if you had been my son, we'd have ended up in jail for what we have done together. There would have been all hell to pay . . .' She laughed and patted my knee. 'It's nice of you to say that, Patrick, and I'll remember it with pleasure.'

She sipped her port. 'Oh, that's good.' She kicked off her shoes and examined her feet as she warmed them by the fire. 'See that? I've got bunions as big as damsons. One on each foot. A matching pair. I wish they were on the bloody sideboard and not on my feet. Your arm is better, is it?'

I nodded.

'The scar is still there. You'll be marked for life with that and yet no medals for earning it. You've come about Kay Roper, I suppose?'

'Yes, I have, Aileen.'

'There's nothing that I can tell you. Nothing.'

'I want to see her. Don't you understand? I want to help her.'

'Well, you can't. I want, I want, I want. It's not what you want, it's what she wants – and she doesn't want to see you, or anybody else for that matter. She wants to be left to herself.'

'Does she have relatives? I saw a woman in her garden.'

'Oh, did you? There are no relatives, only her father and her and now he's gone.' She clicked on the wireless and tuned into a forces record request programme. 'There is something you can do. I don't know why everybody is gone on Vera Lynn. She has a harsh voice, I'm more taken with Anne Shelton. She's a big woman, you know.'

'What can I do? How can I help?'

'She's short on coal and logs. Leave her some bags on the front door porch. No need to ask your mother for it. Save your breath. Poor woman, she's not capable of giving a blind man a light. Call on some of the village women, they'll sort something out between them. Mrs Haycock, Mrs Wherly, Mrs King . . . They'll give something without asking too many questions.'

'Can I see her?'

'When she is ready. Not until. I do her shopping.'

'Is she looking after herself?'

'Nobody can nurse a single woman like she can nurse herself.

171

She's deeply grieved. She's at the bottom of the ocean with it. She needs a lot of time. Time. Kay Roper was the only person in this village who gave me the time of day. When other women would cross the road in order to avoid me, she would cross it from the other side to greet me as though I were Lady Muck. She was such a grand girl.'

'She still is, she still is!' I cried.

Aileen Pugh shook her head from side to side with slow deliberation, sipped her port and murmured to the wireless. 'Oh no, she's not a girl any more, she'll never be a girl again. That's over. All done with. Finish your rock cake, you're dropping more on the carpet than you're putting in your mouth. If you see that woman in the garden – just leave her be. That would be a help ... Passion is selfish ... love isn't. My God, I sound like a deaconess at the Baptist Church. Turn that song up a bit ... I love a good tenor. We appreciate good singing in Wales, you know. He's I-talian, that singer. The I-talians are on our side now – well, some of them are. I wonder if there are coal-miners in Italy? A lot of the POWs here looked very Welsh. Poor buggers – some of them looked as if they hadn't long left school ... Listen to that. He's not had his adenoids out like some that you hear, he's as clear as a bell. You know what people will do when this war is over?'

I shook my head. I'd long since learned to live only day by day.

'They'll breed. They'll breed like rabbits. And you know what I'll do? I'll own a wool shop and I'll sell baby clothes. I know the man in Wales who I'll have with me.'

'Would you be true to him?' I asked.

'He's not a woman's man in the way of sex, and I don't think ... Oh, look at the time – if you are going to call on those women you'd better do it now. They are all in the same row, find one and you'll find the lot.'

11

Poor Ivy, she really didn't want to leave the betting shop. She despises the nursing home – it reflects the aura of her born-again son-in-law. She had never granted him much respect and he always seems to view her as though she were some aged, errant, wilful widow. In another age he would probably have been happy for her to burn at the stake as a witch. The signs, the sad shake of the head, the studied forbearance when he is with her. Who the hell does he think he is? If the centurion at the foot of the cross had offered up his kind of understanding, I'm sure he would have shot down through a hole in the ground. Direct to hell.

I'm the first to admit that she does have a sharp tongue, but she doesn't miss much. She sensed my happiness, if that is what it is. I never mentioned that I had called on Mr Harper or that some sort of feeling was developing between us.

Now I'm back in my bungalow, I feel almost sad to be here. I've walked from the lounge to the hall, into all three bedrooms, and now I'm in the kitchen. All these rooms – the space – it makes me feel just a bit desolate, as though I'm roaming alone in a desert of domesticity.

And yet, as a teenager I yearned for privacy. There were five rows of houses in Cecil Street; each row held twelve or so dwellings. In each house there were two rooms upstairs and two down. A back kitchen was attached, and beyond this stood an outside lavatory and a coal-house. Our bathroom was made of aluminium and hung from the back door when not in use. We bathed on Mondays because this was wash-day and the open boiler served a dual purpose. In this sense, both our cleanliness and our privacy were restrained by economics.

Yes – he called then, he called on that day. Patrick Harper called on us. He couldn't have chosen a worse time. It was inappropriate, to put it mildly.

I was in my third term at grammar school and I arrived home in a foul temper. As far as I could tell, none of the girls at my new school came from homes like mine. None of their mothers swore, none of them worked 'nights' in factories, and none of them had rough hands and false teeth. Some of their mothers did voluntary work like serving tea at the RAF camp: this work seemed more elevated than what my mother did. Girls with fathers away at war were given the kind of respect reserved for royalty. I never mentioned my father's work on the coal-face. I had become not only estranged from my parents, but ashamed of them.

'Janet dear, we are all pleased with your examination results, it's clear that you have made a great effort. However, there are more ways than study to help keep up the good name of the school. Trentfield girls ought never to be seen in the street eating a bag of chips.'

'I haven't been eating chips in the street, Mrs Henneaker.'

'It's not chips, Janet, that I want to talk about. It's your hat.'

My school uniform with its green and gold colouring set me apart from my village and even my home. Skirts and blouses were not worn by other children in our surroundings and none of the girls would have been seen dead in the wide-brimmed felt hat that I was obliged to wear.

Somehow, my mother had managed to buy a second-hand one. Even when I first wore it, it was well past its best. Now – after exposure to many seasons of wind and rain, after being pushed hurriedly into several satchels on countless occasions – its shape defied any millinery composition. I felt dismayed that Mrs Henneaker, our Latin mistress and form teacher, had brought it into the focus of her gimlet-eyed scrutiny.

'Why, only this morning, my dear, I had to be very firm indeed with two fifth-form girls who were being most disparaging about your hat. They said that it would have looked better on Roy

174

Rogers and that you had borrowed it from Johnny McBrown. I don't know these boys.'

'They are not boys, they are cowboys, madam, they are in western films, madam . . .' I began to sob with shame.

'Now, now, dear, there's no point in upsetting yourself, all is not lost. When you get home tonight I suggest that you try steaming some shape back into it. But do be careful with the kettle.'

I got home and treated my mother to a litany of complaints – my clothing, our house, her appearance, her bad language, her smoking, the paper that she had wrapped my school lunch in, the sandwiches that were cut too thickly . . . She bore it all, or seemed to bear it stoically, but when I mentioned the indignities that my father's occupation caused me, she snarled and snatched my hat off the settee and flung it across the room.

'There! That's what I think of your Mrs Henneaker, my lady. If she wants the hat steamed, she can bloody well steam it herself. Or you can. One thing is sure, you are not getting a new one. "Make do and mend" – that's what we are told we should do. You tell that teacher, if she mentions you look like a cowboy again, that your mother is coming up to the school and is going to strangle her with a lassoo. As for you, my lady, you are all airs and graces and bugger-all else. Get yourself into the front room. I've got to dress your Dad's carbuncle. Take your sister in with you – she is your sister, you know. And what's more, whether you like it or not, I'm your mother. And the man who is limping to work in agony is your father – and I'm proud enough of him even if you're not. You can tell Mrs Henneaker that I was bathing your father's arse and you can tell her she can kiss mine before I buy you another hat.'

Memory is a puzzlement. If someone were to ask me to detail all the happenings of yesterday or the day before, there would be so much that I would forget or could not recall or place in a proper sequence of events. Yet there is no blurring of Mr Harper's visit to our house, all those years ago. It's as though some great fog or mist had been lifted from my mind. I can see that time clearly, I can hear what was said, and I can feel what I felt.

I had glimpsed the huge carbuncle which seemed to have spread itself over most of the surface of my father's left buttock. It looked fierce and angry; the flesh, swollen and red, gave off warnings that were volcanic in terms of eruption. My mother began to prepare a kaolin poultice. This was to be followed by a generous application of basilican ointment. I remember those patented remedies – Snowfire Ointment or your own piddle for chilblains, Fennings Fever Cure for any changes in temperature . . . A visit to the doctor bore an expense that few could properly afford and home-nursing was a necessity rather than a choice.

I see that tiny front room in 37 Cecil Street, the newspapers stuffed in the gap under the bottom of the door to the street, the rexine three-piece suite that took up the whole of the room apart from the small sideboard on which a 'shy girl' statue seemed to be skating on the polish. The wallpaper was a heady mass of brightly coloured daisies – and its blossoms seemed to come to life where the damp had caused the paper to balloon outwards from the walls.

Then there is me, or the young girl who was me. I don't like too much of what I view. I see a sulking, be-plaited adolescent who refuses to play Ludo with her younger sister; indeed, she will not even engage in any conversation with her. Instead, she pretends to be immersed in her book – which is Scott's *Ivanhoe*. She is not concerned about its content as she has already read the book twice and over-study has killed her interest in it.

This girl thinks: I should not be here in this cold, poky room. It's not fair that I'm in a house like this – I should be in a semi-detached house. Not one that is part of a colliery row with the front door opening directly on to the street and the back door opening on to a shared yard full of rain puddles, ash and cinders which make it look like a deserted obstacle course. The outlook beyond is no better – the long unfenced garden, and beyond the gardens . . . Oh, the shame of those lavatories. And how had these parents created me? What had I done to deserve a mother who swore and left her teeth in a glass all day Sunday and a father who coughed and smoked Woodbines and who would sometimes fart loudly and say, 'Catch that, our Janet'? This is not a background that I can share with any of the other girls at school. I have lied to them. I have invented a house and a mother and a father that do not exist. I feel no guilt over this deception. Why should I lower myself to their level?

There is a loud banging on the front door which makes the wood creak. The sound reverberates through the wide room and startles both my sister and me. Callers at our front door are rare – only bad news ever comes through it – someone killed, someone injured. 'Who is it? Who is it?' I cry out.

'It's me, duck. It's me, Janet – Patrick Harper. I'd like a word or two with your mother.'

'Wait a minute, I'll fetch her. She's in the back kitchen, wait a minute.'

I hear my father groan in agony as my mother layers the steaming poultice across his buttock. She tells me to let Mr Harper in through the front door; she tells me not to stand and gawp as though I'd been struck by lightning. She will be in as soon as she is finished with her ministrations. She dismisses me as though I were a child of five instead of a young woman who is cleverer than she ever was.

'Come in, Mr Harper. My parents are just finishing their tea. They will be here in a moment or two.'

He closes the door behind him and stands awkwardly near its inside entrance. I do not offer him a chair although there is one vacant.

'It's turned a bit chilly, Janet.' He rubs his hands together.

'We don't have a fire in this room. Except at Christmas.'

My truthful observation seems to increase his social discomfort and he moves his weight from one leg to another. His shyness cripples him. He gets little pity or understanding from me.

'A bad business about Mr Roper, isn't it? The funeral was held up north somewhere. It was private.'

'I didn't know him very well.'

I am so possessed by my own indignation and suffering that I find it very difficult to enter anyone else's. I know that I am being less than pleasant, less than polite, yet I can do nothing to modify my tone or attitude.

'Kay's very upset – deeply grieved. That's why I'm here to see your Mam.'

'Oh?' I look towards him with a vacant but questioning gaze which implies that I am not really the slightest bit interested in his presence – or the reason for it.

I pick up my book and begin to read it as though each line were filled with endless surprises. I exclude him. I begin to feel slight quavers of remorse – since being at my new school I have only seen Miss Roper twice. On the first occasion, I pretended I had not sighted her when she waved from an opposite pavement. A week or so later it had been impossible to believe I was invisible as I found her standing less than a few yards away from me in the cinema queue.

'You are looking well, Janet. Do give my kindest regards to your mother. I enjoy this picture-house more than all the others. Even if the picture is poor the selection of interval music is diverting. It's the only place that I enjoy the organ – but then, there aren't many places where one can hear it, unless one is a church-goer which I am not. How do you like your new school?'

'I love it. I can't wait for the weekends to be over so that I can get back. I have new friends there. We do algebra, French, biology and Latin.'

'How often do you have Latin?'

'Every day. It takes up the first half-hour of every day. We conjugate verbs and do noun case endings.'

'How very useful.'

'I wish my mother thought the same.' I sniggered mockingly. 'She can hardly speak English let alone French or Latin.'

'Does anyone speak Latin? Italian is my favourite language. I love the way it seems to swoop and glide – there is nothing harsh in any of its sounds. I believe your mother drives a crane in the factory, Janet – it's more than I could ever do. I admire her strength and her truthfulness . . . the same qualities that shine in the performances of the star of this film. You like Ingrid Bergman, do you?'

'Why . . . er, yes.'

I hadn't imagined that anyone could make a comparison

178

between Ingrid Bergman and my mother. I was about to mention Gary Cooper when we were parted.

'Good to see you again, Janet – I'm sitting on the balcony. English is not Miss Bergman's first language, but it's no loss, she says so much with her face. Goodbye, dear.'

How dare she treat me in that way? Who did she think she was? My teachers at my new school all had proper degrees and they wore gowns to prove it. If Miss Roper were on the staff of my new school she would have been Miss Nobody. How could I have adored and worshipped a woman who paraded around like a decorated goose? When my mother had mentioned the death of Kay's father I had only offered a passing commiseration. At this stage in my adolescence, I was not just fickle, but deeply embedded in the kind of snobbery which blinded ordinary perception.

I see my mother entering the front room wiping her hands on a tea-towel. There are white blobs of kaolin still clinging to her apron. She apologizes to Patrick for keeping him waiting.

'Sit down, Mr Harper, rest your back. What's our Janet doing leaving you standing there without offering you a seat? Sorry to keep you waiting – Albert has a carbuncle as big as a saucer on his behind and I've been dressing it. It's very painful for him. Agony. He's due on the late shift in an hour or so.'

'There are a lot of people with boils,' says Patrick as he lowers himself into the nearby chair. 'We seem to be plagued with them.'

I feel shallow – he knows now that I lied to him, he knows my pretensions were false, he is truly concerned for Miss Roper. I still remain unable to offer the smallest degree of condolence, yet some part of me aches on behalf of her.

'It's about Miss Roper, is it? Anything we can do?' As she speaks, my mother wipes the blobs of kaolin away from her apron with the tea-towel.

'She needs coal. Mrs Pugh says that she's got less than two or three days' supply left. She wondered if . . . if some of you in this row might be able to help. It was Mrs Pugh who suggested I should tell you. I think it might be more urgent than she says as I've seen no smoke coming from the chimneys today, and there's no way I'd miss seeing smoke, the air being as cold as it is today.

It's bitterly cold, you can feel it hit your throat when you step out. My eyes watered like a faulty tap on my way up here.'

My mother responds immediately. There are no reservations, no qualms as to her own situation. 'Albert's on late shift – but that old pram in the yard will hold a hundredweight. Take the pram and help yourself from our coal-house. I'll let the others in the row know tomorrow. There'll be enough in the pram to tide Miss Roper over.'

'I can't do it today. I'm on "lates" myself.'

Mr Harper is about to suggest another time for this unorthodox delivery, but my mother flings the tea-towel across the back of the settee and I know this is a sign that her mind is made up.

'No need for you to bother further, Mr Harper. I can do it before I go to work – and our Janet will help me.'

I feel sure Patrick Harper hears my sigh of muted exasperation.

'Oh, I'm certain I could ask a couple of mates to come round for it, Mrs Haycock. It's no job for a woman and a girl to be doing.'

'I do a man's job every night save the weekend, Mr Harper, and it will do our Janet no harm at all. The exercise will do her good. She's not the Queen of Sheba, you know. Put your coat and scarf on, Janet – and the old mittens you knitted two years back. Would you have time for a cup of tea, Mr Harper? Albert will make one for you, it's no bother and . . .'

He says that he does not have time, he says he has to get back and pack his sandwiches and change into his pit gear. My mother opens the door for him and I am suddenly aware that courtesy is not based on appearances or social strata – my mother ignores my snobbery, for that is what it is. She does not question it, she seizes it from my bosom and flings it directly into my face.

Perhaps I shouldn't judge that girl, that girl who is me, too harshly. Social class is tightly adhered to in this village. It is very hard for that girl in her struggle to step outside the role her birth has allotted her. She is dissatisfied with her background, but is not sure what new background she wishes to adopt. She feels sure that there is something better than what her mother seems to offer. Prejudices and narrowness seem to be part of both cultures.

How is she able to pick out the best that both can offer? In trying to be part of both groups, she only manages to do the splits and feels pained and unhappy. Such acrobatics are beyond her.

As they push the coal-laden pram along the pavements, she is reminded of a conversation that she has overheard between her mother and her father. She can scarcely call it a conversation – such an exchange was unusual at any time in her house.

Her mother switches off her bedroom light as she and her father make their way towards their bedroom. 'Don't burn money at this hour. Read in the daylight. That's what it's for.'

The girl creeps from her bed after she hears their door close in order to switch the light back on. Her hand pauses before it reaches the switch, her attention is drawn to the love-making noises of her own parents. There are pantings and gaspings, mutterings and small strange cries. The creaking of the bed now takes on an insistent rhythm that is gradually getting noisier. 'Oh, oh, oh, oh . . . don't fetch a baby, Albert . . . oh, oh, oh, oh . . . don't fetch another baby . . .'

It wouldn't have been possible for a prudish child to live in one of these houses. The paper-thin walls left little room for privacy, whether it was sacred or not.

I chuckle to myself when I think of that errand of mercy shared between mother and unwilling daughter, pushing the coal-heavy pram through the streets on that bitterly cold afternoon. It became a ferocious battle of wills between the two of us as to who could push the ungainly vehicle the fastest. Distances were easily sorted out as each lamp-post indicated a change of driver. The chariot race in *Ben Hur* was not fought with any greater competitiveness. I was intent on showing my mother that I could beat her on her own terms and she was fixed with exposing the limitations that learning had bestowed upon me.

Consequently, we both arrived at Miss Roper's door speechless through lack of breath. Our heavy breathing seemed to send vapour signals to one another on the cold air. We stood outside that door and gulped, our exhaustion signifying a truce which – I suppose – was fair.

'Are you in, Roper? Are you there? It's me, Mrs Haycock,' my mother called through the letter-box.

We heard the pad of footsteps in the hallway. We both knew that Kay was standing just the other side of the door. She must have heard us breathing.

'I'm not seeing people, Mrs Haycock. Not anyone.'

I recognized Kay's voice and felt full of remorse and guilt that I had offered so little in terms of gratitude or condolence over the past months.

'Of course you don't want to see anyone, I understand that, it's only natural. Of course I understand it, my love.' My mother spoke with gruff tenderness. 'I didn't expect to see you, I didn't come to pry. I've brought you some coal. Thought you might be low on fuel. Whatever else, you have to keep warm. I'll leave it here for you. It's in the pram. Mr Harper can bring it back when you've emptied it.'

'How kind of you . . . how very kind of you, Mrs Haycock. I've received more love from women . . . What an irony . . . Thank you . . . You are most kind.'

'It was our Janet's idea.'

With this gently spoken lie my mother emerged victorious from our duel.

'Dear Janet – dear girl . . .' Kay muttered and we heard her footsteps as they padded away from us.

We left the pram there and made our way home. I complained that my legs were cold and my mother said that I should wear two under-skirts during the winter as she did. How could I go to school wearing two under-skirts under my gym-slip? What would the other girls have said if they had found out such a thing? I didn't quarrel any more with my mother. I nodded as if in agreement but at the same time dismissed the advice from my mind.

Later, we drank hot, bitter-tasting cocoa and I saw that my mother's cheeks were streaked with tears as she sipped the dark brown liquid from her mug. I knew that she was thinking of Kay and Kay's bereavement. I attempted to offer some measured balm.

'Don't cry, Mam. Don't cry. Miss Roper is more resilient than you might think.'

'How would you know what I might think? I'm not crying. It's the cold that has got in my eyes. I must change and get ready for the factory. That bus waits for nobody. See that you and your sister are in bed by nine – and settle yourself down to some homework. No mare ever won a race that was left to graze.' She laughed to herself. 'I wouldn't mind doing a bit of grazing myself. What a swine this war is.'

That night it was difficult for me to compare Rowena with Rebecca, or to consider how the Angevin Empire was gained and lost; even the simplest geometrical theorem was beyond my powers of proof. My thoughts were with Miss Roper – willing her to return to us all. I had no idea that the woman I knew would never appear before us again.

12

'A lapse in decorum, improper attention to dress, slovenly deport-
ment – all these things, if practised by one single girl, drag down
the good name of the school. Your selfishness astounds all of us.
That you girls could have embarked on such a sortie, and at such
a time, leaves most of the staff here sorely wounded and let down.
An hour's detention is a very light reminder by my reckoning – I
feel you should count yourselves lucky. I hope that you will dwell
on the shame you have brought on yourselves and your fellow
pupils.'

What was our heinous crime? What terrible deed had three
chastised and chastened girls committed? Not only had we been
to see Johnny Weissmuller in a Tarzan film – we had bragged
about it. Poor Johnny was on the list of forbidden things that our
eyes should not look upon; he was considered improper viewing
for 'the better class of girl'. We weren't supposed to imagine what
naked men looked like – such contemplation was thought to be
too horrible for words to express. Male film stars hardly ever took
their clothes off – and here was one swinging from the trees. All
male, beautiful, savage, and – for the most part – naked, but
tender. We had broken the boundaries of the corporate good taste
of the school and now we must suffer for it.

'I cannot trust you not to waste your time. Here are some essay
titles for you. Write them down in your rough notebooks. I shall
only read them out once, so pay full attention. I want at least
three pages. Ready? "Victory", "Why I love Britain", and "The
Great Day".'

I have no recollection of what I wrote on these subjects, which were directed towards and centred on the VE Day pronouncements. I wonder if any girls of my background recorded their own experiences in such schools. I don't think an authentic version of our experiences would have been welcomed at that time.

It was May, and I know that we had gathered some lovely hawthorn blossoms – their sweet, sickly scent made us feel almost dizzy. We were forbidden to bring them indoors as they were said to herald bad luck if taken inside a home. After the announcement there seemed to be an unnatural quiet, not dissimilar to the moments just after an air-raid warning. But then, there was an explosion of human celebration the like of which I have never known since.

All repressed hopes and reservations were cast aside as people ran into the streets and clasped and hugged one another. Kisses were exchanged between total strangers and were not limited to opposite genders. The party – our village party – was not planned. It burst from every door and cascaded on to the main street.

No one seemed proprietorial about furniture as kitchen tables and chairs were handed from every home and placed down the centre of the roadway. Wirelesses blared out different tunes, windows and doors were opened and the village throbbed with activity.

Secret food, hoarded for months, even years, was produced for the communal good and enjoyment. Precious tins of peaches, home-baked cakes, jam – all kinds of jam – corned-beef and fish-paste sandwiches, jellies of every flavour and hue, towering blancmange shapes . . . The tables held before us a feast the like of which none of us children had ever seen before.

I don't know how the conga began, or who started it – but all the village seemed to be part of that long line of dancers. One's hands gripped the hips or waist of the person in front and the motion started. Like some enormous boa-constrictor we glided about the streets. 'I came, I saw a conga, I came, I saw a *cong-a*. We've finally done old *Hitla*, we've finally done old *Hit-la*. Aye – aye – aye, aye – aye – aye.'

Eventually, we settled on the chairs and surveyed the food

185

before us. It was hard to know where to start – but adults saw to it that sandwiches were to be attacked first. The meal seemed to go on for most of the afternoon, but our time was not entirely taken up with eating. We were entertained too. I don't think I've ever seen such a variable group of performers. No other variety show has ever matched its diversity of content. I doubt if any of us children could have guessed the assorted talent that lurked amidst the adults of our village, who had previously always seemed rather dull to me.

The show (for that is what it was) did not begin quietly. It kicked off with a rousing dance number from about eight or ten of the village women. Mr Arkwright played the piano-accordion and an elderly man (whose name I have forgotten) played on the spoons.

Most of the other adults formed a clapping and chanting semicircle around the new-found ladies of the chorus line. 'Ta-ra-ra-boom-de-ay . . . ta-ra-ra-boom-de-ay . . . our cat's had pups today . . . old Hitler's got to pay . . . ta-ra-ra-boom-de-ay . . .' Skirts were lifted up to the chin to reveal acres of dimpled thighs, the sunlight caused suspender buckles to sparkle in the sun and heightened the colours of knickers which had certainly never been exposed to daylight before, at least, not whilst they were still being worn. There were screams and shouts of encouragement as the women kicked higher and higher and displayed satin bottoms and fleshy thighs to public view.

This dance was followed by a raucous version of 'Hands, knees, and bumps-a-daisy', the participants flinging up their skirts and giving the audience a multi-coloured panorama of female back-sides. It was all very shocking, very vulgar – but oh, so thrilling – and, yes, one could say that it was liberating.

Then there was Mr Foster, the milkman, who played on a banjo and sang George Formby songs. I'm sure his version of 'When I'm Cleaning Windows' was more forthright and rude than the original one we had heard on the wireless.

We gasped with horror and awe as Mr Allport's son did vile things with a white-furred, red-eyed ferret. It crawled about the inside of his shirt, round his neck and up and down either arm.

And worse. He let it slide down the front of his trousers. We watched the hidden shape of the creature move about his crutch; we held our breath when it paused there and sighed with audible relief as it made its way down his trouser-leg and out into the open air. We thought he was very brave to risk his manhood all for the sake of our entertainment. Our applause was long and respectful.

Mrs Davenport, Mrs Wilson, Mrs Johnson and other ladies of the Baptist Church choir brought a modifying influence to our street theatre by singing 'Jerusalem', 'Oh Love Divine', and 'Bread of Heaven'.

'Bread of Heaven, Bread of Heaven. Feed me till I want no more. Fee . . . ee . . . ee . . . d me till I – er – er – want no more.' They concluded by singing and miming to a hymn called 'I will make you Fishers of Men'.

I can see them marching about, those Baptist Chapel ladies, casting imaginary fishing lines and chanting, 'I will make you Fishers of men, Fishers of men, Fishers of men. I will make you Fishers of men, if you follow me. If you follow me. If you follow me.'

Some of the men present chose to interpret the message quite differently from its pious intent and had to be called to order by the older women.

Even when the greediest appetite had been satisfied, we still remained seated at our tables, and in the late afternoon one of the miners began to produce tunes from his mouth-organ. They were not rumbustious or rousing, but plaintive and reflective, and in some measure quite sad.

There was a woman called Mrs Wilding, who must have been in her mid-forties. A plump, plain woman who had chosen to wear black ever since the war had granted her a widow's status. Her enforced single state and her lovely voice commanded a deep respect, so there were sh-sh-shushes when she stepped off the pavement to sing.

'If I were a blackbird, I'd whistle and sing
And follow the ship that my true love sails in,

And on the top riggings, I'd there build a nest
And pillow my head on his lily-white breast.'

Men and women cried unashamedly as she sang, so full throated.
This was a time when sentiment needed to be declared, but it was
far from being sentimental. As she sang, we noticed a figure
walking down the hill towards us. There was a newsagent's shop
on its brow which was owned by a man called Richard Richards,
and this small incline was known locally as 'Double Dick's Nob'.

It wasn't easy to make out the identity of the approaching
visitor as the sinking sun bedazzled our view. I discerned that it
was a woman but couldn't determine who she was. Mrs Wilding
was still singing as the woman reached the first of the tables and
stood quite still out of courtesy for the performer and the song.

After the song was over, there was clapping and general
murmurs of encouragement and approval. There were calls for
'encore', 'encore' – but Mrs Wilding seemed unaware of the praise
that we were heaping upon her. Very slowly, she walked towards
the late-comer. There was a good deal of whispering amongst
most of the women. My mother and Mrs Pugh joined Mrs Wilding
– these women put their arms about the stranger and greeted her
with great tenderness. It was as though we were not present. They
linked arms with the woman and seemed to guide her to the centre
of the merry-making.

'Janet, squash up a bit. Squash up. Make room for Miss Roper,
she's come back to us,' my mother ordered.

Mrs Wilding gave some sort of signal with her hand and the
piano-accordionist broke into a tango medley.

As Kay Roper sat down. I made a final assault on a large dollop
of pink blancmange that had been plonked on my plate. 'What a
feast you've all had, Janet. And quite right too.'

So, it really was Miss Roper. No one could imitate that voice. I
have never heard another one similar to it or even vaguely like it.
The voice matched the woman I knew, so did the perfume, but
nothing else was the same. This woman – this Miss Roper –
seemed set in a middle-aged wilderness: she could have been any
age ranging from thirty-eight to forty-eight. Was it possible to

claim so many years in a matter of months? And why should any woman contrive to look so plain? In some ways, I had always attributed a certain kind of romance or glamour to bereavement. It seemed such a commonplace thing then, there was always someone in mourning. Black arm-bands and black clothing had a mystery and allure and loss was tinged with patriotism.

The sight of the new Miss Roper held no such appeal. Sitting next to me was a woman who might well have served out most of life behind a grille at a post office, or as a spinster-like dogsbody who worked within cream walls in a male solicitor's office. Such women existed then: they were single, they offered loyalty and service for a pittance in payment, yet they were derided and called 'old maids' and 'plain Janes'. These were external judgements. I wonder how vivid their interior lives were?

Miss Roper had never before been seen without a plethora of coloured clothing – indeed, the uncharitable or jealous were of the opinion that she had an excess of it. The village's brightly coloured exotic bird had, in a matter of months, changed into a hen thrush that was long past mating.

Now she wore a shabby, woollen, light brown skirt and matching jumper, thick lisle stockings, and flat ultra-sensible, lace-up brown shoes which could easily have been worn by a man and not caused comment. Gone were the bracelets, ear-rings and necklaces. She was bereft of decoration. Lipstick, rouge, eye-shadow – all the 'Hollywood Glow' – had disappeared from her face. She had succumbed only to using a great deal of very pale face-powder which gave her the look of someone who had come back from the dead.

And that wonderful hair – it was now parted down the centre and braided into two small buns, one on each side of her ears, so that only the lobes were visible. From this time on, I always felt she resembled a telephonist – an unpleasant but not unperceptive girl had said that she was using Olivia de Havilland as a role model.

I think – I think now – that the pace of Kay's grief had to be swift in order for her to come to terms with it, and in the process she had become a gross caricature of what she felt she ought to be.

'We've beaten the Germans, Miss Roper. We've won the war – nearly won it, anyway.' It was a struggle to make conversation with her.

'It's not Germans we have been fighting, Janet.' She spoke quietly but in an assured manner.

I wondered if there might have been some mental change as well as a physical one. We had been told daily on the wireless, and in all the newspapers and magazines, that the Germans were our arch-enemies. Had Miss Roper gone mad? I escaped response by spooning a large portion of blancmange into my mouth. She explained without any question from me; she was always good at stating her case.

'We have not been fighting Germans, Janet. We have been at war with Nazism – at war with Fascists. Fascists!' She spat this last word out as though the syllables might cause her tooth decay if held there too long.

'Fascists?' I mumbled. It was difficult to say much more as my mouth still held some of the sweet raspberry-flavoured blancmange.

'Oh yes. They appear like toadstools or any poisonous fungi. No country is ever free of them. Under a guise of nationalism and peacock-like strutting, they spread their cancerous all-conquering messages.' She laughed bitterly. 'Ah yes, and you know – they claim patriotism as the centre-piece of their spores.'

I gulped. 'They sound very dangerous, Miss Roper.'

'They are gangrenous, Janet.' She seemed to look over my head in the direction of the brow of the hill. 'And they will be back. They will be back with their marching, their strutting, their flags, their cruelty towards anyone who they feel is different from them. Yes, I'm sure they will be back – when the time and conditions are ripe, they emerge in any country.'

A chill or tremor of fear seemed to pass right through my system as she spoke and I half expected to hear the thud of jack-boots and see an alien column of military appear over the brow of the hill.

'Your new school is continuing to please you?' she enquired.

'Oh yes. Very much,' I answered, too energetically.

'Glad to hear it. I've no doubt that you will do well – coming as you do, from such a privileged background, you could only do well.'

There was no trace of sarcasm in this observation, which had its desired effect in that it made me take new stock of my home and its surroundings.

The place that I lived in then does not now exist. It is little more than recent history with few statues or monuments left to record it. The pits are all closed, the miners (what are left of them) live in a twilight world of early redundancy without much prospect of future work. Others have left to find labour in different regions – nowadays, it seems as though a fifth of the nation have to be working gypsies in order to live. The village still retains its rural aspect, and on this level the properties that have taken the place of the mean rows of colliery houses are much sought after by affluent workers from cities up to thirty miles away.

Most of the residue of the original inhabitants are now housed on the Marshland Estate. The place is aptly named – it is built over a stretch of low-lying marsh between the railway and the main road on the eastern side of the town. The mist often hides the broken windows and air of dereliction and desolation of the people who live there. The place is little more than a welfare prison from which there is no escape for the people who dwell in it.

In my young days, the furthest most people travelled was the mile and a half walk into the town. I think my journeying to my new school granted me a wider universe than the rest of the village children. Yet, on that celebration day, all our horizons seemed to be enlarged. The festivities still went on long after the tables had been cleared and taken indoors, and at dusk, people walked about the village arm in arm or sat on their front doorsteps talking and singing and laughing.

For the first time in years, night did not bring total darkness. Doors were left open, black-out curtains were pulled back from windows, upstairs lights were left on and our streets were flooded with rays of light. The Church of England, the Primitive Methodists, and the Bethany Baptists as well as the Tin Tabernacle – all rang their bells and the children stayed out of doors.

I walked to Miss Roper's house: perhaps I hoped that all this light amidst the darkness would have some magical effect upon her. Change her back to the woman that I had once known. There were two or three soldiers drinking beer with Mrs Pugh. The windows of her house were half open, the curtains drawn back – she called out a friendly but drunkenly slurred greeting as I passed.

The lights were ablaze in Mr Harper's house and he watched me as I paused and stood outside Miss Roper's place. Hers was the only door in the village that was closed, the black-out curtains remained in place, no chink of light was showing; she remained in a state of siege.

I walked up to the front door, raised my knuckles to rap on it, and then thought differently and let my hand drop to my side.

'She's gone.'

I heard Patrick Harper's voice and turned quickly; he was standing there in the middle of the untarmacked road, his hands in his pockets.

'Gone?' I enquired of him.

'Yes. Kay has gone. She won't come back to me – or you, Janet. You might as well face up to it.'

'I was with her this afternoon.'

'No. Oh no, Janet,' he shook his head to emphasize this point, 'you were with Miss Roper . . . but Kay . . . but Kay Roper, the woman you knew, the woman I knew . . . and wanted to know more . . . has gone. She'll not be back.'

'I'm sorry. It was lovely with her while it lasted, wasn't it?' As I spoke I made my way to his side, right there in the middle of the road. I began to cry and he placed his arm around my shoulder to comfort me . . . then his mother called out to him from their front door and he pulled his arm away from my shoulder just as if he had received an electric shock – and left me whispering the quietest of farewells as he went.

I wonder what his mother would think now if she could read

my mind? If the dead can read the minds of the living then she will be turning in her grave.

I want his arm resting on my shoulder again. No, I want more. I want his head resting on my breast. I want to touch his body. I'm intent on having him. 'Intent on having him,' I'm sure I must have read that phrase in a book somewhere. A nice phrase. Why shouldn't a woman make some of the running?

13

I was in mind to open up the garden centre today – just to sell a few seasonal plants in the shop section at the front. Finally, I've decided against it. We don't talk about Christmas now – we talk about the Christmas period. Christmas Day has been gone for four days now but the people around here (at least, the ones that you see) all look a bit shell-shocked. This holiday has become more of a duty than a pleasure. I sometimes wonder if we ought to have holidays inflicted upon us. We ought to have times in the year when we can choose our own reasons for taking time off.

Well, there's a conundrum if you like. Shot myself in the leg with my own ammunition. If I were to take time off for people I loved or honoured – people who have gone from me – then Miss Roper would have to be included among them. And here she is popping off at Christmas. I suppose in future years I can refer to this period as Kaytime – however I look at it, her death has certainly livened up this mistletoe session.

I was surprised to see the solicitor go in her house this morning: it seemed a bit crude to be calling so early. I wonder if it has anything to do with the inquest. He wasn't alone, there were several people with him. More than I would have thought the situation merited. There were two police officers, one male and one female. If the female hadn't worn stockings and a skirt, I could have sworn she was a man. Accompanying them were four other men who I'd never seen in this area before, and I thought I knew everyone. I called out to them and asked if I could help in any way. 'No. No, thank you.' They answered me with a snotty-nosed abruptness that was only just the right side of being downright rude.

They must have been in there for two hours or more. God alone knows what they were doing. My surprise came close to shock when I saw them carrying great bundles of papers and files out of the house and storing them in the boots of their cars. For one shivering moment I wondered if Kay might have been cheating on the income-tax people. After very little thought, I dismissed this from my mind. She had made her views known on taxation, her mind was set.

'No, no, Mr Harper. I think that we should pay more income tax. Not less. There has to be a deeper and more thoughtful share-out. If you create an underbelly of hopeless, inescapable poverty, you sow the seeds of crime and serious social dissent. Once sown, these seeds are more expensive when reaped than a penny in every pound. If I didn't put anything back into this garden I wouldn't get much of a harvest out of it, would I?'

She was a great admirer of Ellen Wilkinson and women like that and often sounded like them when she spoke – preached would be nearer the mark.

Kay's interest in gardening became close to obsession in that year of 1945. What a year for events. It wasn't only Kay Roper who changed in that year – the whole world seemed to change form. It seemed to be one shock after another and they weren't all pleasant.

On the sixth of June at a quarter to four in the afternoon I was in the back kitchen repairing some floats for a future fishing expedition. It was a warm day and I had left the back door ajar. The wireless was on low and I could just hear the late election results as they came in. The same words were being spoken over and over again: 'Labour elected,' 'Labour elected,' 'Labour elected.' As the announcer stated that it was now certain that Mr Attlee would be forming the next government, I heard not one – but at least three – piercing screams which came from the direction of the garden.

My first fears were for Miss Roper – although I could never imagine her allowing herself to emit a scream. These anxieties were quickly allayed. She stood amidst rows of carrots, a huge straw hat jammed on top of her head leaving half of her face veiled and hidden from me. She raised her hoe and pointed towards the blackcurrant bushes that flowered at the bottom of my garden.

'Your mother. It's your mother. She's behind those bushes. I can see her feet, I can see her shoes, she is kicking out in a strange way, she is struggling. Go to her. Go quickly. Be quick, Mr Harper.'

I found my mother flat on her back, her body convulsing, her legs splayed about in an unnatural way. One of them seemed to twitch. Paralysis seemed to overtake me, I stood there unable to speak, unable to move. Somehow, I managed to call out, 'Miss Roper! Miss Roper! Help me.'

My mother's face was so contorted with pain that she seemed barely recognizable to me. In particular, her mouth appeared to be pulled to one side as though she were making some agonized kind of snarl and there was white froth about her mouth. Spittle dribbled freely from the corners of her lips and trickled from her chin on to her neck. Had the election results caused her such a shock as to bring on a heart attack? There was no history of epilepsy as far as I knew. Still immobile, I stood in the heat of the afternoon and wondered if I was dreaming.

There was no movement from her now. She lay quite still and her eyes gazed up at the sky above her.

Miss Roper must have scaled the fence very swiftly; in thinking back, I have to marvel at her agility and athleticism. She clutched my arm, released it, and then knelt beside my mother.

'Mr Harper! Mr Harper! Get the other side of her. Move! Do as I tell you. Move. Now do as I say.'

I obeyed her. I was grateful that someone else had assumed responsibility for an emergency that I was ill equipped to deal with.

'Now, Mr Harper, put one hand behind her head and try to keep her jaw open with your other hand.'

Again I simply did as I was told and watched with horror and revulsion as Miss Roper's long, bony fingers probed and tugged inside my mother's throat.

'There! There!' she gasped as she flicked out my mother's bottom set of dentures on to the grass. I noticed that the top set had already been discarded.

'Mrs Harper, Mrs Harper, Mrs Har . . .' Miss Roper stopped patting my mother's cheek. She knelt back on her heels. 'She's gone, Patrick.'

'Gone? Gone?'

'Your mother is dead, she is gone, Mr Harper. I had better make a telephone call. You will need help, Mr Harper.'

Even as we stood there the mystery that lay behind my mother's death was revealed to us. A few segments of orange lay in the palm of her left hand and we stood transfixed as the wasps crawled angrily over her wrist and forearm in ever-increasing numbers. I heard Miss Roper catch her breath with shock and my eyes now followed hers.

My mother's bottom lip had swollen in the most grotesque fashion – it ballooned outwards and had already begun to turn blue and purple. The creatures were on her lip . . . and yes . . . yes . . . they were even crawling into . . . and out of . . . her mouth.

'Fetch a blanket, Mr Harper, or a coat – or something. You must be quick, she should be covered.'

Kay pushed me gently as though I were some machine that needed human coercion and encouragement to get its engine started. From then on, she organized everything – the telephone calls, interviews with the doctor. She seemed to be familiar with the business of death.

The coroner recorded death by accident due to choking as a result of wasp stings. What a strange way to leave this world – greedily gobbling oranges behind the flowering currant bushes in order that she might not have to feel obliged to share any of it with me. The countryside can be just as savage as a busy road – it has to be treated and approached with care.

In fact, if my mother had lived longer, I think she would have enjoyed those years of austerity after the war. She loved to skimp and save; her nature left little space for holidaying or celebration.

197

I think the knowledge of my conception must have killed many of her feelings – and now I'm glad that I can at least think of her with some degree of pity. I'm sad, too, that I cannot feel any filial affection for her memory.

At the time, the lack of affection didn't stop me from feeling any less lonely after the funeral and settlements were over. You get used to people that you live with, even if you're not too fond of them, and it's possible to miss them when they are gone. I should know. I remember sitting in this very room, a few months after her death, and thinking that I'd go mad with loneliness.

I'd sometimes go round to see Mrs Pugh – not for sex. She'd placed that out of bounds for me – but just for a game of cards or to hear another voice apart from the ones that I heard at work or on the wireless. It was thanks to her that I met my wife. She didn't introduce us to each other, nothing like that – she asked me to get her sweet ration for her. It was always the same order and only available at Woolworth's in the main town.

There was a counter called Pick and Mix and for a fixed price you could have half a pound of assorted confectionary. Two girls worked behind the counter. One of them was often irritable if you took too long in choosing a few from this pile and a few from that. Understandable, I suppose, as some people took ages bibbing and bobbing over this caramel and that acid drop.

Over a period of weeks I adopted a strategy. I always waited until the bad-tempered one was occupied and then called the attention of the other one. I remember . . . I remember exactly when I first knew that she fancied me.

'Can I change these for an ounce of Pontefracts? I'm sorry to mess you about,' I said.

'Oh, I don't mind. It helps pass the time – it gets a bit boring here some days. Makes your feet ache. Funny, my feet never ache at the dance. An ounce of Pontefract cakes did you say?' She smiled slowly almost to herself as she let the liquorice drops fall on to the scales. She took two off and put on a false frown as she scanned the weight indicator. She smiled again and put more sweets on the scoop than she had removed. The indicator went well over the half-pound. She smiled directly at me before tipping all of the sweets into the paper bag.

'I can't dance very well,' I said apologetically.

'That's not a crime, is it?' She twirled the bag so that the action sealed the contents. 'That's one and threepence altogether, please. I thought I hadn't seen you there.'

'Where?'

'At the dance.'

'Did you look for me, then?'

'I might have done. It's one and threepence, please.'

'If I could dance and I went there, I'd look for you.'

My own brashness and forwardness made me feel suddenly self-conscious and I was anxious to leave the counter as quickly as I could. She seemed to linger over sorting out my change from half a crown and I felt that all the people in the store were watching some great drama being played out. Casual flirtation has never come easy to me.

'There's your change.' She placed the money in my hand. 'If you wanted to look for me, you wouldn't have to go to the dance, would you? I'm here every Monday to Saturday from nine to five thirty excepting Thursday when I finish at one.'

'My name's Patrick.' I volunteered the information as I took the change from her.

'Oh, I know,' she said.

'What are you called?'

'Evelyn. Evelyn's my name and that is enough for now.'

It was more than enough to start our courtship in motion, and I took readily to it. I think what I enjoyed most was the kind of spaniel-like devotion that Evelyn offered to me after our second or third meeting. Some men might run a mile if a girl said 'I love you' on a second or third date. Not me. Oh no, I needed such things to be said. No one had made me such an affirmation before – not in any context. There was no pretence to my Evelyn – no guile. Two months before our marriage: 'Don't fiddle and fumble, Patrick. Let me do it. There, there, it rolls on beautifully if you are careful.'

She regarded my prick without a trace of shyness. 'Are they all this size? I mean, are all men's things as big as . . .?'

'I don't know, love, I've only seen this one.'

'I love the feel of it inside and I like your sounds when you are there.'

We married just three days after her eighteenth birthday. Her parents were not displeased with the pairing. Few brides could move into their own home just hours after their wedding in those days and, what's more, she wasn't pregnant.

There was no question of a honeymoon or anything like that – we took two day-trips. One to Blackpool and one to Rhyl. Evelyn said the sea looked much the same wherever you viewed it – she was never much of a traveller. I didn't need seaside holidays for romance – with her, those first years were all honeymoon for me. No one had ever made me feel important before. Her mother concluded, 'Oh, our Evelyn thinks that the sun shines out of Patrick's arse.'

Evelyn and Miss Roper got on well with each other right from the start, and Kay's gardening enthusiasm transferred to my wife with a deep and lasting infection.

'Miss Roper hasn't bought a single vegetable this year – she's fed herself entirely from the garden. She's stopped eating meat, she's become vegetarian.'

'She's not a pacifist,' I remarked.

Vegetarianism was rare in those days and many thought that a meatless diet might cause malnutrition or something worse. It was considered to be an eccentric choice – not a rational one.

The two of them came to an arrangement with Aileen Pugh: they would cultivate her garden and let her have a percentage of the crops as rental. So it came about that between the three of us, we had as much land as you could find on a small-holding farm. Evelyn continued to work part-time on the sweet counter as well as work in the garden and home. At dusk, on warmer summer evenings, she and Kay would talk together. I can see them now, sharing a bottle of Vimto, sharing the same straw. The bottle passed to and fro.

'There's no choice in films this week, Evelyn. It's the first time in months when I have felt I could not attend.'

'I thought you liked musicals, Miss Roper?'

'I do. I do like them, Evelyn dear. But I cannot watch women dive in and out of swimming pools or spin round and round on ice-rinks. I have nothing against the performers – one can hardly apply the term actress to either of them. I do fear for the hearing of Miss Esther Williams – a well-built young woman. Do you suppose she wears ear-plugs? And how Miss Sonja Henie can spin on the ice with such velocity and then kiss a man immediately afterwards without vomiting down his throat, I can't imagine.'

Of a Saturday during this period, Evelyn would take her lunch-hour break from the sweet counter and spend it with Miss Roper and Ivy Chaplin. They always met at the same place. Ivy grumbled about the venue and Evelyn was not too keen but was too polite to make her viewpoint felt except to me. 'Miss Roper always insists on going to the British Restaurant. There's hardly anybody else there apart from us three. Not surprising – the tea is like dish-water – and often tepid. Miss Roper always says the food is delicious even when it's not. If you disagree with her, she makes you feel as if you have done a disservice to the country by not enjoying what is on offer. Last week we all had scrambled eggs on toast. Miss Roper dived in with her fork first and I could tell from her expression that she didn't like what she was sampling. "Mmm . . . Splendid," she said.

'Ivy Chaplin was not having any of this. She swallowed her first mouthful as though she were taking medicine. Then she placed her fork back on the table and spoke to me – she made a point of ignoring Miss Roper. Those two are right Tartars, Patrick, I can tell you. "Taste it, taste it, Evelyn. If a bird ever produced these eggs it could not have been a hen."

' "Oh, come, come, Ivy. Dried eggs are more nutritious than fresh ones. Like everything else, the taste has to be acquired." Miss Roper didn't give way.

'Ivy spoke to me again. "Evelyn, do bear me out. These eggs could never have started their life off within a hen. I think that they must have been produced by seagulls."

'Well, Patrick, I didn't want to take sides but I couldn't just sit there looking at what was set before me. Apart from anything else, I was hungry, so I took a good mouthful. I must say it was a bit of a surprise.

' "Now, Evelyn, don't be shy. Do you like it?" Ivy had her dander up.

' "I wouldn't say that I like it. I don't mind it, I can eat it. It doesn't taste like eggs. It tastes like pilchards – but of course it doesn't look like them."

' "Pilchards are very good for you," Miss Roper piped up.

' "Really, Kay, you are impossible at times. How can you enjoy scrambled eggs when they taste like pilchards?"

' "By closing your eyes, Ivy dear. You don't have to stare at your food before transporting it to your mouth," says Miss Roper, demonstrating how we should both do it.

'You know, Patrick, when we left there, there was as much food on the floor and table as what we had eaten. Miss Roper said that I looked like a homely version of Rita Hayworth with my hair done like this. Later when she went to the toilet Mrs Chaplin said that my hair looked perfectly in order and she said that Miss Roper could be silly at times. She talked as if Miss Roper were some young girl – she looks older than Mrs Chaplin, and I'd never say she was silly.

'Anyway, I said that I didn't mind looking like Rita Hayworth, homely or not. When Miss Roper got back to us she said she'd ordered a baked apple each for all of us and that it was her treat. I thanked Miss Roper but Ivy Chaplain groaned. Miss Roper never takes any notice of her rudeness, she seems to thrive on it. After she'd eaten half of her apple Mrs Chaplin said, "I'm three months pregnant, Kay."

'Miss Roper patted the back of her hand and said, "You'd better finish your apple then dear." '

Oh, they were good years, those early times with Evelyn. I suppose nowadays some might consider her to have been young for marriage at eighteen, but not then, not at that time she wasn't. Children weren't allowed to be children much past twelve – and even before then they were constantly exhorted to 'grow up'. As far as children were concerned, just at the time when me and Evelyn thought that we'd never ring that bell, it rang.

It wasn't an easy pregnancy. Evelyn was so swollen and heavy she could barely haul herself about the house in that Christmas of 1952 – but she bore it all very bravely and remained in good heart. She wanted that baby – oh, so much – but I couldn't imagine what it would be like to be a dad. I know I was excited and nervous at the prospect.

And there was no excitement on the most important day, the twenty-sixth of January. There was a birth, a baby was born to us two in this house. It was born dead.

Her relatives offered unhelpful comfort: 'Oh, you can try again,' 'It's happened to others,' 'Lose a child and you'll find a child.' The words seemed more suitable for missing out on a prize raffle Infant mortality was higher than it is now, but it didn't make it any easier for us. It was hard for us to be philosophical about the loss. Evelyn seemed broken by it – as though it were her fault in some way. It was silly of me, but I remember hiding or throwing away the daily newspapers before they came into the house. I never gave myself time to read them – all the headlines were to do with that poor man Bentley being hung. Few thought that he had earned the drop, and headlines like 'Miscarriage of Justice' were all over the place. I still find that word gives me the shivers. Miscarriage.

The doctor said that Evelyn would be up and about in a week or so. 'She'll soon be back to normal,' was how he put it. His prognosis was so far out it would never come back. She got up all right – but by March of that year she was far from her usual self.

She seemed to have gone into a world all of her own and there was no place for me or her relatives in it. I called in the doctor again and he said that if things got much worse, I might consider sending her away for a time. It felt as though she were away anyway. I felt so desperate that night that I banged on Kay Roper's door.

She stood in the doorway as if hesitant to ask me in, so I made up her mind for her.

'Can I come in? Can I talk to you, Kay – er . . . Miss Roper?'
She answered me oddly. 'You can come in to talk to Miss Roper
– but not to Kay, Mr Harper. You understand?'
'I think I do. Yes, I am sure I do. Please can I come in? Let me
talk with you . . . there's no one else I can talk with. Only you,
Miss Roper.'
She did not offer me any tea. We sat in the kitchen and I
remember apologizing to her for still being in my working clothes.
She dismissed my apology with a slight wave of one of her large,
bony hands and said that she preferred to see men in their working
clothes. She'd taken to wearing some of the new National Health
glasses and she retrieved them from the dresser and put them on
as though she were interviewing me for a job or something like
that.
She placed her hands in her lap and asked, 'Well, Mr Harper?'
It was almost like talking to someone that I didn't know,
someone who was skilled in the art of listening, and this gave me
more freedom to talk as I needed to talk. I'm sure it's easier to
spill your worst fears or worries to a sympathetic stranger – or
even an understanding one.
'It's Evelyn. Nothing has been right since she lost that baby. It's
got worse day by day, week by week, and now it's months. I'm
nearly at the end of my tether. I can't bear it like this for much
longer. She's only spoken a few words to me for days on end. She
walks about – that is, when she's not in bed – she walks about
like a duck in a thunderstorm. What time is it now?'
'It's twenty minutes past seven, Mr Harper.'
'Twenty past seven of an evening and I tell you, Miss Roper,
she is still only half-dressed. She's sitting there staring at the wall,
staring at nothing. If she's not doing that she's crying. I don't
know whether she's crying for the baby or just feeling sorry for
herself.'
'There's nothing wrong with crying for oneself. Crying on one's
own behalf. I have done it myself, Mr Harper.'
'No, no. I don't mean to lay criticism at her door . . . It's just
that I've come to the end of the line in knowing what to do. She's
not eating very much – just nibbles and leaves what she has

started. She's lost interest in everything. Even herself. She forgets to flush the toilet . . . and . . . and . . . I don't know when it was when she last washed. She stinks. Her mother said so – just yesterday. She got very angry with Evelyn and started shouting all kinds of things at her. I suppose she was trying to shock her out of it.'

'Of what, Mr Harper?'

'Her mood.'

'I do not believe that Evelyn is moody, a less moody young woman I have yet to meet. She is injured. And you don't treat injury with violence or shock.'

'Injured? Injured?'

'Emotionally injured. Sometimes it's called depression. I know, I have experienced it.'

'How is it cured?'

'By nursing – if the cure is to be of any lasting effect. I think you should keep her relatives away from her for a time.'

'Who nursed you through your bad time, Miss Roper?'

'I did, Mr Harper. It had to be me. I had to do it myself.'

'My wife's not capable of it, she's gone down the pit-shaft too far, too deep, to be able to claw her way back into the light on her own. Please help me, Miss Roper. Please help Evelyn – help us – if you can.'

'I'll try, Mr Harper. If you give me the keys to your home I'll call in and see her each day. Perhaps persuade her to spend a little time around here with me.'

'I'll drop a spare set through your letter-box. I'm afraid . . . I'm afraid our house is in a bit of a mess at the moment – more than a mess, it's a bloody tip. I try to straighten things up a bit when I am home, but . . .'

'If I had someone who loved me as Evelyn loves you, I would wallow in squalor, Mr Harper.'

When she spoke, her hands left her lap and fluttered in the air as though she were making this point on a stage in order to convince a larger audience.

For a few seconds, I saw the Kay Roper that I had known in those early war years. However much the exterior of that person had changed or disappeared. I saw that a great deal of the interior remained. She must have read my thoughts: her hands settled too swiftly in her lap. Her retrieval of her previous composure was too abrupt to be convincing.

'I know you can help Evelyn if anyone can. I won't forget the keys.'

She offered me no beverage, but rose and accompanied me to the door.

'It's very good of you.'

'Not at all. Not at all, Mr Harper. Next to my own company, I enjoy and prefer the company of other women, so what I am offering is not entirely selfless as far as I am concerned. I hope that we can move Evelyn forward from this point. From what you say, her retreat has gone on long enough. A breakdown is often the beginning of a breakthrough . . . we'll see . . . we'll see. It looks as if this gloomy weather – this permanent, grey winter half-light – is about to leave us for the spring. Flowers!'

'Pardon me?' I was puzzled.

'Flowers. That's all I said. It was just a thought. Goodnight, Mr Harper.'

My wife's recovery was not immediate but gradual; it was slow and thorough in its evolution. I wasn't anxious to hurry things, I was so grateful to see the small improvements build up week by week. Of course, I have to be brutally truthful, I longed for the day when Evelyn would return to me as a lover – that part of our marriage had ceased.

'Don't touch me. Don't touch me. Not like that, not at all, leave me alone.'

I had mentioned this to Kay Roper.

'You must wait for Evelyn to come to you, Mr Harper. Emotional wounds go very deep – usually much deeper than physical ones. Would you want to impose yourself on someone you loved if that imposition aggravated a wound? I think not. A little more nursing, a little more patience may bring its rewards.'

That spring was the beginning of two transformations. You could say that Evelyn's and Kay's gardens began to bloom in tandem. During the war years it was considered to be just short of criminal to grow flowers where you could plant vegetables and in any case there was an abundance of wild flowers all about us in the spring and summer months. Even by the early 1950s – in our region – if it were a choice between space for rhubarb or a rose-bush, then the rhubarb would probably win hands down.

Miss Roper's garden became a bit of a local talking point. It wasn't just a few vegetables she replaced, but all of them. Her garden was all flowers; they were abundant and varied for much of the year. It seemed miraculous to me that when I returned home I didn't find my wife staring emptily at the wall or out of the window, I did not find her lying sleepless and tearful in bed. More often than not, I would see her working side by side with Kay Roper in the garden – it was as though their bereavements were being put into the soil as some kind of fertilizer, the strength of their sorrow producing a flowering all about them.

There was an excess of blooms, and it was Kay Roper's idea to put up the small sign, 'Cut flowers for sale.' By mid to late summer the sign had been enlarged to read, 'Cut Flowers for Sale. Wreaths, Bouquets, and Sprays made to order.'

They were self-taught as far as the wreath-making went. I'd find them in the kitchen with bits of wire, clippers, and straw-coloured raffia binding, and reference books from the lending library. They snipped and weaved as they talked. What's more, my wife had begun to smile again.

Ah, that was an evening of revelation. It must have been September or early October. It seems a bit daft for me to sniff at this thought, but when I came in that day – that early evening – the bitter but captivating scent seemed to pervade not only this kitchen, but the whole of the house. Evelyn and Kay Roper were twisting the wires and snipping off unsightly ends – one worked on a cross shape, the other on a heart. They sat around the table, Kay Roper, Evelyn and Ivy Chaplin. The talking didn't impede Evelyn or Kay Roper from working.

I was welcomed warmly enough. I brewed myself a cup of tea and one for Ivy at the same time. I sat on the back doorstep to drink it as I didn't want to interrupt their work and it was a pleasant way to take some air after being underground all day.

There's something really lovely about the way women talk to each other amidst themselves, particularly if they are good friends. Somehow I think the quality is lacking in men – and it's a bit of a sadness, I think. The three of them talked with great bunches of chrysanthemums lying all about them. There were Pennine Jewels, vivid orange and sharp on the eye, masses of pink Ringdove, and the soft, sweet Cloudbanks as well as smaller bunches of single-petalled Redwing.

'The funeral's tomorrow. A big one. This is the largest order we have ever had. There's eight wreaths and seven sprays to be made up. Do you think I could make up one wreath entirely from the Redwing? We've more of those blooms than any other.' Evelyn seemed alive and full of energy.

'It's obvious they can make up the heart,' Ivy observed. 'Talking of hearts, have either of you heard that Janet Haycock is marrying in three months' time?'

'Yes, we have the floral order,' Kay replied.

'Well, Kay, that sounds callously commercial coming from you. I'd have thought you might have proferred some sweeter comment than that. Janet is very fond of you. She was your favourite pupil – one of your successes, if you like – and all you can do is make her future wedding sound like a business item.' Evelyn giggled at Ivy's retort. 'You could at least say that you hope she will be happy.'

'That passes without saying – of course I hope Janet will be happy.' Kay bent and selected some Redwing chrysanthemums and concentrated on trimming the stalks but continued to talk. 'Yes . . . yes . . . I hope Janet will be happy but I have no faith in the fulfilment of such hopes.'

'I wonder what your reservations are about, Kay? Janet is a sensitive, intelligent girl. A pity she didn't go on to university. Her mother wouldn't let her go on to sit for her Higher School Certificate – the woman told me so herself. Some mothers can be very selfish.'

'Selfishness has nothing to do with it, Ivy. It was an economic decision. Mrs Haycock had no choice – Mr Haycock is ill. His sick pay cannot support the home. Janet seems happy enough at the library. I have no reservations about Janet.'

'You have some about him? About the man, Miss Roper?' Evelyn enquired.

'Some conjectures. Some question marks. Yes, I do,' said Kay. I am sure they must have forgotten about me sitting there on the step. Either that, or they didn't mind me hearing what was being said. I'd heard groups of men talking about women any number of times – particularly when a working shift was over – but this was the first time I'd heard a group of women talking about men. Had they forgotten I was near? Was it a question of out of sight and out of mind? Or did they want me to hear what was being said? Ivy was intent on defending Janet Haycock's choice of mate – in the long term she was proved wrong.

'I can't see what objections you have to him, Kay. He's just started teaching at the new primary school in Peacock Lane and his looks would turn any girl's head.'

'They wouldn't turn mine.' Evelyn laughed as she spoke.

'Ivy, your teacher-malaise of talking too much and listening too little seems to be returning to you. I had reservations not objections – and if you really wish to know, my reservations were not of a material nature. Janet will always be able to earn.'

'I know what you mean, Miss Roper.' Evelyn stripped away some leaves from a stalk with one quick movement of her hand. 'He looks too romantic to be real.'

Ivy made a chuckling sound not unlike a disgruntled hen. 'My husband is romantic and real and . . .' She paused and spoke more quietly as sadness crept into her voice. 'Or at least he was . . . I wonder if he will ever be rid of duodenal ulcers? I'm sure that they are a legacy of the war . . . I have the sinking feeling that his working life will never be up to much. It means I have to return to teaching. I'm afraid the calling is necessitous rather than vocational. The thought of working in the new large school alongside Mrs Pickett daunts me.'

'Why not learn something very different? Start on something new?' Kay suggested.

'Oh, no, no. I could never teach infants. Never. My own daughter represents all that I wish to know of that world.'

'I wasn't thinking of infants – not in that way. I was thinking of more war legacies. Had you ever considered teaching the blind? They are short of teachers in that sphere as the numbers of blind children have increased enormously. They need education – they are entitled to it. They need care and nurture, they need a special skill. Why not retrain, Ivy?'

'It's something I'll think about, Kay. Thank you.'

'I wonder why there are so many blind children? I mean, why have the numbers increased so much?' Evelyn seemed to be asking the questions of herself, but Kay provided the answers.

'Syphilis. Many men returning home from the war passed the legacy they had picked up whilst they were away on to their wives. The wives passed it on to their unborn children. There is a varying degree of innocence to all the victims of such a secretive war wound.'

'I wouldn't say that the men were in any way innocent.' Ivy made no attempt to veil her indignation.

'Men have their needs, Ivy. You know this only too well. There must have been situations and periods of time for some men when only a saint would not have resorted to some pleasure or satisfaction of the flesh. In my heart, I cannot judge them.'

'It's because you wilfully chose to be a spinster, Kay – only a spinster could view men in such a liberal way.'

'I'm not a spinster, Mrs Chaplin, and I wouldn't want to be married to a saint.' Evelyn spoke nervously, as if it required great effort to make her point of view known. 'I think . . . I think . . . in such a situation . . . I would still love Patrick . . . er, I mean . . . I wouldn't judge. I wouldn't judge.'

The conversation rested and all that I could hear was the snipping of the clippers and the rustling of discarded leaves and fern. I wanted to make my way indoors but there was something about this quietness between the three of them which defied interruption. It made me feel the conversation was continuing in spite of them all being mute.

'Well, you two have launched me on a new career.' Ivy rose

from her chair. 'No, don't get up, I can see that you're both busy. It looks as though the two of you will be at it until the early hours of the morning. I can find my own way out.'

'Why not make a start now?' Kay enquired of Ivy.

'A start on what?'

'Oh, your career . . . close your eyes . . . use your sense of touch . . . experience the darkness that your future skills will attempt to lighten.'

As I re-entered the kitchen, I watched Ivy, hands outstretched, feeling her way past the furniture and into the hallway. She negotiated the steps up to the front door without mishap and I thought Kay and Evelyn might utter some encouragement but they continued to concentrate on their flower assemblages. It wasn't until the door closed and Ivy was well out of earshot that Kay spoke. 'She'll do it. And she'll be good.' Evelyn nodded confirmation and continued working.

Some men can never seem to make up their minds about women working. Many of them only seem to want their women to work if it suits them. All I wanted at this time was for my wife to be happy and well, and this present situation seemed to suit her. 'I'll be up to Bedfordshire if you two don't mind. I'm on early shift in the morning so I'll have to be up and out by five.' It wasn't unusual in those times for mining families to be all abed by nine of an evening.

'We could be working here very late . . . the early hours of the morning . . . even if we are lucky.' Kay surveyed the mass of unbound flowers all about them as she spoke.

'I'll try not to wake you when I come up, love.' Evelyn smiled in my direction as she made her point.

I know I felt a little resentful in leaving the two of them there together: I think I was jealous of the satisfaction they got from their industry. They were enjoying their work and I was disliking mine more as each day passed. On some days I woke in dread of the day's labour before me. The pit-cage, the darkness, the maleness, and the enclosed nature of that subterranean world were beginning to get at me. In spite of feeling sorry for myself, I always managed to go to sleep as soon as my head touched that pillow. I'm sure physical fatigue would still be the best cure for insomniacs if they'd only give it a try.

At some point in the night I entered the most pleasurable dream that a man could ever have – my wife was making love to me . . . she was astride me . . . her hair brushed my face . . . the fingers of my right hand lingered and pressed on the nipple of one of her breasts whilst my mouth suckled at the proud fount of the other one. She writhed and bobbed over me at her leisure, leading my prick into the very depths of herself. Both of us were calling out strange sounds in mutual ecstasy before I realized that this joy was no dream but a reality. After we had both come and were both spent it was time for me to go to work.

Evelyn came downstairs with me in the early light of the dawn and I knew that she had returned to me once again. The funeral sprays and wreaths were all tidily arranged about the kitchen, the cards of condolence all neatly attached. 'If we all put our minds to it, we could live off this.' Evelyn made an arc-like movement with her hand which encompassed the night's work.

About a month or so later, I gave notice at the pit and joined the two of them. I learned to drive a van, I built the first greenhouses, I planted seeds and worked side by side with my wife and with my best friend and it all fell into place. When Aileen Pugh went to open a wool and baby-clothes shop in Cardiff, we bought her house. We now had enough land and property to grant us a good livelihood.

I still love plants – there's great peace to be had from growing things – but I'm buggered if I want to talk to fuchsias, rhodendendrons or roses. I need a human landscape, I need to talk to . . . I need to see Janet Haycock again. Soon.

14

In the 1960s, when any number of people seemed to be trying to find 'their true selves', my husband of five years' standing lost himself. He'd left teaching to become a student yet again – he'd murmured something about doing a job with social work connotations but unrelated to any kind of institution. I was left with a child (placed in a day nursery) and an income from my library job that had to keep us all as well as supplement his grant.

As the university terms progressed, he came home less and less and as the intervals of absence became longer his appearance somehow seemed to grow more beautiful. He was a tall man, wide-shouldered and narrow-hipped. The fashion of the day enhanced his looks to the point where both women and men would look at him with appreciation. For some reason, I knew that when he bade me farewell at the beginning of that summer I would never see him again.

He stood there in tightly fitting, wine-coloured flared trousers (so unsuitable for travelling), a dark blue open-necked shirt dotted with mauve and yellow daisies and sandals which seemed to be nothing more than three or four leather thongs which held the soles to the bottom of his feet.

Dark brown, lightly curling hair parted directly down the centre of his scalp tumbled in thick lustrous locks and settled comfortably on his shoulders. A long face, an aquiline nose, and full lips were further sanctified by ice-blue eyes which always seemed to be fixed on a point somewhere beyond me when we conversed.

On this last occasion he had grown a beard, and I remember

thinking that he looked like one of the picture-book versions of the disciples – or even Christ himself.

'I know you will understand, Janet – it's just that I have a deep need to travel. I can't quite explain it . . . but . . . but I feel claustrophobic here in the village. I need to have plenty of space . . . I need mystic communion with strangers. I need to say hello and goodbye all in the course of a day. Maybe even an hour . . . I need . . .'

'I, I, I!' I remember shouting at him. I'd never done this before – no, it was quite the opposite. I'd not stopped at loving this man – I worshipped him. When I married him I felt enormous gratitude that someone so beautiful should want to choose me as his wife. Most of the village thought that I had made a 'good catch'. There were only two dissenters to the match – my mother and Kay Roper.

'Couldn't you just live with him for a time?' Kay had remarked in an offhand sort of way.

'He ought to be marrying himself,' my mother grunted and said no more except, 'It's your bed, your making, I'm glad I'm not sleeping in it.'

For the most part, I slept in the bed that I had made – alone. On the day he left, I watched him pack his duffle-bag with great care. His smile of compassion (for that is what it looked like) made me feel sick. He asked me to let him have five pounds to put by for any emergency; he said that he'd return it when the university term started again and his grant came through.

I gave it him without comment and all he said was, 'See you then.' These last three words were very precise as I never set eyes on him again. This was a false idol whom I had worshipped.

In October of that year, I received a postcard from Barcelona extolling the beauties of the Ramblas and the Gaudi architecture. In the spring of the following year there was a card from Fez in Morocco. Finally, three or so years after this, a card – featuring the motel from where it was sent in San Diego – bade me final peace and love.

By this time, I could only laugh at his pose: his pretence towards a pursuit for spirituality was only a veneer for his love of himself. I'm sure his most successfully erotic moments came from him

214

masturbating himself in front of a large mirror. Now, as of this moment, I don't think of him with any trace of rancour, in fact it's hard to grant the memory of him any reality. I know why he has come into my mind this New Year's Day – I slept with Patrick Harper last night and it was good. It was also the first time that I have felt loved in that way. What a game of chance marriage can be . . . innocence isn't always a virtue . . . and there is no bliss in ignorance.

Patrick made me breakfast this morning – just cornflakes and toast and marmalade – and I sat next to him at the kitchen table. I had borrowed his dressing-gown to come downstairs in and as I drank my tea he slipped his hand inside the gown and placed it on my breast and said he'd always like to lay his head there.

'Would you like some marmalade?' I asked.

Then we both broke into laughter before talking, not about Kay Roper, but about one another.

Mr Barraclough, Miss Roper's solicitor, has asked us to meet at his home tonight. I'm collecting Patrick and Ivy Chaplin and we have to be there at seven. It seems a little odd not to be seeing him at his office.

'I have some news which might well prove upsetting for all of you – at Mrs Chaplin's age, I don't want to say anything which might shock her if she is in frail health. Perhaps it might be advisable if you relay the information to her after I have given it to you.'

I explained to Mr Barraclough that it would take a great deal to shock Ivy Chaplin and that I couldn't imagine any news, no matter how distressing, that I would wish to keep from her. In Ivy Chaplin's case, physical debility was not mirrored by emotional frailty.

Word will be out tomorrow. Mr Barraclough says that it is sure to be in some of the newspapers, if not all, but he is hoping that none of the sensation-seeking tabloids will make it headline news.

He has advised us not to give interviews to any reporters, even if we are offered money. I don't think he need have any fears on that count – none of us are poor and the reading of the will leaves us more than comfortable. Everything that Kay owned is to be shared between the three of us and there are few complexities holding up its swift implementation.

'I, K. Roper . . .' the will began, and Mr Barraclough read it out aloud to us. Apart from Miss Roper leaving much more than we had envisaged, there was nothing in the papers which might shock us or give cause for concern and I wondered why Mr Barraclough seemed so tense and agitated.

'Please remain seated for a short while as there is something else that it is my duty to relate to you. Would anyone like a drink?'

We shook our heads but he took his offer as an excuse to pour himself a large gin and tonic from the array of bottles and glasses on the sideboard. He took two large gulps from his glass as if he needed the alcohol to release his tongue from some kind of dental clamp.

'I have made out photocopies of the will for all of you – and it would be as well if each of you retained one for safe-keeping.' Mr Barraclough distributed the papers as he addressed us and then settled himself behind a dark mahogany desk. He drank some more gin, coughed and began to speak in an undertone.

'I would like to draw the attention of you all to the opening words of this will. It says, "I, K. Roper".'

'Nothing unusual about that. It was Kay Roper who made it out.' Ivy always sounds sharp even when she's speaking normally – her manner tends to be abrupt.

Mr Barraclough continued in a voice that was little louder than a stage whisper. 'The letter K in this case . . . the letter K pertains to Kenneth Roper who was born in Scotland.'

'Did Kay have a brother?' Patrick enquired with obvious surprise.

'The Kay Roper that you knew was the K. Roper who wrote this letter.'

'I don't understand you, Mr Barraclough.' I felt my voice falter.

'Kay Roper was in fact – in body – Kenneth Roper.'

'You mean . . . you mean to tell us that Kay . . . that Kay was a man?' Patrick sounded aghast and I felt too bewildered to say anything. It was too much to absorb.

'I'm afraid that the person who lived amidst you all as Miss Kay Roper was in fact a man – not a woman. I'm sorry.'

'What splendid duplicity!' Ivy exclaimed and then broke into peal after peal of chuckles and cackles and helpless laughter. I had to pat her back eventually so that she could get her breath back.

Patrick seemed badly affected by the news and didn't share Mrs Chaplin's mirth. He went quite pale and I felt deeply concerned for him when he buried his head in his hands.

'To all intents and purposes, Mrs Chaplin, it was a noble duplicity. At least, there were good reasons for it. In times of war, I suppose all kinds of sacrifices are made. Some of course are of such a rare and unusual nature that they cannot be revealed until . . . until they could all but be regarded as a history. History is full of quirks.'

'Thank God Mrs Pickett is dead. If she were alive, this piece of news would have pole-axed her.' Ivy began to chuckle again and I felt that the news might have caused her mind to wander a little: I couldn't see how Mrs Pickett could be too upset by the revelations.

'You make it sound as though Mr Roper in parading as Miss Roper was carrying out some kind of duty,' I observed.

'I think you have made a fair appraisal – apart from the moral conclusions some people might wish to draw.' Mr Barraclough sipped his gin.

'Well, we were short of teachers,' said Ivy, 'short of everything, but teaching wasn't her main duty, was it?'

'*His* main duty. *His* duty,' Mr Barraclough corrected gently.

'Oh, don't *his* me. I shall always think of K. Roper as a woman. K. Roper will always be a *her*. A tassle between the legs means nothing to me at my age.'

Patrick sighed audibly. He had taken his hands away from his face but still looked distraught. I remained bewildered and Ivy didn't seem to be worried at all.

'But it's . . . it's . . . it's so unnatural.' Patrick managed to speak.

'Not for Kay, it wasn't.' Ivy was economical in defence of her friend.

'I can't understand where duty came into it. Mr Barraclough, can you let us know what these duties were? It might help us.' I looked in Patrick's direction.

'Only what I know myself. During the war K. Roper was employed by what are now known as the security services. His record in this field was . . . apparently excellent. Unblemished.'

'You mean Kay was a spy?' I couldn't keep the note of disbelief from my question and Patrick groaned.

'You could say that, yes – but more in an operational sense.'

'It's nonsense,' Ivy declared. 'What spying could dear Kay do in Batsford? And what so-called operations could she be involved in orchestrating? There was no enemy there to fraternize with.'

Mr Barraclough appeared to be most calm now and it struck me that he was actually enjoying all of this. It was as if he were allowing us to savour titbits from some wonderful meal that we had never been able to fully partake in.

'Wasn't there?' He threw the question out in casual fashion. This caused the three of us to look at each other in a strange way – as if we were searching for some guilt or close secret that might transgress our friendship. This uncertainty did not last for long: the singing drifted back into my head . . . back to Sorrento.

'Italians.' I spoke confidently. 'There were Italians, Kay was in contact with them.'

'It's true, she was.' Ivy lost no time in confirming my submission. 'Mrs Pickett had it on her list of complaints against Kay. She said that she had seen Kay conversing with one of them on at least three occasions and had seen her hand a packet over to him at one time. I said it wasn't uncommon for local people to give the prisoners of war cigarettes now and again. I disliked Mrs Pickett, and I still dislike the thought of her even if she is dead.'

'Your suppositions are correct. K. Roper was part of a group of undercover workers who worked with Italians who supported the allies during the war. There were a great many of them who felt less affection for Mussolini than we did. K. Roper was part of what we called our Mediterranean Strategy. For the most part, this involved supporting the partisan movement in Liguria and creating internal mayhem in Italy. In order to strengthen the allied advance K. Roper was "fed" information by Italian prisoners sympathetic to us who had been "planted" in various camps.'

'How do you know that?' Ivy asked.

'I was a prisoner myself, Mrs Chaplin – I survived internment by the Japanese. Prisoners of war – or at least some of them – continue to fight. Intrigue of one kind or another is often a reason for staying alive.'

'Did her father . . . er, his father . . . K. Roper's father, did he know about all this?' Patrick asked. He seemed a little more comfortable with himself now.

Without asking, Mr Barraclough poured him a drink from the sideboard and spoke as he handed Patrick the glass.

'The man sharing the house with K. Roper was not in any way related to him.'

Patrick gulped on his drink. 'You mean he was not her . . . his . . . father?'

'Exactly. K. Roper was without relatives – hence all of you being beneficiaries. One could say that you were as close to any family ties as K. Roper ever got. The man you knew as K. Roper's father was merely a colleague.'

'No. Not merely a colleague.' Ivy's tone was unusually tender.

'I assure you, he was,' said Mr Barraclough. 'He visited Italy many times during his stay in Batsford, making contact with the partisans and other operational groups who were working with the allies. He was not related to K. Roper.'

'He was related to Miss Roper.' Ivy gently insisted. 'He was her lover, I'm sure of it.'

'There's no proof, no evidence, no documentation left behind of such things ever happening, Mrs Chaplin. In a small village – or town – homosexual tendencies would surely have been noted by someone. K. Roper, as far as anyone can judge, remained chaste.'

At this point, Patrick spluttered over his drink so that I had to pat his back to aid his recovery. Ivy shook her head vigorously in disagreement with this point of view.

219

'Kay Roper could not have talked about men in the way she did unless she had known one. And I mean "known". I'm glad that she did, I don't care a damn about her physical geography. Somebody must have found her contours interesting. Dear Kay.' Ivy turned to me. 'Get us both a drink, Janet. Sherry for me. You get it – we don't want Mr Barraclough bobbing up and down like a cork any more.'

'As I have said, Mrs Chaplin, there's no proof that such a relationship existed.'

'I'm an avid reader, Mr Barraclough.' I found that I had given myself whisky, not my favourite drink, but it did seem to strengthen my personal resolve. 'As far as espionage is concerned . . . it does seem that men and women of homosexual persuasion have always been used by most countries.'

'I don't doubt it,' he replied.

'But why?' Patrick asked.

'They were considered expendable.' Ivy snorted disapproval. 'If they were lost, or if they disappeared into thin air, who would mourn them?' Ivy sounded bitter in her cogitations.

Mr Barraclough closed our meeting there and then, just as formally as he had begun it. Kay Roper's entire estate was to be divided equally between the three of us. Her only funeral direction was that her ashes should be placed somewhere in the garden centre. The locks and bolts were to be removed from Kay's house and we would all have access to the property within a fortnight to three weeks.

I acted as a taxi-driver as the three of us made our way home. Patrick sat in the back and remained silent for most of the journey; in contrast, Ivy was in high spirits. The astonishing news seemed to have granted her new powers of rejuvenation. Ivy was not upset by the shocking revelations, but delighted by them.

She began with a chuckle. 'Oh, oh, that little madam. No, she wasn't little by any standards of womanhood, was she? But that Vanessa Redgrave – lovely actress – she's a big girl too, and she's all woman – got children to prove it. I always thought that Peter looked a bit on the young side to be Kay's father, I wouldn't have minded going a lot further than the quickstep in his arms – if I hadn't been married. My dear Ralph would have laughed at all this. Perhaps he's laughing now – if the dead are allowed it. Bless him.'

I glanced at my watch as I had promised the superintendent I would get Ivy back to the home before ten. It was already twenty past.

Ivy was unconcerned. 'Oh, don't worry about Miss Bible-Witness, I'm booking myself out of that place when all our business is settled. I can afford to – I'd rather die on my feet than my back. If I let myself die in that place they'll find a cluster of moth-balls for cremation not a body.'

Ivy began to hum a tune. 'Do you remember that song?' she asked. I said I remembered the tune, but couldn't fit the words to it.

'Don't let your brain go, Janet – not now when you're just discovering your body again.' She'd guessed about Patrick and me. I said nothing but let her continue. 'It's called "I'll Get By". Bing Crosby made the popular recording of it, but Kay sang it in the style of Alice Faye. Oh, I can't wait to see my son-in-law's face when I give him the news.'

'Break it gently, Ivy,' I murmured as I pulled the car into the driveway.

'I said that I will *give* him the news. Plates are broken. News is given. I hope I can tell him before he sees it in the press. I've no intention of being gentle. There's no need for me to elaborate on the story, the plain facts will send him spinning to his knees.'

Miss Bible-Witness received us as Ivy and I knew she would. She opened the front door just as we were about to press the bell. Ivy had seen the curtain twitch and had said that the Lord's bridesmaid's eyes were upon us.

'Ah, I've caught you before you pressed the bell. Most of our guests have been in bed for an hour or more and we don't like to disturb them.'

Ivy offered no apology, she just said, 'It's half-past ten, I'm not due to change into rags for another hour and a half.' She turned towards me and cackled, 'We'll be in touch tomorrow, Janet.

What a day it's been, I wouldn't have missed it for the world and...'

'Shush ... ssh ... ssh, Mrs Chaplin. The other guests are sleeping.'

The biblical janitor oozed concern.

'Oh, shush your bloody self.' Ivy was beyond intimidation. I heard her words as the door closed.

15

Even if the contribution to the whole is relatively small, it's a good thing to feel useful if you are as old and physically decrepit as I am. I've put a stop to the pilfering in that I discovered the thief.

Many of our potted plants seemed to be floating through a hole in the ozone-layer. No one could account for their disappearance. In particular, the primulas and cyclamen seemed to escape our hospitality void of sale.

The woman was a regular customer – she would call at least one day a week, usually just before closing. She was always expensively dressed, but in an overtly sensible way. Good quality blouse, skirt, and pearls brigade. My suspicions were first aroused by weather conditions. Why did the woman always carry such a heavy-looking anorak over her arm even on the hottest of days? Days when the heat was pulverizing some people.

The swiftness and skill of her well-practised action caused me to feel some grudging admiration for her. The hand shot forward and a diamond ring sparkled in the sunlight. In one smooth movement the plant had left the tray and disappeared into the recesses of the anorak hood. Within minutes she had repeated the operation a second time – and continued to stroll about the garden-centre grounds apparently lost in adoration for the plants surrounding her.

We decided not to prosecute. Poor woman. She needed psychiatric help – she was a member of the county council too. We just accepted renumeration for our past losses and that was that.

There was quite a rumpus when Kay's news was announced. Janet and Patrick refused to talk to anyone – but I took on all comers. I have to admit that, for the most part, I enjoyed it all. I hadn't had so much attention for years, and I dare say I won't get it again.

I gave interviews to three newspapers and several women's magazines, I talked on 'Woman's Hour' on the radio and I was even interviewed by Jonathan Ross on television. It was wonderful having cars come to collect me and the pay was good. My son-in-law has practically disowned me and that's a bonus by my standards: I'm long past the stage of feeling dutifully obliged to see people I dislike. As soon as Kay's will was settled, I booked myself out of that morgue for the living they call a nursing home and came here. I have a daily help visit me, an unmarried mother from the Marshland Estate – a rough-tongued, warm-hearted girl. We get along fine together.

I've happiness again (of a kind). It's sad that dear Kay's death was the cause of it being granted to me. We scattered her ashes here in the garden – it was a very private ceremony. Only Janet and Patrick and I were present.

Afterwards we had tea; Janet had made a cake. She fancies herself as a bit of a cook, but I found it rather dry and could only manage a few mouthfuls. It had the texture and taste of vanilla-flavoured sawdust. I slipped most of my slice into my cardigan pocket so as not to injure Janet's feelings. Patrick lied and said it was delicious. I felt a bit in the way as he was looking 'goo-goo-eyed' at her. Not that she discourages him.

I excused myself and said that I'd like a little air – just a moment or two. No, I didn't need help, I could make my own way into the garden. I managed to crumble the cake in my fingers and throw the crumbs near the rose-bushes where we had cast Kay's ashes.

Half an hour later, when we were on our second cup of tea, Janet cried out in spontaneous anguish. She pointed towards the view from the french windows.

'Oh look! Look what's happening.'

A flock of greenfinches were twittering and arguing angrily with three or four sparrows. In between the shrill chirping, all the birds were pecking furiously at the ground. Kay, or what was left of her, was being eaten.

'How horrible!' Janet exclaimed.

'Oh, I don't know, I'm not so sure.' I spoke with as much reassurance as I could muster, knowing that I had unwittingly fed Kay to the birds. 'She'll pass through their systems and come up as a daisy, or a field of poppies.'

'That's a nice thought Ivy,' Patrick concluded and we let the birds get on with their meal.

Patrick has called to see me no less than three times today – not entirely out of the goodness of his heart. Janet's gone on a day-trip to London and says she won't be back until late. He's very stricken with her and is like a chick without a hen when she's not fussing about him.

He says she's visiting an elderly aunt. I know she's lying: having lived in this area all my life, I know that there are no brothers or sisters on her father's or mother's side of the family down there. It's bound to be a small lie, or one of no significance, as Janet is incapable of any large kind of deceit or intrigue. Sometimes I wish she were – a little subtlety might not come amiss.

I've got to know her ways . . . and without any doubt, she is closer to me than my own daughter. I enjoy her imperfections – yet I haven't managed to dissuade her from wearing some very pungent perfume. She's very heavy-handed in applying it, she's like the Chelsea Flower Show on legs. Even a room of heavily scented wallflowers fails in competition when she is floating around. Funny habit for such an intelligent woman.

16

It is almost an hour before my train arrives but I don't feel put out. It's quite pleasant here in the station buffet watching the commuters come and go – people meeting people, people asking people questions, people saying goodbye, and people saying hello. All of this is only half-absorbed.

I'm not interested in looking at an evening paper. The other half of me has to quietly assess my thoughts and feelings concerning the day's events. In one day, I have discovered what lay behind decades of suffering – and I wonder how on earth it could have been borne alone. I suppose it had to be.

There was little left behind in Kay's house that might give any indication as to the details of her past life. Patrick had said that the police and fellow-travellers had emptied her home of bundles of papers long before we were allowed entrance. We had hoped to find some photographs or small mementoes which might have given us some inkling or inroad into Kay's secret life. There was nothing – and I felt quite cheated and angry about this. Mrs Chaplin appeared unconcerned and Patrick could not veil his sense of relief.

I turned my anger on him as it couldn't be expressed anywhere else. 'Why are you so smug? I thought you were fond of Kay? There was a time when you were more than fond of her.' I could see I was causing him some discomfort but I couldn't check my tongue. 'Tell me, tell me, did you ever make love to Kay? Did you?' Perhaps this was an unconscious jealousy on my part. Lovers are often jealous of their partner's past. Poor Ivy gasped.

He did not answer me but stared down at the carpet as though he were examining its pile. Just as I was about to apologize for my outburst and withdraw my question, he looked at me with such sorrowful eyes.

'I can honestly state that I never made love to Kay. I never made love to Kay.' He smiled in sad recollection, more for his own benefit than for ours, and added, 'I never kissed Kay. There.'

Last week – only last week, when not involved in any kind of search – I came across some old magazines (mainly *Picturegoer*) and newspapers as I was clearing out the bottom of the airing cupboard. A postcard had managed to affix itself to the inside cover of one of them. It was moored between pictures of Ingrid Bergman and Roberto Rossellini. 'The Swinging Sixties – Carnaby Street' was printed across it with different views of the shopping area depicted on either side of the caption. I peeled it away from Ingrid's breast. It is here now in my raincoat pocket.

> Trattoria Maggiore,
> 42 Sekforde Street,
> Clerkenwell,
> London EC1

Dear Kay,
I wondered if you might want to contact me again after all these years. I have thought of you often but felt you would not like me to get in touch for obvious reasons. I don't even know that this will find you. You may have moved. If this card causes you further injury then cast it away and do not reply. Perhaps time has healed some of your wounds and left you unscarred. If so, then let us meet.

> Yours, Enrico Trebaldi

My first impulse was to share my discovery with Patrick and Ivy – but for some reason I withheld it for the rest of the day. By the third day, I knew that I wanted to keep this communication to myself until I had found more out. Just like some toddler at the solitary stage of learning, I did not want to share – I wanted to keep this part of Kay all to myself.

I researched the background of the address before making this journey. To hear some people talk one would have thought that immigrants only started entering this country in our own lifetime – some would have to bite their lips if they knew that an Italian enclave was started in Clerkenwell way back in the Middle Ages. Yet it surprised me to find that by the nineteenth century much of Clerkenwell was known as 'Little Italy'. The last war seemed to cast a darkening shadow on many Italians in this community as the majority of them were classified as 'enemy aliens' – some were sympathetic to our cause. 'Clerkenwell is an area that has seen great changes in its development. Just before the Second World War it was an area which reflected the lives of the many poor immigrants who lived there, in the main of Italian extraction . . .'

There was nothing poverty-stricken about the look of the Trattoria Maggiore. However, if one looked between the spaces of office buildings one could see that the area must have once held a village-like charm. I arrived at one o'clock and the place seemed to bustle and hum with well-dressed young men and women who exuded an air of working arrogance and confidence that I found somewhat daunting.

Before I left home, I thought I'd chosen my clothes carefully. I have to confess that I have far too many clothes, I buy something new almost every week. Well, to be fair to myself, it's not usually brand new as I give a lot of trade to charity shops. Cancer Research, Oxfam, Help the Aged – they all receive regular custom from me. There are any number of shops like this and something in one of them is bound to catch my eye.

Patrick just regards it as a foible but Ivy is a little more disapproving. I wonder if it's anything to do with my childhood – or compensation for my miserable marriage? Shopping for clothes always cheers me up a little and if I feel I'm contributing to a charity at the same time as I am indulging myself, I never feel any guilt.

I had toyed with the idea of wearing one of my black coats but felt that this might put a tragic, sombre air to my visit, although I could have lightened its effect with a lapel brooch and a trailing coloured shoulder scarf. Instead, I chose my latest acquisition – a bright yellow, well-cut overcoat with large patch pockets. I'd bought it just a week before at the Spastics' Centre and the colour came out beautifully when it was cleaned. I thought that I looked very smart in my shiny black shoes, black handbag, and gloves to match. I had sought Ivy's approval and half twirled in her presence, as models do.

'Do you like my London outfit, Ivy?' I was so confident of her approval and appreciation that I twirled again as I spoke.

'It's cheerful, dear, I'll say that for it. Nice and bright. You don't see coats that colour nowadays except on lollipop ladies and men who work on the railways.'

Ivy can be very cutting at times and I think she was feeling a little resentful about my day's outing. It's understandable, as her journeyings are clearly over.

Just after one o'clock I stood on the pavement outside the Trattoria Maggiore – the name, beautifully sign-painted in gold-leaf on a black background, could not be missed. The large plate-glass window was uncurtained and revealed a substantial clientele which kept the three young waitresses permanently busy. Two be-tubbed bay trees stood on either side of the entrance door and the day's menu was displayed within a glass frame on a side wall.

I paused before entering, felt some misgivings about going in and finally chose to do an about-turn and cross to the other side of the road. What could I say to Enrico Trebaldi if I did find him there? It was unlikely that Kay's death was unknown to him. Most of the press seemed to have recorded it in one way or another and Ivy increased the coverage by giving interviews about Kay as if she were a great film star or something like that. She even gave an interview to a sex magazine and her son-in-law hasn't spoken to her since. Surely Enrico could have come up to Batsford and found out more if he had wanted to? Was he still alive? Had he been forbidden to renegotiate a contact with the past?

My curiosity managed to overcome my apprehensions. I recrossed the road and entered the restaurant with the kind of resolve one musters on a visit to the dentist – this might be initially painful but there will be relief afterwards.

The place was crowded. The diners sat about round glass-topped tables placed on either side of the aisle which ran the whole length of the long, oblong-shaped room. The chairs were of the modern, shiny steel variety and the same metal was used in the central table supports, the floor was carpeted in pale green, and the walls were white and void of pictures. Placed in the centre of each table were narrow vases, each of which held two or three carnations.

I closed the door behind me and waited for one of the three waitresses to direct me to a seat. I could see that there were one or two places vacant, but wherever I eventually sat I knew I would be an unwelcome guest in the grouping.

As I stood there, my nerve began to fail me. I could see that none of these people were over forty – the men or the women – or if they were, their attempts at age-abatement were highly successful. They seemed to be able to absorb a great deal of alcohol – and this in their lunch-break. No table was without a bottle of wine or bottles of European beer with gold wrapping paper around the necks. Many of the women wore jackets with exaggerated shoulder-pads, sometimes balanced cloak-like over plain but beautifully cut designer blouses.

They all talked animatedly to one another, causing a constant buzz in the atmosphere. They paid no attention to me. I saw one of the waitresses register my presence with a faint nod. Quite suddenly, I felt like an unwelcome refugee in an alien country. I felt ashamed of my glorious yellow coat which now seemed to cover me as though it were a tent or some garish marquee enveloping me at a garden party.

I had no place in this temple to present chic and stylish living. As the waitress spoke to me I placed my gloved hand over my port-wine mark on my brow – an action that I had not taken since I was a teenage girl.

'I'm sorry, but we are all full. All the places are booked. It gets a little quieter before we shut. We close at three.'

Grateful for an excuse to leave, I accepted her words without question. I stumbled out on to the pavement. My cheeks burned with shame and embarrassment and I was glad of the opportunity to take a brisk walk. In my aimless journey, I saw a wider cross-section of people and after ten minutes or so I felt I was part of the world again and not a redundant woman in a garish coat. I hadn't noticed which direction my legs had taken me but finally paused when I got to Farringdon underground station.

I had every intention of leaving the traffic-congested city to disappear into the bowels of the underground – to make my way home to familiar comforts and company. It would be simple enough to think up an excuse to explain my early return.

'I'm sorry, madam, the lines are closed. King's Cross – another bomb scare. You are advised to take an alternative route . . .' At least the railway official had been courteous.

More from nervous tension than need, I went into the nearest café, which displayed a sign that read 'Counter Service Only'. I asked for something on toast, and was given a choice of tomatoes, eggs scrambled or fried, beans, mushrooms or grated cheese. I shared a table with two young be-turbaned Indian bus-drivers who sought my assistance with a number of obscure clues regarding a crossword competition. In spite of their turbans, they spoke with London accents and told me that they were born in Bethnal Green. I felt a lot better for taking a little food and chatting to friendly strangers and left the café in better spirits.

The bomb scare was still in operation and my thoughts seemed to carry my sauntering feet back once more to the Trattoria Maggiore. I could see that the restaurant was empty. Inside, the one remaining waitress was busy checking till-takings at the far end of the room close to the kitchen. I sat down at the table nearest the entrance and I had time to remove my gloves and unbutton my coat before the same waitress I had seen before stood at my side.

'I'm sorry – we are closed, madam.'

I glanced at my wrist-watch. 'But it is only a quarter to three. You said three. You said you closed at three.'

'We close a little earlier today.' She shrugged her shoulders.

Perhaps it was the shrug, the studied insolence, that made me persist.

'Couldn't I just have some antipasto and a roll of bread and a glass of wine? I won't be long. Thank you.'

She returned with my order and ostentatiously placed the bill on the table at the same time, making it clear that my presence was being tolerated but not welcomed. She also made great play of hanging a 'Closed' sign on the inside of the glass door as if she were placing a portrait in the National Gallery.

I took tiny mouthfuls of sweet-tasting ham and sipped the dry white wine. I could hear voices coming from behind the swing-doors next to the cash-till – presumably these led to the toilets and storage rooms. The language being spoken was Italian. I could not understand what was being said but the tone was high-spirited and congratulatory and there was some laughter interspersed between exchanges. I heard the name Enrico and took another sip of wine.

A short man, who must have been close in years to my own age, pushed his way through the swing-doors for all the world as though he were setting foot on a stage in full view of an audience. He handled a tray which held a magnum bottle of champagne and three glasses. He called out in mock pleading for the other person to join him.

'*Subito. Su-bi-to.*'

I remained an unnoticed and silent witness as he arranged the bottle and glasses on the table-top for some kind of celebration. As Ivy often says, 'It's somebody's birthday every day.' The waitress sat nearest to the wall. He did not sit down but called out again for the third member of the party to join them. '*Subito. Su-bi-to.*'

There was no mistaking the casually dressed but distinguished-looking elderly man. I knew immediately who he was. In spite of the walking-stick that helped support a lame or rheumatic right leg, despite the head which now displayed more scalp than hair – what hair remained was of a light, sandy, grey colour. There was an air of immense charm about this old man. I knew that I was in the presence of Peter Roper.

He greeted the woman openly in Italian, and added in English, 'I like your hair, Fiammetta. You have changed the style, it suits you. Most becoming.'

Then he placed his hand on the shoulder of Enrico who looked up to him from his sitting position. He bent forward and kissed

Enrico on the cheek and looked into his eyes. I had seen that look before. I had seen him look on Kay in the same way. And now, I knew what it meant – or had meant.

Enrico helped Peter to his seat and deftly hung the walking-stick over the back of his chair. As he turned, I studied him full face. He had a full head of white hair, cropped short, but still managing to curl about the ears and over his brow. The eyes were still lustrous – large, soft, dark brown . . . I saw them again with tears spilling from them . . . I saw the hand – and the holly clutched in it . . . I saw those rows of desks . . . I saw the young girl that was me . . . I heard the music, the click of the gramophone . . . I remembered the kiss . . . and the blood. I saw the complete picture.

Dear Kay was not bereaved. Her loss – for that is what it was – could not be so easily accepted. Adultery is probably forgivable if you love someone dearly enough, but this was a deeper and more profound kind of betrayal.

I no longer felt nervous sitting there. I had decided not to declare my identity. Not to speak. As I picked at my food, I even began to make excuses for them – after all, the war and its aftermath caused so many fractures and repercussions in thousands of people's lives. Should I forget all this?

The exploding cork of the champagne bottle caused me to start so that I almost dropped my fork. Peter poured the bubbling alcohol into the glasses. He raised his glass first and the others followed suit.

He offered the toast: '*Brava Alessandra*'. The glasses clinked as they touched.

'*Brava Alessandra*,' the other two echoed him.

And then, in unison – '*Brava Mussolini.*'

I spat a half-chewed piece of mortadella back on to my plate as they drank. My head seemed to swim, I felt dizzy and my throat and mouth had become dry. I recovered myself by drinking the rest of my wine and by taking in great gulps of air. I thought of Kay's words . . . 'they will be back, they will be back with their marching and . . .'

The duplicity was on a greater scale than ever I could have

imagined – Kay had known only when it was too late. Or had she? She had suffered – suffered terribly. They must have known of her death. Was it accidental? I asked myself.

I stopped all this questioning – the answers became uglier the more I dwelt on them. I tried to look at the group dispassionately and as I looked it occurred to me how damned respectable they appeared. It was this show of respectability and decorum which caused my whole being to course with a controlled rage that I had never experienced before.

I searched in my purse and found the exact sum of money to pay my bill. I would not have to wait around for change. I put on my gloves, buttoned my coat and took up my handbag.

I had almost reached their table before the waitress noted my progress. She smiled weakly and took up her position behind the cash-till. I gave her the money together with the bill. I did not smile nor did I speak.

It was a small gesture – but I felt I had to do something. On making my exit I affected to stumble over the walking-stick. Both my arms shot forward on to the table to prevent my cinematic fall. The champagne bottle and three glasses crashed over – much of the liquid gushed and fizzed its way into Peter Roper's crutch. Whilst they were fussing about him with tea-cloths and flannels I discreetly made my way out of the building.

How do I feel now? Sad but . . . but satisfied. I have decided not to reveal anything about today's events to Patrick or Ivy. I'll keep this all to myself, just as Kay kept things to herself. It brings her closer to me.

Although Patrick has assured me that his association with Kay never veered towards the romantic, it has not stopped him murmuring her name in his sleep as he has lain at my side with his hand cupped about my breast.

Even so, he'll never know her as deeply as I do now, not even in his dreams. He will never know that sometimes I whisper her name back to him. And he couldn't – he couldn't possibly have loved her as much as I did.

The train is due in twenty minutes. It will be good to be home again. I'll do some baking tomorrow. Ivy loves my cakes.